Praise For Jon Armstrong's *Grey*

"Jon Armstrong's debut novel puts a fresh suit of stylish clothes on the beloved body of cyberpunk, skewering high fashion, consumerism, and... the public fascination with celebrities..."
— *Locus Magazine*

"If F. Scott Fitzgerald had ever imbibed himself into a science-fictional state of mind, subsequently pouring his talent for vivid images and acid observation into a futuristic dystopian extravaganza, the result might very well read like Jon Armstrong's debut novel. This formidable newcomer has given us, in Michael Rivers, a grey Gatsby who will revisit your reveries long after the last page is turned."
— James Morrow, author of *The Last Witchfinder*

"*Grey* is a truly extraordinary and original work--a deft and raucous mash-up of William Gibson and J.D. Salinger by way of Fellini. It'll change your outlook, your brain chemistry, and your wardrobe."
— Catherynne M. Valente, author of *The Orphan's Tales*

"*Grey* is a fascinating book. It's a fusion of the quasi-apocalyptic corporatism of Alfred Bester's *The Stars My Destination* with *Bladerunner* and a big hunk of *The Umbrellas of Cherbourg*."
— Jay lake, author of *Trial of Flowers*

"Two thumbs up... I couldn't put it down."
— Cherie Priest, author of *Four and Twenty Blackbirds*

"...a stylish, weird, funny, and inventive debut."
— Tim Pratt, author of *The Strange Adventures of Ranger Girl*

GREY

GREY

JON ARMSTRONG

Night Shade Books
San Francisco

For my parents, Carole and Russ Armstrong

One

Nora and I finished our fried whale and plum sandwiches, our cream coffees, and the cocoa and coca pastries, and sat in a comfortable silence as landscapes of buildings and millions of well-wishers whirred past the windows at six hundred kilometers per hour. Halfway on our train-date, after the conductor blew the massive, buzzing horn, and the waitresses in their black-and-yellow-striped honeybee uniforms, complete with dangerously sharp-looking stingers, cleared the dishes, Nora closed her right eye and gazed at me with her left; I, in turn, did the same, and it was like we were the perfect couple.

This was our fourth and last date before our marriage, and while the whole thing had been arranged between our parents to complete the merger of our families' companies, I could not have imagined or wished for someone as wonderful as she. Standing just an inch below my six foot three, with shiny black hair, a light walnut complexion, and obsidian eyes, her features were wide and open like an innocent doll, but she was also intelligent and witty. Most impressive of all was that she, like myself, loved the fashion magazine *Pure H*. We quoted from it, dressed and struck poses like the models, and felt that we were just like the beautiful and tragic people of our dreams.

Two of her attendants, all in black, helped Nora from her chair and adjusted her clothes as she walked. Her long, grey, satellite-cotton coat had spherical metal buttons with craters exactly like the moon. Beneath her grey suit, her shirt had a high collar like mine, and the material looked so smooth it could have been made of fine powder. The cut and tailoring was impeccable, of course, as she worked with October 13th, the best woman's tailor in the world.

Since the date took place on the inaugural voyage of a new, super-luxury Bee Train, which circled the Pacific Rim, Nora and I were obliged to tour all the cars with a camera crew. She seemed to enjoy the nature car best. And it was a calming space with its small trees, shrubs, and manicured lawn where sat an arrangement of lemon and lime chaise lounges. Before we exited, she stopped to pet one of the tigers, and I watched the gentle curve of her gloved fingers against the striped fur. Growing up, Nora had studied classical dance, and unlike the wild and useless gyrations of my youth, her training had given her a supple, athletic grace which permeated all her movements.

The way she stroked the beast, reminded me of just how elegant were her gestures. During our first date, in the city of Kong at the top of Convolution Tower before a thousand cameras and five oceans of lights, as we had sampled white rhinoceros tartar, black truffle sugar, and fugu tarts, it had been her grace which most impressed me. And later as I reviewed the recording, I watched her charcoal-gloved hands move like two elegant sea nettles undulating in warm ocean currents. When she held her wine glass, her spare pinky hovered effortlessly to the side; when picking up her silverware, her fingers curled around the metal slowly like miniature constricting snakes, and at the end of our date when she waved goodbye, she cupped her hands slightly, with her fingers together, arched, and tranquil.

During that first date, we just glanced at each other shyly. I had been nervous and not because of how many people were watching or what it meant to the companies, but because I knew I was in the presence of a rare person. We said not a word until moments before we began our post-date interviews. She leaned toward my ear and whispered, *"Embellishments."* The breathiness and sexiness of her tone was one I hadn't heard on any of the recordings I had reviewed prior to our date. I shivered. And her word—her single, perfect word—was luminous. Quoted from an ad in *Pure H* for a company that sold plutonium buttons, it read: *Embellishments. A week of green rain.*

The ad's photo[R6] is of a couple in identical charcoal frock coats, vests, and boots laying side by side in an elaborate garden of trimmed bushes and flowering poisonous lantana. Their dry eyes stare blankly. Their skin is ashen, and their lips, blue. Between them their hands are both upturned and yearning, but unconnected. Perhaps their rigor mortis caused their previously held hands to pull apart, but whatever it was, now the lovers are tragically separated by a fraction of an inch. My advisor had called the ad gloomy and morbid, but the way Nora said the word so sensually, emphasizing the *bell* syllable, made it evocative, even anticipatory.

The Bee Train began to decelerate and unfortunately that meant our date was ending. As our attendants gathered our things, and we pulled in the new station where Bee Train employees stood at attention all along the track, their striped uniforms forming what looked like a black-and-yellow staff of noteless music, Nora and I readied ourselves to meet the press.

We stepped before the doors as the train inched into place. Beyond the translucent cement walls of the station, I could see hordes of people filling the streets. All of our dates had been mobbed. In fact, our second, held in the desert metropolis of Seattlehama, forced the city to close down because so many tourists and fans had clogged the streets.

"I wasn't sure about you," she whispered.

Her hushed voice surprised me, and I was afraid she was saying something bad. "Sure about what?"

"Even in your grey suits," she said, gazing at my chest, perhaps noting the fibers in my dark tie, taken from the bras of one hundred alcoholic teenage girls, "I figured you were still garish and loud."

"No," I said, wishing, as I often did, that my life had always been quiet and grey. "That was years ago."

She smiled knowingly; then her expression turned cold. "But I had no idea how lonely you are."

I felt exposed and broken. "I didn't know either," I said. "Until I met you."

Her gaze circled my face as if studying me, judging the sincerity of my words. "What I want … " she began slowly, her lips beginning to tremble, "is to be alone … alone with you." She glanced away, and I saw her cheeks flush. "You?"

"Yes," I said. "That's exactly what I feel. From the first photo I saw of you … from the first report I read, I sensed that we were parts of each other."

"I was afraid to meet you, at first."

She hadn't admitted to anything like that before. "Why?"

Swallowing, she said, "I was afraid of what you would mean. How you would change me and make me who I am."

Her words were exactly my own feelings and I craved to touch her, to finally make contact with the surface of her body, but just as I raised my right hand toward her face, the train doors slid open, and the cool air of the station poured over us. Part of me wanted to slam them shut, take the controls of the train and head back to the wide circular track. We could live in constant motion, in the seclusion of the nature car, and never have to take another step in the rest of the world. But then I thought of a story in *Pure H* of a man who lived his whole life on a train. At eighty-three, when he is finally forced off, he stumbles on solid ground and cracks his skull.

"Will we?" she asked, so quietly I barely heard. "In this awful world, will we?"

She meant: Would we find silence, solitude, and love? I took her gloved hand in mine, inhaled her delicate sassafras, sandalwood, and ambergris. "We will," I said, as I led us from the train. We walked past the bowing Bee Girls and the conductor in his three–foot-tall, blue-and-white-striped hat. Frankly, I was unhappy that our dates were so commercialized, but Father was hungry for any publicity angle and glad to take their cash. With a nod, I thanked him, and wished he and the Bee Train Corporation good luck with their launch.

Camera crews scurried around us as we made the too-long trek across the new glass and titanium station, christened, as it was, by our presence. At the atrium doors, we paused for just a second. The new station was quiet, hollow, and still, but beyond the doors, the stage, and the podium, we could see thousands of reporters and tens of thousands of fans waiting for our comments and post-date impressions.

Nora and I glanced at each other, and I thought I saw weariness in her. Once we were married, I told myself, we would be able to submerge beneath the scrutiny of the millions of camera lenses, the critics' judgments, and the multitudes of opinions, but today, we had our duty.

When we stepped outside, the crowd's noise rushed over us like a tidal wave. Lights flashed. Everyone began cheering, clapping, and shouting. When we started toward the podium ten feet away, Nora pulled her hand from mine.

She did it gently, but the feeling it gave me was that I had done something wrong, that she was annoyed or had changed her mind about me. As I frantically tried to remember the agreed-upon blocking, but couldn't recall if we were supposed to be holding hands now or not, I stared forward into the cameras and tried to pretend that nothing unusual had happened, that my heart hadn't just been cracked. But as I tried to smile, I was sure I could hear the servomotors whine as the cameras all zoomed in on my flushed face.

When I turned, Nora was tugging off the charcoal chenille glove from her left hand. I saw a metallic flash of what looked like a tiny surgical robot, and then an inch line of blood welled across the creases of her palm.

Although her hand and blood were in color—of course—it was just like an image from *Pure H* in an ad for a top-of-the-line,

Invisi-Pearl™ finishing-stitch machine. The photo^{R6} was a close-up of a wounded woman's hand resting on wet sand. Beneath the image, the copy read: *The moment became her life.* My advisor told me that the hand was that of a dead woman and that *the moment* had passed, but as Nora held her hand for me to see, clearly, she believed the moment was approaching; and moreover, that the wound was evidence of a struggle that the hand had endured on its journey to this climactic moment.

I loved her hopeful interpretation! Most photographers around the stage pushed, shoved, and jockeyed for position to capture the image, but a few, who obviously knew *Pure H*, lowered their cameras in respect and awe.

And then Nora, whose eyes were quivering with tears of what I imagined were joy and pain, held her bloody hand toward me. That was how she felt: she wasn't just offering the warm smoothness of her skin, but the river of her life, the solution of her heart.

I felt a jolt of excitement as my fingers met her soft and warm flesh. At first, I clasped her hand as gently as one might a dove. Her fingers curled around mine and when our palms touched, I felt the heat of her blood. A moment later, I squeezed her gently and spread the wetness between us. And had I known what would happen in the next ten minutes, I would have never let go.

As we stepped before the podium, a moderator, a short, stocky man who I recognized from some interview show on the channels, pointed to a reporter in the crowd and asked for the first question.

– Nora, does that mean you're in love?

Her grip tightened around my fingers, and I imagined the question embarrassed her. In the delay before she replied, I wondered if I should speak for her, to defuse the awkwardness.

"Love is an important subject to ponder," she said into the pipe organ of microphones before us. After a sly glance toward me, she nodded once to the crowd to indicate that that was her answer.

– You were rumored to be involved with a robot. Is it true?

– Nora, do you cut yourself?

– Is your father on ARU?

The MC asked them to go one at a time, but questions came from every angle.

– Show us your hand again!

– Are you really a purebred, Michael?

– Do you endorse Hershey-Decker Industries whose ad you quoted?

– What are you planning for your wedding night?

– Nora, are you sterile from the 'Ceutical Wars?

– They say five women actually write *Pure H*. Think that's true?

– Doesn't your dad hate you, Michael?

– Did you two secretly marry last week?

– What's that blood thing mean?

"The blood *thing*," said Nora, emphasizing the word as if to mock the reporter's ignorance, "is just for Michael. I would never let someone touch my insides without feeling the enchantment I do toward him."

I loved her word *enchantment*. It felt mysterious and yet solid, as if carved from a block of fragrant eucalyptus. I knew I couldn't be more lucky and blessed, and tried to keep my eyes focused forward and clear, like a good foot soldier, but I could feel the saltwater rise. When I wiped my eyes with a handkerchief, more questions rained down on us despite the little man trying to maintain order.

"One at a time," he pleaded.

– Are you crying?

– Michael, when will you take over RiverGroup?

– Are those tears of love? Or is this another of your dad's crazy schemes?

– You're breaking a billion girls' hearts, Michael! Sure she's the one?

– Are you both virgins?

– Michael, they say you still secretly dance Bäng. Is it true?

– Nora, will your family company become a unit of RiverGroup or merge completely?

– Is your father's DNA mutated?

– What's it like to be with Michael Rivers?

– Have you two done it?

– Are those nude photos in *Sir Princess Zonk* really you, Nora?

– Will you deflower her at the product show?

– How much are you both worth?

We fielded the proper questions as best we could, but they kept coming faster and faster. Meanwhile, the moderator became so flustered, he started shouting. The reporters screamed back. I decided to try and calm the crowd and released Nora's hand. At first, our palms stuck, then the seal was broken. Stepping before the microphones, I raised my arms, and said, "Thank you, all." I tried to smile and say it nicely, but the mass of reporters began to push in on the barricades, and soon a dozen family police, in their protective orange satin suits, were pushing back. People started screaming. The next moment a fire burst out and someone was engulfed in flames.

Nora's attendants quickly covered her with a protective net and carried her off to her green and gold Loop limousine. I wanted to go after her, make sure she was okay, say goodbye, and gaze into her left eye so she would know that I felt precisely the same as her, but after I took one step, it felt like a knife stabbed my hand. The force whipped my arm backward and almost knocked me over. As I turned to see if one of the family security satins had accidentally hit me, I was surprised to see Joelene beside me, covered with a fine spray of blood.

Joelene was my tutor, my advisor, and my best friend. She was a good five inches shorter, with loose, curly, light brown hair, a slim mouth, and thin, amethyst eyes. "Joelene," I said, afraid the blood was hers. She had the strangest, saddest expression. "What's the matter?" I asked, as the pain in my hand turned white hot.

Besides Nora's blood that had dried in the wrinkles and creases of my palm, now a dot of my own blood welled up in the middle. For an instant, I thought it perfect and symmetrical. I glanced after Nora as if to show her, but when I turned my hand over, I saw that the back was bloody too.

The wound went all the way through as if I had been shot. I was about to ask Joelene what was going on, when my left hand was violently snapped backward and another spray of blood atomized in the air. I cried out because the pain was excruciating. Bones had been shattered and tendons severed.

Joelene's face was now covered with a heavy splatter and she was grimacing and blinking fast as if it had gotten in her eyes.

"I'm shot!" I said, pulling my hands toward my chest to try to comfort and protect them. How could this be happening? I was first son of RiverGroup, *the* security company.

"You'll be all right!" she said.

Before I could move, I felt a horrific stab in my right foot and screamed. Then I felt the same blast in my left. The tops of my shoes were cracked open like tiny bombs had gone off.

My knees buckled as my body felt clumsy and heavy. I shuffled forward trying to stay upright, but couldn't keep my balance. I began to fall and on the way down, felt someone try to grasp my waist. If there was an impact, I didn't feel it, but then my face was flat on the ground. The pain in my hands and feet burned like the white flame of a welding gun. The salty smell of blood filled my nose.

All around, I heard screams. Joelene shouted the word *ambulance* several times. A siren began to whine and at first it rose and fell like a perfectly formed and pure white sign wave. A moment later, though, the tone turned harsh and the smooth wave I had been imagining became rough and jagged. The siren began to fade, and the wave shrunk to a single point of green light. It held for a moment then disappeared.

Two

What appeared to be the same green dot hovered before me in a vast nothing, like a single jade-colored star in a night sky. I wasn't sure if just a few seconds, hours, or days had elapsed, but I felt I might be in a different place. Concentrating on the green point of light, I felt it was me or was just like me—a tiny entity in the middle of nothing. I wanted to reach out to it and comfort it, if such a thing were possible.

Then another green pinpoint of light emerged and gradually became as intense as the first. I felt glad because the first star wasn't alone. It had a companion.

Then a third dot appeared, and I hated it. I didn't want it to interfere. But soon more dots bloomed from the darkness. Clumps appeared, then dozens, and finally hundreds filled in. The first two were lost in an emerald cloud that looked like the vapors of a nebula. The cloud became opaque and filled my vision from top to bottom, left to right.

Without warning, slashes of yellow and gold cut the cloud to shreds. Molten masses of bloody reds and petroleum blacks bubbled up. The brutality and vividness frightened me, and from whatever state of sleep or dream I had been, my consciousness rose a level.

The mass of glowing dots was actually a huge screen hovering inches above my nose. From the black a lavender froth emerged and then hundreds of orange abscesses erupted like a disease.

"No," I said, squinting into the blinding light, "stop!"

Grape vortexes swallowed up the orange and vomited acid greens.

"Relax, Mr. Rivers," said an amplified voice.

"Get this thing away of me!" I said. My fingers touched cold metal as I tried to push the screen away, but couldn't budge it.

"Quiet please. And do not touch the equipment."

"Where am I? Where's Nora?" The greens mutated into a brittle red, like a giant scab. I slapped the screen and the pain in my hand jarred me further awake.

This was color therapy! Father ranted about how wonderful it was. I was in some sort of a hospital or spa—which explained the medicinal and alcohol tinge in the air—being exposed to the glaring horrors of photochromism. Then I fully woke, and as if remembering who I was, closed my right eye. The atrocious hues became a thousand soothing shades of grey.

"Mr. Rivers," said the voice, "open both eyes. The therapy will be more effective! Mr. Rivers do as you're told. Open your right eye, please."

The giant screen slowly faded to black and pulled away. I relaxed. At least I didn't feel like it was suffocating me.

Footsteps approached. A bald man in a long emerald coat appeared beside me. I could see thick black hair in his nostrils. Leaning down, he peered into my right eye with a lit device. "Tsk!" he said, as if admonishing me. "Burning the cones is illegal."

Only those few who are fully committed to grey have the procedure. Last year, without my father's knowledge, I found a neuro-ophthalmologist in Saru Pauro who performed the delicate operation. While I lay sedated, a microscopic sodium laser destroyed all the cones in my right retina. When I healed and the bandages were removed, my right eye, with only its rods intact, perceived nothing but the creamiest black, white, and grey.

I told the man with the hairy nose, "I want out of here." Instead of answering, he examined my left hand with another device. "Where's Nora?" I asked. "Is she all right? What happened?"

"All I know," he said, still peering through his contraption, "is that the bullets were also illegal. Curiously, they released drugs that healed the wounds they caused." He eyed me angrily, as if all of these infractions were my fault.

As he moved to my feet and examined them, I sat up and saw that I was naked except for a green cloth with some complicated orange and gold logo that covered my crotch. "Where am I?" I demanded. "Where are my clothes?"

Touching his ear, he seemed to listen to something. "Someone is here to see you." With that he headed across a yellow floor so polished it looked like he was walking on his upside-down twin. The room was round and the walls were covered with enormous photos of people who looked like they were in terrible pain. He exited through a door covered with the face of a woman whose mouth was wide open and had blood splattered over her forehead and cheeks.

"Can you bring my clothes?" He disappeared through the bloody woman's face without acknowledging me. "Hello? My clothes please!" Shouting drained me. I felt dizzy and flopped back. I would rest for a moment, I told myself, then get up, and find my way out of here.

The door opened. I expected the man with my clothes, but Joelene and her upside-down yellow twin came in. Both wore long dark coats, high-necked shirts, and held bundles under their right arms. Her change of clothes made me wonder how long I had been here. I was going to ask, but when she came to the side of my bed, I saw tears in her eyes.

"You look good," she said, suppressing a sob. "I have your clothes."

Joelene had never cried before. She had always been strong and efficient. As she laid out a slim, silk-goat wool charcoal suit, a pressed, white cotton shirt, black briefs and socks, and a new pair of shoes, I asked, "What's the matter?"

She shook her head. "I'm sorry to see you like this." Her violet eyes met mine, and then she glanced down at her hands. "I'm very sorry."

"Thank you," I said, touched. "Is Nora okay?"

"Everyone is fine." She straightened the collar of the jacket. "Healthwise." Running a finger over the fabric, she added, "Isé–B ironed this for you." Isé–B was my favorite competitive ironer. The shirt was beautifully done, and while I could see his trademark creases, I felt she was avoiding something.

"Healthwise?" I asked, worried that there was something else.

She shook her head quickly, and said, "Last night millions of girls held a candlelight vigil. They're drawing pink dots on their hands and feet." Her smile lasted for an instant and then a melancholy returned. I could see circles beneath her eyes, and her cheeks paled. However long I had been here, she had probably been awake, gathering information, answering questions, and figuring out what to do. "You and RiverGroup are the only news on the channels."

"But what happened?"

"It was a breach."

Every six months or so a bomb exploded in a distant hospital, a little-known CEO was kidnapped, or an illegal blimp was shot down in Europa-9. But breaches rarely happened to the strongest families, and they never happened to RiverGroup. We were the ones who established all identities and kept track of all the information. I said, "That can't be."

"The gunman … " she began, her finger still traveling back and forth on the collar of the shirt, "was … a … freeboot."

Freeboots had been the worst outlaws. They were people—if you could call them that—who didn't have identities, names, families, numbers, papers, or anything. When I was a boy, new stories of them popping up in boardrooms and bedrooms circulated weekly. "But aren't they all gone now?"

"Despite the official declarations," she said, "they exist. I doubt there are more than a hundred, but it's impossible to tell. They live off the system, completely beyond the laws. Forty years ago, though, they helped defeat the Pharmaceutical Warlords and allowed the families to take control of the cities. At that time they were admired. They were the artisans of anarchy." She stopped fiddling with my shirt, straightened, and faced me. "The slubbers and the warlords are the official enemy, but the freeboots are worst. And from all the information I've been able to gather, I believe your shooting was an act of retaliation."

"What did I do?"

"I don't think it was about you in particular—although RiverGroup's role in security and identity is fundamental to the families—you were just a high-level target in retribution for a series of fierce attacks on the freeboots last year." She exhaled and her eyes fell again. "I am sorry."

"Well," I said, not quite sure what all of this meant besides a huge nuisance, "what happened to the freeboot?"

"At first, the reports were that the freeboot was killed by family satins, but now it seems he escaped."

"How?"

She shook her head. "They're very elusive. And no one was prepared."

Whipping a hand around the room—the awful images and the now black therapy screen, I said, "I want out of here. I want to see Nora."

She didn't move.

I waited several seconds for her to speak then began to panic. "She wasn't shot was she? Please don't tell me that!"

"No! She's fine. She's perfectly fine … " Her voice trailed off. Joelene was not usually this reticent.

"Is there something bad?"

She took a breath, looked me in the eyes, and said, "The marriage is off."

My marriage to Nora was to signify the merger between RiverGroup and her family's company, MKG. Father had invented the scheme a couple of months ago. Although RiverGroup was still number one, we were losing customers because we hadn't introduced anything new in years and our market share had slipped to just below fifty percent. Our biggest rival, MKG, had an innovative approach, and Father's idea was that together, RiverGroup and MKG would dominate the market. As for me: I didn't care for business, or code, or promotions, or money, or any of it. And in the beginning, I didn't want anything to do with his marriage-merger scheme, but when Joelene and I began to research Nora, I couldn't believe how intelligent, beautiful, and serene she was. And then we met and I learned that she was colorless, that she was the epicenter of grey, that she was my conclusion. "Well," I said, saddened, but not devastated, "that's not good, but when can I see her?"

"The marriage-merger is off," she repeated.

"I heard you! I just want to see her as soon as I can."

She spoke slowly, as if reluctant. "You cannot."

"I have to see her!" I laughed because I was so unused to Joelene not understanding. "Marriage or not. Nora and I are one. You saw what she did with her hand. We're grey. We're perfect together!"

"Let's get you dressed," she said, with a sigh. "We're going to meet your father back at the company compound."

"I demand to see her immediately!"

"The merger is off!" She spoke louder than she ever had before. An instant later, I thought she was going to cry again. "Sorry," she said, dabbing her eyes, "I didn't mean to raise my voice. It's just very difficult. And please understand that we won't be able to monitor her on the channels, send messages, or communicate in any way. Her family's company is now RiverGroup's enemy."

When what she said sunk in, I felt like I might weep. I had survived the bullets, only to find my world ruined. An old photo[S7] from *Pure H* came to mind. It was of a man suspended in a vat of clear balls and his whole body was held in place and dimpled like a giant golf ball.

"I'm very sorry, Michael," she said, softly. She started to reach toward my foot, as if to stroke it, but then pulled back, probably because I was still undressed. "Listen," she continued, "after such a devastating security breach, MKG can't merge with us. It would be a public relations disaster. Frankly, RiverGroup is in great trouble. The company's stock has fallen from 63,000 a share to less than 300. We're teetering on collapse." After pursing her lips, she added, "As for MKG, there is no communication between the two family companies. Nora's father, Mr. Gonzalez-Matsu, held a press conference just minutes ago and announced their new direction."

I met Nora's father for a few seconds before our train-date. He was like my father—one of those loud, old-fashioned men who was almost impossible to embarrass, obsessed with volume, speed, money, and the culmination of everything bright, garish, and vulgar. He wore a glowing violet suit, a shirt that blinked green and gold, and large, gold, oil-burning earrings that left smoke contrails when he moved.

"He did this!" I said, sure. "Before we got on the Bee Train, I bowed my head to him, but he just glared back like he hates me. *He* had the freeboot shoot me!"

"I don't see it," she said, shaking her head. "There must be a weakness in RiverGroup security code. After all, it is supposed to track and monitor information that should have prevented this very thing."

Slapping a hand onto the bed, I said, "I just want Nora."

Joelene lifted my legs and spun me on my butt like a mother maneuvering a baby. Picking up the black underwear, she said, "Your tailor has improved the cloth's temperature control system." Joelene slipped my underwear over my left foot and then the right.

"No, it can't be," I said, imagining Nora floating away.

"It can change from indoor temperatures to outdoor heat in one point three seconds," she continued. "That's a third of last year's model, and for the wearer, it means complete comfort."

She sounded like a brochure. Respectfully turning her head, she pulled up the shorts and simultaneously flicked the color spa's green logo-cloth away. "He's also improved the wrinkle control."

"I want to see Nora!" I said, as if mounting one last attack. "I want to be with her, Joelene, I have to see her now!"

She glanced toward the system camera in the far corner of the room. "We're going to survive," she said, soothingly. "Things will work out, Michael. I promise."

Although I didn't know how things could work without Nora, I trusted Joelene. She was the reason I was in a position to meet Nora and understand her significance and brilliance. Until my heart attack when I was fourteen, I was barely a person, let alone a fashionable and grey one. Until then, I danced at the PartyHaus every night before the cameras and what were said to be ten billion fans. Then, on one particular Saturday night, while performing my famous routine, I died.

Wearing gold leaf pants and a hunter green, sheer shirt with gold epithets and ice buttons, I rode an elevator to the center of the polished dance floor. When a spotlight hit me, I began by slowly raising my hands and face to the burning light.

As the massive crowd cheered, the DJ transitioned to my anthem, *Adjoining Tissue*, by HammørHêds. During the intro, I rolled my arms, legs, and head like I was a bit of seaweed undulating in a gentle current. It was a tease and the tens of thousands of partiers on the fifteen balconies of the PartyHaus knew it. They screamed my name as if they couldn't wait. Finally, when the cannon drums started firing, I began.

Back then I had a choreographer, two wardrobe consultants, several hair and makeup stylists, and a team of strength and agility trainers. Because of the forces from the massive, fifty-foot Cold-Flame speakers on the dance floor, the untrained were regularly knocked unconscious, maimed, and even killed by the percussive blasts. I had mastered the beats like a karate-surfer riding tsunami waves.

In my routine, I did splits, hand-twirls, punch backs, double-triples, and my own triple and a half front. Before *Adjoining Tissue* finished, the DJ started transitioning into *Kuts* by Dr. Ooooo. The FX for this part of the routine called for a shower of razors, like deadly snowflakes from far above, and as I deftly avoided them both in the air and on the floor, a few other brave partiers began to join me.

One, a young woman known as Elinor W, wore a brilliant blue costume that covered her from head to toe except for cutouts for her eyes, chest, and crotch. I remember how she got into her groove, then looked up to smile at me. In that split second, she lost her concentration, and like an ax cleaving a block of wood, a razor sliced into her left eye. She screamed and fell as more razors lodged into her legs and body. I continued my program while paramedics dragged her away.

When I think of myself back then, especially, how I didn't even slow my routine for an instant, let alone stop to help, I can see how hollow and unhappy I was—a boy who was very good at one thing, but derived no pleasure from it. Worse, down deep I think I despised the world that adored me, as I was little more than a marionette in Father's marketing schemes.

But soon after Elinor W was taken away, something happened. What I like to think is that the guilt and self-hate built up so much in my chest that my heart began to seize. In the middle of *Engraved Blööd* by The Bürning Spines, the ice buttons had melted and my shirt hung open, revealing my puffed chest. Admiring dancers surrounded me like worker bees. Each time a drop of sweat flew from my forehead or torso, they dropped to the floor, and shoved and pushed for the chance to lick it up.

The first sensation of my heart attack was in my jaw. A strange, cool numbness made my teeth buzz, but I ignored it and figured it was the strength drugs or some odd harmonic from the speakers. But gradually, the coldness traveled into my eyes and brain like a slow, thick liquid. Then the chill traveled into my arms and legs and turned dark and leaden. I slowed, lost my rhythm, and one of the beats slammed into me hard. I tried to regain my groove, but was knocked back and forth like a pinball. As I lost consciousness, the colored lights high above grew so bright they seemed to shine through my skin and into my emptiness.

They say the crowd rose to their feet and screamed in adulation, until they realized that toppling over backward and slamming my skull on the floor wasn't my newest move.

Two days later, when I woke, I heard a tremendous cheer and slowly realized that I was in a hospital bed, in the middle of the dance floor, and that the place was packed with ten thousand watching my every twitch. I had never felt so vulnerable and exposed. I insisted that I be taken away. My house was quickly reconstructed, made quiet and dim. The silence felt good, so I told my choreographers, stylists, consultants, and trainers to leave me. I lay in bed and did nothing. One of the doctors, concerned about my low spirits, brought me a magazine. I remember paging through the thing, at first fascinated, since I had never seen one before. Gradually, though, I became discouraged and angry as I couldn't read a word or even recognize a single character.

I decided I had to read and begged for a tutor. Father refused because he wanted me to resume dancing as soon as I could, but when my body wouldn't respond to the healing drugs, he acquiesced, if only to shut me up.

All of the candidates came in party clothes—feathered shoes, fog bras, chrome nose-plates, gelatin shirts. I liked them all, then at the end of the second day, a woman with violet eyes came in a dark tailored suit, a shirt that matched her eyes, and black shoes with tiny grey stitches around the slender sole. I laughed since I had never seen anyone dressed so drearily. Maybe it was impish curiosity, but instead of telling her to go, I let her answer the interview questions like everyone else.

All the party people I knew were full of bombast, like Father. They shouted and swore, bragged and boasted. Joelene did none of that. Instead, she spoke softly, but with a fluid and powerful ease. At the time, I felt like I had discovered a new type of human. I hired her because she fascinated me, and I knew she would irritate Father.

Two years later, I could read and felt like I was becoming a person. Then she introduced me to *Pure H* and everything changed again.

Published every other month, the magazine is one-half meter square and printed on the most luscious and expensive paper made. It is a joy to touch and hold. But the most extraordinary thing about the magazine is that one anonymous person produces it. Although I'd heard speculation about who he might be, I preferred to enjoy his art without worrying about identity. He photographed every photo. He wrote all the copy. And each issue was a complex puzzle to be savored and deciphered.

I became grey. I began listening to the silence DJs, like Love Emitting Diode, Huush, and ZZZ. I discovered my tailor, Mr. Cedar, and began wearing grey frocks, vests, and suits made of colorless moon and satellite wool. And by then Father and I had come to hate each other.

"Look at these creases," said Joelene, as she held up the gen-cotton shirt. Indeed, it was beautifully ironed. And at the bottom of the right tail was Isé–B's fanciful signature of wrinkles.

"Generous of him," I said, as I put out my right arm. While I loved it, it was small consolation for all that had happened.

"Patience." She added, "*Miniature city flickers.*"

The photo[R5] that accompanied that copy was of a translucent house at the edge of a dark, piney wood. A woman stands in a clearing. Her twisted hair is powdered a light grey, and her ball gown by H. Trow is a beautiful alpaca-silk and platinum draped creation that creates a perfect hourglass. Her face is young and fresh. Her eyes are tart, her lips, moist. Something about her posture—the way her back is arched, her legs bent—makes her look burdened with melancholy, perhaps even pain.

When I first saw the image, I thought a spotlight or some

illumination was creating a halo around her, but as I studied the print I decided that it wasn't just light but flame. The delicate corona that surrounded her looked exactly like the nearly invisible flames of an alcohol fire, and I decided that the photo[R5] was taken the split second before the heat began to singe her hair, skin, and eyes.

Behind her, beyond the translucent wall, stands a man in a black suit and black tie. Although the details are hazy, clearly he is facing toward her. But the way he holds his head both cocked to the right and angled too high, he appears at once blind and yet cognizant of her. At first I assumed he was her killer, but after careful study, decided he was her lover and that he too is dying. His right hand is the clue. His fingers are tense and gnarled in what seems like both grief and regret. On the floor beside him are several sharp dark shapes, like shards of a glass. He drank poison and dropped the glass as the toxins had not only immediately blinded him, but have begun to astringe his veins and muscles, moving from his extremities toward his heart.

When I had finally deciphered the photo[R5], I sat and stared at it for a long time, frightened and disturbed. I discussed it with Joelene, and she explained that it was about the beautiful inevitability of entropy, the wilting of flowers, the browning of leaves, the cooling of cream coffees, the fading of color. Then I understood that I, too, appreciated these things. I sought them out and savored them. But as Joelene slipped the jacket over my shoulders, and I felt the servomotors create perfect folds and wrinkles as I moved, I knew I could never appreciate a world without Nora.

Three

Joelene and I rode back around the globe to the RiverGroup family compound in the speeding silver teardrop that was my limousine. For the first few minutes, I reviewed the post-date interviews, but soon, I switched off the screen and stared out the window at the scenery rushing by. But that motion reminded me of the Bee Train and of my last date with Nora, so I closed my eyes.

"Nora is at Slate Gardens," said Joelene. "For cold baths, mud, and mourning."

I refused to look at the photos or her family's publicity release. Joelene read part of it aloud, and it sounded like something a phalanx of lawyers had produced. I counted the word *regrettably* five times.

As the car exited the Loop, the super highway that only the upper echelon of the families could use, and we wound our way through the baking desert southwest, my feelings shifted from despair to anger. Of course it wasn't Mr. Gonzalez-Matsu, nor was it as Joelene had said, a terrible and inopportune breach. It was Father! It was his ineptitude, his incompetence, and his dreadful strategies. Like so much of what had gone wrong in my nineteen years, it was all his fault.

The access road began to rise above the garish city of Ros Begas, into the Rockies where a valley had been dug in a mountain and the RiverGroup compound had been built. Just as the car came to the top of the lip and started down, a ray of sunlight glinted off the huge glass dome that protected the buildings from the sun, the insects, and the carbon dioxide. Beneath stood the dozen mismatched buildings that made up our little city. Some were windowless warehouses with flat roofs. Several were covered with wooden shingles as if they were trying to be old-fashioned ski lodges. Around the edge were smaller office buildings. Most were glass; a few had metal skins, one was stone. Dead center, sat the black and gold, now abandoned, PartyHaus, with its wide stairs, Ionic columns, and crumbling friezes.

As the car slowed before the garage, I could see attendants, cooks, maids, and workers running toward us. Some were wailing and crying as if I were a coffin containing myself. They clustered around the car, and as I exited, I said, "Thank you. I'm fine. I'm fine, everyone."

Joelene jumped in front to shield me as a tall orange family satin with a golden visor subdued a maid who was tearing off her clothes to expose a complicated set of sharp-looking bands and wires across her chest and crotch. "I'm the one, Michael. It's me. I'm the one who really loves you!"

Years ago, when I danced, I told myself I enjoyed these hopeless displays, like the time an army of teenage girls, dressed in lanolin wools, marched up from the valley, surrounded the compound and demanded all my dancing outfits, toiletries, shaven hairs, and a week's worth of excretions. Now, all of it embarrassed me. As the woman was taken away, Joelene and I hurried in the other direction to my building.

Before my heart attack, my house had been rather like an enormous egg carton inside, with a dozen different rooms. The floors of each room were speaker heads and the place reverberated day and night with heavy bone-jarring thuds and squealing highs. Besides the music, each room was decorated with a theme, like the blinding red light room and the dead lamb room. When I demanded to be taken from the PartyHaus to somewhere quiet and dim, the place had been gutted. Over time, I had decorated and now it had polished muslin walls, black iron floor tiles, and just a few upholstered pieces sat here and there. Two surveillance cameras, little more than black bugs, were mounted on the walls. And while they were there for my safety, I had positioned my bed, desk, and couch out of their range.

Once we were inside and Joelene had shut the cast-iron front door, I felt like I wanted to get in bed and bury myself beneath a hundred layers of wool. I started toward my bed only to jump back in surprise. My mother lay there.

She was a few years younger than father and had at least as much surgery, but seemed older. Her skin was dark and had a leathery quality. Last time I saw her, a year ago, her hair had been long, straight, and hung to her waist. This time it was frizzed like a giant tumble weed and dyed a hundred different colors. Her robe of a dress looked like something a cavewoman would wear. Made of a patchwork of small tanned pelts, I could see tiny rat claws here and there. The bones in her face were beautiful and proud, but now she looked like a former beauty queen who had been forced to fend for herself in the wilderness.

While I felt bad for her, and I had tried not to let Father's poisoned opinion influence me, I distrusted her. Every time I saw her, she wanted something. And not just that, but she always got shrill and hysterical like her generation.

"Thank goodness you're ok!" she said, as she leaped up and came toward me with open arms. "You have to leave," she said, as she hugged me. She smelled of barbecue smoke and soap. "Leave before it's too late."

"Mrs. Rivers-Zssne," said Joelene, pulling Mother's arms from me. "I don't believe you're authorized to be here today."

Mother stepped back and glared at my advisor with her wide, fearsome sage-colored eyes. "I am!"

"May I see your pass, please?"

"A mother needs a pass to come and hug her son! And to

think that we were supposed to be the perfect family. What a lie it all was!"

"Regardless," said Joelene, smiling stiffly, "I must see your pass."

As embarrassed as I felt for my mother, my advisor was right—especially after a terrible security breach.

While glaring at me as if this were my doing, Mother pulled a card from her pouch. Somehow she'd been able to bend the hard plastic. After straightening the crease, Joelene checked her screens. "It *was* valid," she said. "It expired one hour ago."

"I spoke to his father," said Mother, trilling her fingers dismissively. "He said I could have a word with my poor, injured son."

Joelene handed back the pass. "No disrespect, but you did not speak directly to his father, and we are extremely busy. Additionally, I would advise you to hurry if you want to, wisely, avoid Mr. Rivers senior."

"If you don't mind!" bristled Mother. "A moment, please."

Joelene didn't blink. "If you're asking to be alone with Michael, I'm afraid that won't be possible."

I wanted to tell Joelene that it wasn't necessary, that I'd be fine, but I knew she wasn't going to budge. She probably felt responsible for the freeboot's bullets.

"It's okay," I told Mother, "we can talk. She's family."

Mother's face paled; her mouth shrunk to a dot. "Don't confuse family. *She* is not your family. She never will be. Your real family loves you. And they desperately need you," she said, her tone shifting into her familiar pleading. "They're waiting to meet you. They've been waiting for so long. It just breaks my heart." Mother covered her face and began to sob. "I'm so sorry for everything! I'm so sorry!"

"I feel fine." I held out my hands with their tiny scars for her to see. "I'm healthy." I thought that was the answer to the question she hadn't asked.

Mother wiped her face, glared at Joelene, and hugged me

again. I put my arms around her and, up close, I could see that a multitude of tiny metal and glass charms had been woven into her rainbow hair: birds, hearts, aphids, cars, sunglasses, phalluses, and what looked like a tiny caribou stared back at me.

"You really must leave," she said, sniffing. "It's not good here. It's all about the wrong things, and your father uses everyone and anyone he can. Look what's happened to you." She took my left hand in hers and rubbed my palm with her thumbs.

"It was a random breach. I'm perfectly fine." The words came off my tongue too easily and I regretted that I was, after two minutes, trying to appease her so she'd leave.

"Come with me," she whispered. "Come be part of Tanoshi No Wah."

"Ma'am," said Joelene, stiffly, "please."

"We live honestly, and we're not ashamed," continued Mother. "We show ourselves. And I'd love for you to see who you really are."

"Please," said Joelene, raising her voice.

"The families and their laws are pollution to the human spirit. They're all hypocrites! We're trying to do what's right."

"Mrs. Rivers, we're late for an appointment!"

"Think about it, Michael. You're not part of this anymore. You've changed from the beast you were. Change a little more, and you'll see what I mean. Come with me."

I couldn't imagine her life in the slubs, eating grilled rats, living in tents. In the shows, she sang, stripped nude, and ate fire, I'd heard. "I found someone." I said, not sure if she knew of Nora. "I'm in love."

She shook her head frantically, but one of the charms in her hair spun around and hit her on the nose. "Trust me," she said, grimacing and rubbing the spot. "There's nothing to love in the families. They're evil and ruthless. They're all dead lumps of stolen flesh! Come with me. You need to find your real family."

By now, Joelene's face turned red. "Mrs. Rivers, I'm warning you!"

"Please, Michael!" She put her hands on my shoulders. "It's time you came home. They're waiting. They adore you. And you'd make such a lovely addition. You could dance with us."

That was the worse thing she could have suggested. "Mother," I said, squirming away. "You know I don't dance anymore."

"Fine!" she said, angrily. "Don't dance!"

"It's time for you to go," said Joelene.

Mother combed her hair from her face and regained her composure. "I always thought you would be a poet. A lovely poet. But you don't have to do anything in the show. You could be my assistant. Wouldn't that be nice? You could hold my clothes while I strip."

"Mother!" I said, flummoxed. "I don't want to perform. I don't want you doing it either!"

"Mrs. Rivers," said Joelene, wedging herself between us. "Leave now, or I'll be forced to call security."

"Michael, come and find out who you are."

"That's it!" Joelene pushed mother backward. "You must go now."

"How dare you touch me! You're just like all of them. You're sucking his blood. You're just using his talent and fame!" Mother had that crazy look in her eyes. A second later she clenched her fists and lunged at Joelene as if to pummel her. Joelene was stronger and knew the fighting arts. In one second, she had Mother in a headlock and called the satins.

"Let go of me, you bitch!" screamed Mother. "Let Michael come with me and find out the truth!"

"Mother!" I said, wishing she wouldn't be like this. "I know the truth."

"Let go!" she said, thrashing in Joelene's grip. "Let go or I'll bite."

Two especially tall, satin beasts, with angular but impassive faces, rushed in and grabbed her. One held her arms; the other,

her legs, and they carried her out as if they were dealing with so much meat.

"Get these things off of me!" she shrieked.

"Joelene's only trying to protect me," I said, as they came to the door.

"Your father is a mutation!" she screamed. "Ask him what that means! Ask him!"

The door slammed shut.

Plopping onto my grey wool couch, I slumped forward and told myself that I hated her. Every time I saw her, she wound up screaming and ranting. I had the worst parents. They were loud, obnoxious, selfish, and awful.

Joelene sat beside me and stroked my shoulder. "Eventually," she said, "we *will* talk with her. She is a good person. It's circumstance."

"I don't want to see her ever again."

Joelene's hand slid off my back. "Judith Rivers-Zssne," she pronounced Mother's name slowly as if she were going to define the words, "has led a difficult life. As have all the women who have been with your father. I know she loves you, but she expected too much from her marriage and ... " After she glanced at me gently, she said, "She probably thought you would save her."

"Me?" I asked, as if it were absurd. "From what?"

"Unhappiness," she said, staring into space. Her eyes found mine. With a shrug, she added, "Years ago, your mother tried to fight the system. She petitioned the families to let her change her identity. Of course, they refused, as that's wholly illegal—tantamount to treason. Since then, she's done the best she can."

I didn't want to think about Mother and her problems. I didn't want her in my bed when I came home, and I certainly didn't want her asking me to hold her clothes while she stripped. I said, "She scares me."

Joelene folded her hands in her lap and tilted her head in just that way she had when regurgitating her facts. "Reports indicate that she's taking a combination of self-administered color therapy and an illegal and powerful painkiller, strengthener, and mood shaper: ARU."

"ARU?"

"Actually, it's an amazing and useful drug." She frowned. "The families have exaggerated the dangers of everything the 'Ceutical Warlords make. Whatever else they are, the slub rulers are masters of biochemistry." I thought she was going to continue in that vein, but she shrugged. "In any case, your mother's group, Tanoshi No Wah, is losing money. You would be a huge draw, of course."

"Everyone just wants to use me," I complained.

She pursed her lips as if she were going to speak, but stood abruptly. "We have a meeting."

Instead of being driven to the business building across the compound, Joelene suggested we walk along the oxygen gardens and the reflecting pool. It sounded like a good idea, but the temperature-regulated air and the filtered sunlight didn't lift my spirits. Instead, I felt crushed under the vast, ashen sky. While nothing that had happened was Mother's fault, her tantrum made me feel doomed. I would never escape my family. I would never escape their wishes and their desires for me. As we approached the wood-shingled office building, I asked Joelene, "Why?" knowing she would understand.

She stopped before the door and spoke quietly as if telling a secret. "I have diverted some of your discretionary funds to Tanoshi No Wah to try and help your mother and her friends. They have a lot of medical needs, and I believe they're poorly managed. It's the best we can do now."

I didn't even know I had discretionary funds. "But why is she with a carnival in the slubs? Why did she leave us for that?" I felt she did it to embarrass me, like everything else she did.

Joelene glanced to her right as if she were trying to think what to say, but then she stood there, as if momentarily transfixed.

I turned to see that she was staring at the PartyHaus. At one time it had been the crown jewel of the compound, but now its black and gold Rococo façade was matted with dirt and dust. From the roof were long, pale green lines of oxidation. And at the top of the stairs, the enormous front doors were splattered with droppings as thousands of birds had made nests in the intricately carved fornicating animals. It was a combination disco, hotel, brothel, and amusement park where I had spent the nights of my youth at one hundred and fifty beats per minute.

When Joelene's eyes met mine, I felt that we both had the same mood: a nebulous sense of defeat, under-painted with the caustic dread of seeing Father.

Finally, she nodded toward the door. We entered the building, and found meeting theater five. The three-hundred-seat auditorium was empty, dark, and cold. Joelene located the controls, and as she turned on house lights, I sat in one of the orange, over-stuffed chairs toward the front. Above the stage hung an enormous, glowing estimator clock—a family antique. Across the top it read: Hiro Bruce Rivers Arrival Time. Below were the stylized, red numbers.

"Joelene," I said, at once relieved and annoyed to see that it read: one hour and thirty-three minutes. "I'm not waiting."

"That can't be right," she muttered as she opened a screen and checked with his people. "They say five or ten."

As if the estimator clock had heard, the glowing numbers on the clock's face flickered then read fourteen minutes eighty-one seconds and began counting down.

"The freeboot who shot you," said Joelene, reading from her screen, "is suspected to have been from Antarctica. The family council reports that the medicated bullets were prototypes stolen in Europa two weeks ago. They suspected he was a lone gunman. What little has been discovered suggests that he trafficked contraband including ARU AND other pain caustics."

The details of my shooting bored me. They changed nothing. They brought Nora no closer. "What does Father want?" I asked, not sure I wanted to know.

"We'll cover your health, debrief your date and the aftermath. He may want to strategize. And it's possible he might apologize." Joelene shrugged as if to say the last was unlikely.

"It's his fault!" I said.

"It's no one's."

"He ruined the company."

"That," she said, stretching the word, "is a different issue."

"So, it is his fault. RiverGroup should have protected me! That's failure. It was the most important day of my life! The most important moment in history! Just when everything was so perfect!" I put my head in my hands. As much as I detested everything that had happened, I hated to whine like a spoiled child. The clock's numbers twinkled, and now it read fourteen days, five hours, and sixty-three seconds. "Look at that," I said, standing, "he's not coming."

"Wait," said Joelene as the lights sputtered and blinked. Then it said five seconds. Four seconds. Three seconds. I flopped backward into the chair. An instant later, though, the clock read five minutes and was counting up.

"This is impossible!"

The clock numbers flashed, then spun backward again to four seconds. Three seconds. It skipped two and stayed on one for half a minute.

Just as I gave up and started to stand again, the house lights went black. An announcer's voice boomed, "Straight from the highest profit quarter on record, President, CEO, CFO, COO, CIO, CPO, Chief Programmer, and all-around Super Code Bastard, give it up for Hiro Bruce Rivers!"

As a catastrophically loud drumbeat kicked in, and we covered our ears, orange and blue fireworks exploded across the front of the stage. At the back, a figure rose from the floor before a giant vibrating blue RiverGroup logo. For several beats, he stood there, his head down, his arms flexed, as if posing like a monster wrestler.

When a throbbing, super-deep bass and a whining singer, who sounded like he was either in a state of ecstasy or dreadful constipation, started, Father came to life. He jogged forward and pumped his fists victoriously. A spotlight came on as a cast-iron phallus-shaped podium rose to meet him at the front of the stage. Horns and guitars blasted, the voices wailed, and I thought I heard the words *cunt spaceship.*

Now Father sashayed back and forth with exactly the same moves he'd been doing for years—a combination of pelvis thrusts, head bobs, and a lot of sliding to and fro on his foot-tall, green-glass platform shoes.

"Slap me! Slap me hard!" he cried as the music—apparently his latest anthem—ebbed away. "That's *You're My Cunt Spaceship* by TastyLüng," he announced, beaming his smile toward the back of the amphitheater as though the house were full. His grin slowly waned in the silence. Leaning forward, he peered into the darkness. "Hello?" he asked, as if afraid he was alone. "What the hell? Anyone out there?"

I was tempted to say nothing, hope he would decide the place was empty, and go away. Instead, I said, "You ruined everything!"

His eyes darted toward me. "I'd like to fire the whole fucked-up piece of fucking shit company!" First he threw a stack of papers into the air, then hugged the podium and thrust his hips into it. "We're fucked! What do you want me to tell you? It was the weirdest and worst possible thing at the worst possible moment." Papers rained down on his head as he implored, "How we gave a fucking freeboot an identity and let him right in the middle of our fucking press conference, I have no fucking idea!"

"It's your fault!"

"Me?" He laughed. "We had everything nailed down—everything completely checked, then out of nowhere—wham! A fucking freeboot with a fashion rifle. And I thought you were dead when you fell over! That was fucking scary. That was shit-in-thong time! And why he shoots your hands and feet, I don't know. Nothing makes any fucking sense! We've been checking everything, but I can't find any answers." As if he were shouting at the world, he tilted his head back and cried, "Fucking freeboots!"

My father was an inch shorter than I, but he still worked the machines so his arms where bulky, his legs, sculpted, and his neck, thick. His clothes were as putrid as his taste in music. Today, he wore a long, tailed, green-plaid jacket over a vibrating orange and black shirt, long blue pants with little video screens all over, and the aforementioned platforms. As for his hair, he dyed it dark brown and had it permed into a tight Afro. It looked exactly like moist chocolate cake.

His hairdresser, Xavid, with his snow-capped hairdo and huge square glasses, came running onto the stage, and began to gather up the fallen papers and hand them to Father. Xavid then quickly patted Father's Afro here and there and headed off.

"Anyway, I feel for you, son! I do. I was watching that date—and holy fucking shit was it boring—but whatever! I was there with my girls, my snacks, and we were all cheering and going on, and then I couldn't fucking believe a freeboot! They should all be rounded up and fried in oil! Motherfuckers."

"They're off the system," said Joelene, with surprising annoyance. "That's why they can't be located and *rounded up*, as you say."

Father leaned far forward and squinted. "You're here, too? Jesus fuckercakes, Michael! Can't you fart without her anymore?" He smacked his face with one of his thick hands. "God, son, what do you have in your ball sack? Muffins?"

"I want Nora back," I said.

He shook his head. "You know what I think of MKG, Mr. Gonzalez-Matsu, and that Nora—who, I have to say, seems like the biggest priss hole in the universe? They can suck one of my anal enchiladas!"

"Don't say that. I love her!"

"I don't know why. She's as dull as skim milk!"

I hated his relentless verbal attacks. "You never understand."

"Thankfully!" he muttered. "Anyway, glad to see you're better. That color-therapy blasts, doesn't it?" He paused, as if waiting for me to agree, then shrugged. "Anyway, believe me, someone was behind that shooting. There are too many things that don't make sense. Like where are the bullets and how in the hell he could shoot the top of your feet?"

"The freeboots," said Joelene, "despite the families' miserable view on them, do have some highly advanced weaponry."

Thrusting his pelvis, Father said, "My highly advanced weapon can't pee around a corner!"

"The commission is looking into the possibility of guided and disintegrating munitions."

Father threw his hands into the air. "Anyway! It was a total disaster. Especially for us, because we're the idiots who are supposed to keep track of those maggots. But forget all that crap for a second. We have to act before the company goes down the toilet, and I've got something lard." Stepping to the edge of the stage, he turned to the wings and hollered, "Watch this dismount!" Until then, I hadn't noticed his film crew, but there, in the shadows at the edge of the stage, stood his silvery-haired director and the cameraman. Father had everything recorded for an auto-documentary that he was always reediting. Last time he screened it, it was five hundred hours long. Next to the crew stood his hairdresser and his assistant, Ken Goh, who wore his usual loyalty-proving orange and blue face paint.

Then Father jumped from the stage, landed on his green glass platforms, and proclaimed, "Still got it!" Snapping his fingers, he bellowed, "House lights!" He swiveled one of the other chairs around, and plopped down. "First, a few announcements." Nodding toward his hairdresser he said, "I just promoted Ken to Financial Distribution Officer and Chief of Positives. And Xavid, who shows lots of ambition, will be our new Chief Financial

Officer, Chief Operations Officer, and Chief of Brains. Take a bow, guys!"

Ken gave two thumbs up and winked at father. His hairdresser bent at the waist. When he straightened he smiled, rolled his eyes up in his amber lenses, and said, "I'm just so fucking smart, aren't I!"

Father laughed. "Oh yeah, tell the world! Got to let them know. So, they're working hard to sell our stupid assets just so we can keep going."

"My extreme pleasure!" said Xavid.

"Meanwhile," continued Father, turning back to Joelene and me, "we look like the world's biggest idiots—like we can't even wipe our own asses—*and* instead of MKG and your dumb-ass Nora schmora from bitchora for the product show, we got tons of empty dick."

"Stop talking about her!" I told him.

"It was categorically not her fault," added Joelene. "Nor has MKG been implicated in any way. The family commission has exonerated them."

Because it was poignant, fitting, and guaranteed to annoy Father, I quoted copy from *Pure H*. "*Her sadness replenished.*"

Father slowly turned toward Joelene. "The day he started worshiping that stupid *Pure Ham* magazine, was the worse ever!"

"*Pure H*," I corrected.

"No," he said, with a laugh, "the H *has* to stand for something. So maybe it's *Pure Hell* or *Pure Halitosis!*" Turning to Ken and Xavid, he asked, "You hear that? *Pure Halitosis!*"

"Funny!" exclaimed Ken.

"Witty," agreed Xavid.

I thought about getting up and leaving since this was pointless.

"Whatever one's fashion tastes," began Joelene, "*Pure H* is a remarkable fusion of influences with a brilliant and elegant sense of individuality."

"Holy fuck!" he bellowed. "Shut up and hold onto your dicks!" Eying Joelene, he added, "Hold 'em real tight!" She stared back coldly, and it occurred to me that she had come to loathe him just as much as me. "We've got someone else." He winked at me. "Someone scorching hot!"

I sat there and stared at him. It was like my brain couldn't make sense of the light and sound emanating from him. And even when he handed me a screen, I couldn't interpret the image.

"Her name is Elle Kez," he said. "She's the granddaughter of Konrad Kez, the real estate gazillionaire. He died in that stupid blimp accident and his company went under, but she's all blue blood and all. Anyway, Xavid knows Chesterfield, her uncle and he's go experimental security-code model. It uses some micro-organic rRNA chip thingy that is supposed to be super-stable and … then … it … um … " He threw his hands into the air and turned to his men. "It's real complicated and shit, right guys!"

"Experimental!" called Xavid.

"That's it! Anyway," he continued, "we can demo it at the product show and keep our biggest customers, like BrainBrain, SLT, iip-2, and LETTT from leaving. They're all calling me and freaked out because they're afraid a freeboot is going to jump out of their closet and shoot their balls." Father laughed sadly. "It's not easy to talk them off the ledge, but this will help. We need something new. You with me?"

"Sir," said Joelene, "this seems quite rash. Are you sure?"

With his upper lip curled, he asked, "Am I sure? I don't know! But we can't show any weakness now because we're just about dead." He turned to his crew to scoff at Joelene. "The guy who runs Ribo-Kool is Chesterfield Kez, and he's lard." He let out a breath. "Look," he began again, "even if Ribo-Kool's thing is a big ol' green turd, it's going to save us for the product show."

The photo he had handed me finally turned into a discernable image. It was a girl who looked about my age. She might have been pretty, except that she was terribly over-done. She had fake, gold hair, green eyes with heavy pink mascara, and lips covered with thick, violet paint. Her nose was pointy and pinched, as if she were wearing an invisible clothespin on the end. Worse, she was laughing and had her mouth so wide open you could see a half-inch of gum above her white teeth, a glistening, golden, made-up tongue, and a uvula hanging in back. Dressed in a fluttering mass of polka dots, and what looked like a white furry, little ear-bot hanging from her left lobe, she looked like one of those flighty, imperceptive, and giggly girls who read *CuteKill*, *Ball Description*, or *Petunia Tune*.

"Don't worry if she looks like more than you can handle," said Father to me with a sly grin, "I've got some fully charged sex-pods you can borrow."

I scowled at him.

After a laugh, he said, "Anyway, you're going to go on a big publicity date with her to get a buzz going, then we'll have you two French or something at the product show. They'll love it!"

My jaw went soft. He was serious. This was his solution. I wanted to laugh at him, or somehow cut his notion in half with one perfect word. But all I could do was imagine Nora floating farther and farther away.

"Michael is devoted to the family and the business," said Joelene. "But he is still suffering from both the trauma of the attack and a broken heart."

"Trauma?" shouted Father as he stood and climbed back onto the stage. "You want trauma? I'll give you a trauma." Toward the back of the auditorium, he shouted, "Crank up *Massive Bladder Tumor!*" An instant later, the sounds of drums began firing and some male singer wailed in pain. Father treated us to his same dance moves he had just five minutes before.

Holding my hands over my ears, I closed my eyes and waited for the cacophony to stop. When it did, and I opened them, Father was standing before me. Dumping the rest of the papers in my lap he said, "Tomorrow. Eight o'clock. That's the whole deal."

I saw logos of what looked like more sponsors, blueprints of what was probably the meeting place, pie charts, diagrams, bullet points, and pages of contracts. I let the papers slide off my legs as I stood. "I can't do this."

"Bullshit!" He bared his teeth like an angry dog. "We don't have a choice! Everyone's laughing at us. Our stock is worth half a bug fuck." Waving a hand toward Xavid, he added, "We're selling everything just so we have electricity."

With a shrug, I said, "I won't do it."

"You will!"

"I refuse."

"I'll make you," he said, stepping forward. "I'll make you do it, you little shit!"

"You will not."

"Sir," said Joelene. "This operation of yours is a surprise. Can't we have time to recuperate and figure out our next step?"

"It should be a surprise! It's a genius surprise. I thought of it in my own head! And if we don't we're dead. Right guys?"

Ken pumped a fist. "Otherwise, we're dead!"

"Expired!" chimed Xavid, as he tickled his hands over his oily shirt.

"Just today," continued Father, "we lost seven thousand customers. Seven fucking thousand! I've been on the phone begging the buggers not to leave, but they're so fucking stupid, it's real hard." As Ken echoed the words *fucking stupid*, father got in Joelene's face. "And you! I'm tired of your worthless input. I want to see you working *for* RiverGroup."

She stiffened. "I am Michael's tutor."

"Yeah? Well, tutor him this: He's going to fuck Elle's stinkin' hole at the product show or you're finally out of here. You got that?"

I wanted to tear his head off. "I'm not doing it!" As I spoke, tears ran down my face. "I'm out of this horrible family." I could barely see as I stumbled past him, around the stage, past Ken Goh, and past Father's idiot film crew and back outside.

I ran to the garage, got in my car, and said, "Europa-1," to my driver. We started moving, and as I strapped myself into the seat, I added, "To the MKG complex … to Nora."

Four

The two-lane highway that traveled around the world roughly at the Tropic of Cancer rose high above the desert, cut through mountain ranges, floated over oceans, and was *the* way to get around the globe fast. After we exited the compound and wound our way down the slope, we came to the desert floor and then began to curve around Ros Begas, toward the long entrance ramp. No other Loop cars were out, so it felt like I was the only one in the world moving, and I liked that. As each of the sixteen vacuum-arc motors started, wound up to speed, and then kicked in, I was agreeably pushed into the seat. Although I was stylistically against speed, I couldn't help but feel a surge of adrenaline and allowed myself to enjoy it because I was heading toward her.

From the outside, my car was shaped like a giant teardrop with the fat end forward and the back slowly tapering down to a needlepoint. The metal skin was covered with millions of little fibers that felt velvety when it was still, but vibrated at high frequency when the car was in motion. It had something to do with aerodynamics, but I wasn't sure. Dozens of skinny tires protruded below and made the whole thing look like a fat centipede. Mine, like the other RiverGroup Loop cars, was painted the company orange and blue, and on the stabilizing fins, like the dorsal fins on a fish, were the logos of the company, products, and those of our strategic partners.

Soon we were on the Loop nearing full speed. The white road and the orange guard walls on either side were a blur, but the distant mountaintops passed in stately fashion. We had left the city and were traveling through the slubs, where millions of tiny orange and yellow houses and small square buildings covered the landscape like so many bits of sand. A few of the taller and steeper mountaintops were bare, or unicorned with a transmission tower. All around, in the valleys, the air was thick with a grayish haze.

"Four point three," announced the driver.

Releasing myself from the safety seat, I stepped back to the bathroom and leaned over the toilet. Nothing came up, but I wished I could have vomited what was supposed to make me part of my family—whatever nurture, or DNA. Finally, I stood, unhappy that I couldn't rid myself of my lineage so easily. At the duralumin sink, I splashed water on my face then studied myself in the mirror. First I closed my left eye and lamented the pinkish tone of my cheeks and ears, which made me appear bothered and anxious. But when I closed my right, and the flush faded away, I felt I looked stronger and in control. This black and white version was the real me—the me beneath the hues.

Once I got back to my seat, I checked the camera views of the road flying past us. They were clear, but just in case, I asked the driver, "Anyone following us?"

"Negative, sir," was the answer through the intercom.

"Nothing?" I asked, surprised.

"Negative."

Maybe this was all it took. Maybe Father finally heard and understood. Years ago, he had finally accepted that I would no longer be the dancer he wanted me to be. Maybe today he understood that I could not and would not date Elle. And maybe he saw that our only course of action was reconciliation with MKG.

The rust-colored mountains gave way to flatter and flatter vistas covered with a crazy quilt of house developments, shopping malls, sweat shops, all interspersed with fields of corn. In the distance, a cloud of greenish vapor tinted the horizon.

At night, much of the slubs were black, but a few dots of electric light or bonfires mirrored the dozen stars in the sky. During the day, it was ugly, limitless, flat, and dull. Worse, it made me feel insignificant.

I wished Joelene were with me. She would surely applaud my daring. Several times lately, she had congratulated me on puzzles solved and initiatives taken, but this was the boldest yet.

The car began to slow, but we hadn't even come to the Gulf Coast yet. I glanced at the red emergency stop button, with its big white E, at the front of the cabin, as if I had accidentally pushed it, but of course, I hadn't. "Driver," I said, "what's the matter?" A second later, Ken Goh's blue and orange painted face filled the screen.

"I know you just had a terrible ordeal," he said, "and I feel very *very* bad for you, but your father and the company are under tremendous pressure right now." His eyes, nostrils, and mouth were outlined in dark blue, the rest was orange so that he looked like a tangerine skull. "He is trying. He really *really* is."

"He is not."

"No, he is." Ken had worked for Father for more than a year, but what he did besides agree with everything Father said, I didn't know. My impression was that there was nothing inside of him. He didn't care what he kissed, how many times, or how bad it tasted. "I know you'd agree that he's brilliant and yet modest." Ken smiled, and across three of his front teeth the letters Y E S were stenciled in blue. "Trust me, he knows your situation and feelings."

I snapped off the screen, but he turned it back on from his side.

"See," he smiled a big YES smile, "your father predicted that you'd turn me off." Leaning in, Ken whispered, "He knows. He's much wiser than you might think." Scrunching up his citrus face, he added, "Sure, he's got a temper. And sometimes it flares up badly. But all great men have fits. I think it is part of being *that* great." He turned to his left. "Right?"

Xavid and his huge square glasses leaned in. "Elle is a peach. Squeeze her and you'll get nectar."

I had liked Father's previous hairdresser. She was a tall, bosomy matron of a lady who was always complaining about the horrible styles he wanted. But he got rid of her. Xavid was a scrawny little man who dressed mostly in oily, black sealskins. His huge amber eyeglasses made his eyes look yellow, watery, and distorted. For some reason his lips were always an odd bluish color, as if he lacked oxygen, and his little whitish tongue often darted out of the right corner of his mouth like a feeding sea worm. Mostly, he was just creepy and odd.

I clicked it off again, waited for them to come back, but it stayed dark. Just as I decided they had given up, Father's face appeared.

"Hey, Michael," he said slowly, "I know I was loud before. I've got a talent for loud." He laughed and held his smile until it slowly wilted. "Anyway, I know you're not into Ültra, or Heâd, or Bäng anymore." He paused as if to lament my transformation once again. "Look," he said, his voice quieter, "I know you're unhappy about being shot … and everything about that … you know … and that MKG girl and everything … "

He couldn't even say Nora's name. I reached to turn it off.

"Wait! Hold on! I'm upset too. I really am. And you know what I think? I think that freeboot was nothing more than dick fuzz!" He held his grin as if waiting for me to agree. "Look," he continued, after he decided that I wasn't going to play along, "the deal is—the company needs you. We've got to have something for the show. So come on back home, we'll sit down with your little tutor and we'll get this all hammered out."

"No." The word came out easily and I was proud of myself. In the past, I had had trouble standing up to him. To the driver, I said, "Full speed, please."

"Elle's not so bad," he continued. "You see the stats on her tits?

They're pointy!" His eyes lit up. "Remember there was a girl who looked kind of like her from the PartyHaus? She had that kind of nose." He flicked up the end of his with a finger.

I did not remember, nor did I want to. "Driver," I said into the intercom, "increase speed now."

"No," said Father, speaking louder, as if commanding my attention, "I'm pretty sure you said something about her once. You have to remember! She was the one who swallowed everyone and everything." As he always did, he got too close to the camera, and his face became distorted so that his nose looked like the front of a blimp. "Sheila! Wasn't that it? Remember her? Slurping Sheila we called her."

I glared at him. Dividing her name into two faux syllables, I said, "No-ra."

"Shut up!" he exploded. "Don't even say her fucking name! From now on, I'm banning it."

I reached out and flicked the off switch. Nothing happened.

"Ha!" Father winked off camera. "Lard work, Ken."

"Please," I said, "go away."

"MKG is our enemy. Two minutes ago Nora's dad was on *Profit Ranch 5000*. The bastard said we're community butt plugs!"

"I'm sure he'll apologize if we just explain."

"No explaining! No apologizing! They rejected us, and now we're total enemies."

"We can go back and explain that it was no one's fault."

"Stop with the explaining!" He flung his hands into the air. "They want to bury us. I'm telling you, they were behind that damn freeboot. They're against us."

"Against us!" echoed Ken from off camera.

"I'll talk to Nora," I said.

Father began laughing so gutturally at first I thought he was retching. "Oh, boy! That's a big mug of flush water!" Turning to his guys, he said, "We're saved! He's going to talk to the pud-girl for us. He's going to have her go tug on her daddy's trousers, and he'll fix up everything!" Then he leveled a stare at me. "You're dumb," he said sadly. "I'm sorry, but it's the truth. I thought you wanted to become smart! Your tutor has taught you dick spit!"

I wanted to scream at him, but that would mean loud had won. "I am not your son," I enunciated. "I'm not a Rivers anymore."

With a big roll of his eyes, as if I had to be fooling, he said, "Come on! You don't have a choice there!" Then he leaned in, bumped his nose against the lens, and left a greasy spot. "If you want to get all quiet, and still, and grey, and whatever ... fine! But you are Michael *Rivers.* You have your duty so get your ass home! Get ready for your damn publicity date, and that's it."

I pushed the off button as hard as I could and managed to get the screen to shut down. To the driver, I said, "Full speed," and an instant later, the acceleration pushed me back into my seat.

It felt over. I was no longer Hiro Bruce Rivers' son. I was no longer Michael Rivers, and I no longer had his worries. The only thing I felt was the anticipation of seeing Nora. Of inhaling air she had breathed, of touching her face, and gazing at her with my grey eye.

Then the car began to slow again. "No!" I said, "don't stop. Speed up!"

"Sorry, sir," was all the driver said.

"Keep going!" I switched to the next seat and jabbed a finger at the screen. An instant later, I saw Father. Now he held a glass of that horrible sweet, black, fermented carrot liquor he liked. "Let me go!"

"Oh, you're going," he said, as he tilted the glass and let a glob of the stuff ooze into his mouth like tar. After he struggled to swallow, he said, "And if you're out, then you're really out!" His foot flew up at his screen and it went black.

I asked the driver to continue to Europa-1, but outside, I could see the baffle brakes open up and the air began to howl. "Please," I begged, "for me. For Michael Rivers, please don't turn around." Red and yellow emergency lights began to spin all over the car.

A siren, like a slide whistle, sounded and a deep voice repeated: *Warning—remain in your seat for safety.*

Thirty seconds later, we had come to a stop. I turned and looked behind, afraid another car was coming. I didn't see anything, and as I looked around at the enormous flat lands that spread out on both sides and the road that split me down the center, I started to feel a strange dread. I was no longer on my way to see Nora, but I also felt that something else was about to go terribly wrong.

On the monitors, I watched the driver get out of his cockpit at the front and come around to the side. I'd never seen a car stop on the Loop before, and wondered if maybe we were having mechanical troubles. "Everything okay?" He didn't answer. Instead, he opened the lock on the large side door and slid it open. The air that rushed in was humid and hot and smelled like rotting garbage. "Is there a problem?"

My driver was a short man with watery eyes and gentle, worn fingers. He wore the blue and orange RiverGroup uniform. The awful blue pants, with a long, padded, orange codpiece that snaked down the right leg, were leftovers from a previous product show—a costume hand-me-down. With his head bowed, he said, "Master Rivers senior says you must leave."

"Leave?"

"Step out of the car."

I wanted to laugh. "Where am I supposed to go?"

Shaking his head fearfully, he said, "I'll lose everything, sir."

Pushing myself up, I stepped to the threshold. The direct sunlight felt like it would caramelize my skin in a minute. While I didn't want to get out of the car, I wasn't going to call Father and plead. Besides, stepping onto the Loop—something I never fathomed doing—was a call of his bluff. The drop to the roadway was three feet. I always entered the car from the garage platform, but was sure I could make it down. As I lowered my right foot, a line of copy from *Pure H* came to mind. *A sad fog. We jumped anyway.*

I landed awkwardly and fell into my driver's arms. "Excuse me!" I stepped back and straightened my jacket and tie. Standing on the road's white octagonal tiles—that had never been anything but a blur before—I found I could no longer see into the slubs. The orange safety walls on either side blocked the view. And although the road stretched to the horizon in either direction, the feeling was claustrophobic even with the sky and the blaring sun overhead. After a second, the ventilation fans hidden in the shoulders of my jacket turned on and kept me comfortable.

"There!" I said into the interior so Father could hear on the system. "I am out, but now I'm continuing to Nora." I turned to ask my driver for help getting back in, but he was heading to the pilot's door.

"Excuse me," I said. "Do we have a step or something?" He climbed into the small round opening at the front and closed the door. "Hello!" I said, knocking. "I'm still out here!"

At the nose end, the car was ten feet tall. Halfway up was a curved black windshield eight feet across and eight inches tall. Trying to peer through it, I asked, "What are you doing?" The engines, which had been idling, began to rev. Banging on the windshield, I said, "Open the door! I'll die out here."

The car lurched forward, and I twisted out of the way before it ran me over. As the big teardrop body taxied forward, I beat on the side with my fists. "Stop it! Stop the car!" The vibrating surface felt like sandpaper, but when the engines engaged, it slipped ahead like a big blue and orange fish into the rippling heat.

"You can't do this to me!" I screamed after it. A moment later, I laughed because I had never fathomed that my driver would do something like this, but of course, ultimately, he worked for RiverGroup and that meant Father.

Glancing around for security cameras, I said, "Joelene, can you see me? I'm on the Loop. I don't know where I am, but please come now. My driver left me out here." The problem was I didn't see any channel cameras anywhere. Turning, I said, "Joelene! Please help me!" I knew that the Loop was not completely on the system, but there had to be a camera somewhere.

In the direction we had come, skittering headlights appeared in the boiling heat. For a second I panicked then decided it had to be Joelene. Or Father. Either way, I would be rescued from this reeking oven. Although I saw emergency yellows blinking, the car was still coming fast. And the sound—a high-pitched whine like a tiny but powerful drill—was getting louder by the instant.

Terrified that it would flatten me like a mosquito, I threw myself into the other lane and covered my head with my arms. As I clenched my eyes, a blast of air flattened me against the opposite wall. An instant later, I heard a tremendous crash.

Out of a murky, purple darkness, I woke. I was lying on my stomach, nose flat against the burning tiles. My head felt like it was on fire, and I could barely pull air into my lungs. My right elbow throbbed, my neck was stiff, but I was alive.

In the distance, I heard the whistling of another car approaching from the other way. Crawling on hands and knees, I scurried to the far wall and covered up. As it howled past, I was smashed into the corner, then whisked up, and tossed across the tiles like a piece of paper.

I didn't black out, but landed on my back and slid for what must have been fifty feet. When I came to a stop, I stared up into the sky where the clouds spun around a center point. My head ached and my left leg felt broken.

Thinking I heard another car, I pushed myself up and saw lights coming from both directions. If I wasn't run over, the opposing blasts would rip me in half.

Ten feet away, I saw an orange tarp tied to the wall as though covering a repair. If I ran toward it, grasped one of the ropes, maybe I could somehow vault over. Although my legs ached, I got myself up and started for it. After two steps, I swear a bone in my left broke, but I kept going.

As I neared the tarp, I knew I couldn't jump over and wondered if I should just fling myself at it in desperation. Then I saw that the far end was loose and that the tarp covered an opening. Planting my right, I clasped my hands over my head, and as if I were diving into water, leapt at the hole.

The two cars whipped past at that instant and the sonic boom shot me forward like a flesh and bones bullet. The plastic-coated fabric smacked my face and wrenched my head far to the side. Then I was flopping head over foot down a sandy embankment and couldn't tell which way was up. I thought it would never end, and then all motion came to an abrupt stop with a splash.

I lay in rank water that stunk of excrement and made me want to retch. Sitting up, I expected to find fractured bones protruding from my chest like a rack of lamb gone awry. And although my hands looked like they had gone through a zester and were well seasoned with sand and grime, I was okay. In fact, Mr. Cedar's suit was clean dry. Of course, I had never been sitting in sewage before, but I couldn't believe how clean it was. Dipping a sleeve into the goo, I pulled it out and watched the fabric shed the mud and sewage like water on waxed steel. Surely, its strength had saved me.

Slowly, I crawled to dryer ground, collapsed, and caught my breath. I had survived the fall. I was off the Loop and away from the cars' whirlwinds, but I was also off the system, beyond the security cameras, and farther from the families than I had ever imagined.

Then I started to cry. Although alive, I was doomed. And I wasn't going to see Nora! So much for touching her hand, or feeling the heat of her blood again. And so much for my declaration of independence! Now I was nothing more than a hurting body sitting in sewage somewhere in the slubs, waiting to die under the burning sun.

In *Pure H* issue seventeen, a nothing of a salary man decided to become immortal. After an exhaustive study of his options, he submerged himself in a geologically perfect bog and dies knowing that his body will become a fossil in a billion years.

I heard voices and laughter. Twenty yards away, in a muddy lot between what looked like abandoned warehouses, stood a dozen men. Half wore ill-fitting silvery jackets. The rest wore what looked like shiny white plastic bags. Their translucent khaki and brown pants hung like skirts. Most wore belts of rope or thick leather. Many had hair on their faces and what looked like purplish patches of skin.

All I had ever seen of the slubs were images on screens: gangs of marauders in silver, whites, and beiges, the massive, dark factories, the hordes of bugs, the wretched workers, the running noses, and the miles of polluted cornfields.

The men laughed again. Then, I heard glass breaking.

Pushing myself up, I realized that the lower left pant leg had become stiff and thick. It was like my suit had sensed that I'd cracked a bone and turned itself into a cast. I'd heard of such things, but was surprised that my tailor had outfitted me so.

Turning, I gazed up at the Loop atop a steep, sandy embankment. Before the men noticed me, I wondered if I could climb up, and walk beside it until I found a camera. Surely Joelene was monitoring the system for me.

Making my way back from where I had just come, through the mud, wasn't easy. I couldn't put much weight on my left leg, and at one point, my right sunk in so far I wasn't sure if I could pull it out. What I had to do was fall back into the gunk and slowly wiggle it free. Several times, I stopped to rest and let what felt like white-hot embers of pain in my left subside.

When I got to the base of the Loop, I doubted I could make it. It was thirty feet high and steep. After I took a breath, I started to climb, but when I dug my fingers into the sticky soil, black roaches scurried out of holes as if I had disturbed their sleep. I got maybe three feet before the soil let go and a half-ton of it avalanched down.

After slapping the bugs from all over, digging dirt from my eyes, nose, and ears and spitting the stuff from my mouth, I tried again. This time I went slower, but my climbing had brought out so many waterbugs I spent half my time flicking them off my arms and legs. When I got four feet high, the earth let go again and half-buried me in a mound. Once I had pulled myself out and cleaned off, I felt sick. I vomited blood, and knew I didn't have much time.

Turning, I watched the men. One had taken off his silver jacket and was waving his arms about as if explaining something. The sleeves of his undershirt—if that's what it was—hung to his knees like long pillowcases.

The undershirt man began wrestling one of the others in white plastic. They pushed each other back and forth and shouted. When the plastic man fell, the others cheered. I feared they were going to start kicking him or pummeling him, but a moment later the fallen man was helped up. They all laughed as though it was fun.

They were people, I reminded myself. They weren't unlike me. They just lived in a different place and wore different clothes. Some of them had to be friendly and polite.

Pulling myself out of the sand, I stood, and started limping toward them, avoiding the deeper water and mud and muck. When I was ten feet away, the one in his undershirt pointed at me. He had frizzy-looking light brown hair, round, bloodshot eyes, a thin crooked nose, and a patch of oozing purple skin on his forehead. Up close, I could see that his undershirt was a ghastly nonwoven that looked as rough as unfinished oak plank. Just below the neckline was a small, blue bug-looking thing with text below that read *M. Bunny*. Pointing at me, he said, "I thought I recycled you!"

The others laughed.

I tried to smile, but felt instantly ostracized. One of them in a silvery jacket pointed to my suit, snickered, and nudged the man next to him. Another said something about my bride throwing me in the ocean and I wondered if they knew of Nora. *Pure H* issue seven had copy that read: *Mechanical Man. Exquisite*

Oceans. After swallowing a knot in my throat, I said, "Hello. I'm Michael Rivers."

"Who?" asked the man I presumed was Mr. Bunny.

"First son of RiverGroup."

"No!" said another. "What shitting team you with?"

"He doesn't shit. That's why his jacket is that color!" answered someone else.

They all laughed.

"I fell from the Loop," I continued. "Can anyone help me back?"

"He's the enemy!"

"He stinks!" said another, covering his nose.

"I used to dance," I said, hoping they might know me from my PartyHaus days. "I was on the channels." None of it seemed to register. Instead they giggled and pushed each other like schoolboys.

"He's ill and delusional," said one.

"Could be high-fructose psilocybin!"

"Wait!" said Bunny, as he looked me up and down. "He thinks he's the one who dressed in gold."

It was true. I had a twenty-eight-carat-gold outfit. "Yes," I said, glad he remembered if disheartened how.

Bunny stepped beside me, and as if introducing me to the group, said, "You slubber idiots, it's the evil banging-boy. In the deadest jacket ever seen with his diseased face in need of serious recycling!" He got them to laugh again.

I tried to smile to show that I didn't mind, but worried that no good was going to come of them. I wished I had blacked out in the mud and suffocated.

"That's not him!" said another, who had hair all over his face. "That kid was the richest pill ever. He'd never be here."

"Yeah," concurred Bunny. Wiping his dripping nose with one of his huge sleeves, he asked, "Who are you, and who do you shit for?"

"I need to get back to the families," I said, as a ripple of fear, like gamma rays passed through me.

"I don't want to hear any *families*!" The thing on his forehead oozed a yellowish puss, and he smelled like rancid frying oil.

"If he came off the Loop," said someone. "Could be soaking with p'thylamine!"

"Satins will zap a slubber dead if you get up there," said one of the others. "They electrocuted my uncle. Half his body was burned away. Couldn't get anything for him."

I retreated a step from Bunny and tried to make eye contact with the other men. "Will someone help me?" No one spoke. "I could assist you," I suggested. "I know we're supposed to be foes, but I could have some clothes tailored for you." They looked at each other and laughed again.

"What's wrong with our knits?" Bunny wanted to know, as he primped his sleeves and smoothed the stiff spunlaid material over his belly.

"No, nothing," I said, taking another step backwards. "Sorry. Um … my family company keeps information … and … identity and …" Bunny glared at me as if I wasn't making any sense. My voice trailed off.

"Michael Rivers," said a female voice from farther back in the group. A short, chubby woman in red shorts, a sparkling red bra, and a small, white plastic jacket stepped forward. Her hair reminded me of Mother's from last time—a stiff, multi-colored muddle shaped like a garden shrub—only hers was so laden with tiny silvery trinkets, it sparkled and tinkled like an enormous charm bracelet. Around her otherwise naked belly was a wide red plastic belt with a large button in the middle. "I heard he's getting married to that Gonzalez-Matsu girl next week."

"I *was* going to," I said, "but there were complications."

"Complications!" roared Bunny. "There's going to be more than complications when they grind your ass into pâté and spread you on bunny crackers!"

Everyone laughed except the woman. Instead, she peered at me suspiciously.

"I *am* Michael Rivers," I told her, and thought I saw a glimmer of recognition in her eyes. I quoted, "*The moment became her life.*" Her expression darkened, and I cursed myself for thinking she knew *Pure H.*

Tilting her head to the right as if sizing me up, she said, "You look like that boy."

"If he is," said one of the men, "he is a big pill."

Bunny said, "Pay for all of us to do Kandi's hole."

"Shut up!" she snarled.

"I was playing!" he said. "Next time you're at the clinic, get a humor implant!"

Curling a lip, she said, "No more for you. Never again!"

"I was just joking!"

While the other men made cooing sounds, Kandi stepped forward and asked, "What are you doing here, honey?"

"I don't know," I said, glancing at her belt. The thing in the middle wasn't a button but a plastic lid attached to her stomach.

She noticed my eye-line. "You want it?" she asked, with a sly grin. "You have to wash, honey." She licked her lips and smiled.

It felt like the cooling system in Mr. Cedar's suit had given out. "No, thank you," I stammered, ashamed. I knew what it was: she had a vagina implanted where her bellybutton had been. Back when I danced, some women had it done, but it was terribly out of fashion in the cities now.

Meanwhile, the men were laughing at me again. Someone had said *virginity*. Another said *spilling Grandma's gravy*, whatever that meant.

"Can't you help me," I asked the woman. "Please?"

"You got money?" she asked. "You with Segu or Bunny or what?"

I glanced at the logo on the front of Bunny's shirt, but didn't know what she meant. And since I didn't carry any money, I didn't know what to offer. Touching my chest, I said, "What about my Mr. Cedar jacket?"

She curled a lip. "That thing?"

It was Bunny who touched the fabric. "Weird thing is," he said, "you're covered with shit, but the knit is all sweet and pretty."

While I wanted to tell him that it wasn't an awful knit, I thought better of it. "It's self-cleaning," I said, hoping it might impress them. "It also has a temperature control system. My tailor is famous. He's from outside Seattlehama. It's probably worth ..." Since I had never directly paid, I had no idea. "Maybe seventy-five billion?"

I saw green and red bits of food on Bunny's tongue when he laughed. "You're a fucking round sugar pill. Stupid and blank."

"I'm not sure exactly," I said. "My family buys them."

His fist came at me in a blur and hit me in the gut. Next, I was on the ground trying to get air back into my lungs.

"Don't be stupid," he said, wiping the drip from his nose. "I'm intelligent, disease-boy! And your ugly, gray, sick jacket isn't even worth a good shit."

As the woman came to my side, she said, "You've got a bad testosterone imbalance!" to Bunny.

"Fuck you!" he screamed, then opened a small jar and tossed several tiny emerald tablets onto his tongue.

When the rest of the men teased Bunny, he hit the back of the woman's head and knocked her across me. As three others helped her up, I saw that the lid on her belly had fallen off. Inside was a wrinkled daffodil of purple and pink flesh. I turned away as she grabbed the lid and snapped it back on.

"No looking," said Kandi angrily. "That's ten right there!"

"You contaminated whore!" said Bunny. "I'm taking him in for recycling. You take all your fake cunts and get out!"

"Go have a cell storm!" she scoffed. From a beaded red bag, she got out a pill and popped it into her mouth. As though it gave her strength, she stood, and said, "Don't get near me." She grasped my arm, yanked me up, and nearly dislocated my shoulder. I tried not to cry out. "Come on," she said, tugging my hand, "we're going."

"No, you're not!" Bunny grasped my other arm and the two of them played tug-of-war with me. I lost my footing, and when she let go, fell face first in the mud.

Then I heard shouting and feet going in all directions. Pushing myself up, I saw three large men dressed in orange satin skiing down the sandy embankment where I had fallen. Family satins! I was saved.

The one in front, who wore a helmet with a gold visor, hoisted a clear fashion rifle to his shoulder. He fired. An orange streak zipped through the air. To my right, I heard a soft thud. Someone in the distance screamed. Then it was quiet.

"Michael Rivers?" asked the satin in the gold visor, as he stepped before me.

"Yes." I coughed. "Thank you."

Grasping me under the arms, he lifted me, and threw me over his shoulder. From there, I could see Kandi face up in the mud. Blood covered her implant. No! I thought, not her!

The Loop was blocked in both directions and an air-conditioned tent had been set up. To the left sat Ken, Xavid, and the film crew on folding chairs. On a puffy, orange, over-inflated marshmallow of a couch were Father and one of his women, like king and queen of the Loop. In his right hand he held a glass of his fermented carrot gunk. With his big pink straw, he idly poked at the stuff.

He wore white pants with little blinking blue dots all over them, a red shirt with RiverGroup logos and fornicating bunnies, and a tiny, frosty green vest that looked like it might properly fit an infant. His current girl had orange hair, blue lips, and the sort of haughty, upturned nose that he preferred. Her frilly, awful pink and green dress ended at her midriff so the whole world could see the orange-painted treats inside her translucent bloomers. I didn't see Joelene and figured he forbid her.

The satin had set me before them on a wooden crate. My whole body hurt. My right elbow throbbed as if it were shattered. When I wiped my mouth, I saw a brilliant smear of blood on the back of my hand. And even seated, I had trouble keeping myself upright. All I wanted was to be put out of my misery.

"So," said Father, "how's things?" He laughed, winked toward his ever-present film crew, and then nudged the girl who had become absorbed with a tiny golden robot that lived in her navel. Seemingly annoyed that he hadn't gotten a big laugh, he said, "Hold this, spaceship!" and thrust his glass at her. After glancing at the hole in the Loop wall, he asked, "What were you thinking? First, it's illegal to go into the slubs. They are the enemy. The families are gonna fine us big for this. And second, they're all drugged-up savages down there. It's hell. There's no system, and there's not one good satin."

Pointing at Gold Visor, I said, "He killed that woman!"

"He did not!" He stood and stretched his back. "Besides she's one of those stupid bellybutton whores anyway. That's like *so* old!" Then he turned to the right, held his chin with a hand, as if trying to look philosophical or letting the camera soak up his profile. "What we're doing—and I'm saying this because you don't seem to be catching on—is we're talking about family. And we *are* a family. I'm the dad; you're the son. It's a natural thing for us to be at odds at times. It's how it goes with fathers and sons." He glanced at the girl. She nodded weakly. "And as I see it, the funny thing is, we're the same in so many ways. I know you don't see it, but I do."

"Is she really ok?"

"You used a fuckin' tranquilizer?" he asked the satin.

"Sir!" Was he replied.

"There!" said Father. "Anyway, my dad, Alexander Rivers, built RiverGroup—"

"I've heard this a trillion times," I interrupted.

"A trillion and one!" he screamed. "Anyway, Dad was a fuckin' genius. He invented the little box; he programmed it so it kept things secret and secure and just right, and soon, everyone had to have one. And low and behold, RiverGroup becomes so big the controlling families have to let us in. We're part of the system: we vote on the rules and kick ass when necessary. We're lard. Hard lard." Shaking his head sadly, he added, "He was so completely super-super smart! Do you even understand what he did?"

I nodded, because I wanted him to stop. My head and spine were throbbing. "Where's my advisor?"

"You don't need her! Be a man for once." Squinting, he paused. Then his eyes shot back and forth. "Right!" he said, snapping his fingers, "anyway, Dad invented a way to completely cloak something. You could send it from A and it arrived at B, but in the middle, it was gone. It was vanished. It literally did not exist. Or you could put whatever you needed in the box and no one but you could get it. No one. Ever. Completely and totally secure because until you looked inside, it didn't exist." He laughed. "I think about how crazy genius that was every single day." He waved to Ken and Xavid and asked, "Right? Dad was a super genius?" Ken gave two thumbs up. Xavid nodded vigorously, then pushed up his huge amber glasses. "So, there's money and power, and more money, and more power and then … and then came me!" Holding up his arms as if to the gods above, he screamed, *Then came Hiro Bruce Rivers!*"

His arms flopped to his sides. His head fell onto his chest. "I had to come along and fuck it all up. Even before the freeboot shot you, I had done a pretty good job of ruining the whole damn thing." He shook his head. "I'm the biggest idiot in the world!"

"No, you're not!" said the girl, with her bottom lip sticking far out.

"Thanks," said Father, coochie-cooing the girl's chin.

Ken spoke up. "It's a difficult time. Very difficult time."

"You've done exceptionally!" added Xavid.

"You guys are too much," he said, exhaling a deep breath. "I wouldn't be here without you two!" He faced me and continued.

"So anyway, Dad croaks. We have him cremated, sprinkle his ashes on a bunch of naked high school girls playing volleyball, and I take over. And since that instant—since that *exact* instant—everything went butt rocket." As an aside, he added, "All you can argue is how fast." Then he laughed at himself. "So, my fabulous, giant, and genius point is," he said, as if trying to regain his momentum, "I'm sorry. I screwed up. But I can't let the company turn into fuck water. I want you to have something when I die, and merging with Ribo-Kool is the only way."

He had admitted that he was an idiot before, but it never prevented him from being an idiot again. "Let's go back to MKG."

"Nooo!" he screeched like a baby. "Don't say those three letters! I hate them. And you know what the new rumor is? They're gonna make a big announcement soon, like they think they have a big booger on their finger and want to show the world!" He turned to his girl, "Right, my little pünta?"

She giggled obliviously and then pouted. "It's stinky out here."

"Yeah … stinky!" he said inhaling deeply and appreciatively, as if odor were his own invention. A second later, he dropped to his knees. "Look here, son, I'm begging you. The company really needs your help." He smiled a big phony smile. "You'll do it?

"No."

"Do you see my knees on the ground? That means I'm begging you. I'm really begging you!" After a beat, his shoulders sank and he sat back on his haunches. "Fine. I grant you, it's not *real* begging. There is a difference. In real begging, I'm just on my knees … you know … begging." He scrunched up his mouth as if he thought he was being clever. "Here, if you don't do what I want, I'll throw you over the wall and let those slubbers slice you into hors d'oeuvres."

My head hurt so much and felt so heavy I could barely keep upright, but I did my best to stare back at him.

"But technically, with the knees on ground, it is begging. And you can tell people I begged you if you want. Right, guys?"

"Tell them your father begged you, Master Rivers! Big deal, that!"

"Extra-extraordinary," said Xavid.

"Anyway," he said, "we've got an agreement, right? You go on your publicity date with Elle—pretend to like the bitch if you have to—but be nice, and at the product show you say good things, and smile for the cameras. Do that and I'm not going to dump you back into slub hell. That's our full agreement."

I glanced toward the hole in the Loop wall. I wouldn't last for more than minutes there, but I didn't want to go back. I couldn't betray Nora and our dreams.

"You hear me?" he screamed.

I wished a Loop car would run him over—or both of us.

"You hear what I'm fucking saying?" The veins on his forehead and neck bulged. "Say something! Open your fucking mouth and push some air over your vocal chords."

"No!"

Father snapped his fingers. In an instant, Gold Visor picked me up by my ankles and held me over the Loop wall. At first, the rush of blood to my head felt good, but soon the pressure made my eyeballs feel like they were going to burst. Then my stomach felt like it was going to slide down my throat.

"Which is it?" asked Father. "Are you going on the date, or should I have him drop your ass?"

Beneath me, I could see the sandy embankment, the rank water, the dirty square where the slubbers had been, and the body of the prostitute, where swarms of black flies now crawled over her face and bloody abdomen.

Five

Strolling down the long spiral hallway leading to Mr. Cedar's showroom had always been a cleansing and meditative retreat. Usually, I spent an hour or two meandering down the polished glass path, stopping along the way to push the buttons on the wooden booths and observe motorized fabric strength or abrasion tests, or to study mannequins dressed with his latest designs, treasures from his design past, or selections from his burgeoning historical collection.

That day, however, I did not walk as the doctors had advised me to let my leg heal. So, I rode atop an annoyingly bright green frog scooter—a single steady-wheel chair and handlebars—that the medical staff had given me. Motoring straight to the sugar maple and hammered palladium doors, I arrived in one minute flat.

His assistant, Pheff, in a charcoal suit, textured white shirt, and a cream tie, said, "Welcome, Mr. Rivers. He's expecting you." Usually I met with my tailor in his gallery, where currently a dozen black robot mannequins, each impeccably dressed in his latest creations, mimed the actions of daily life—drinking coffee, strolling through indoor parks, and posing for cameras, but this time, Pheff led me to a black door in back. After entering a long code into a lock, he released several bolts and pulled it back slowly.

I had not been in Mr. Cedar's design studio before and felt

honored. The air had the tangy aroma of new fabric and starch. Down the center were a dozen wide, flat worktables piled with bundles of material, projects in various stages, boxes of notions, and all manner of tools. Along the interior wall, I saw sewing machines, de-weavers, and other muscular-looking equipment, some with large knobs, lit dials, and levers. The exterior wall was some sort of a translucent material from floor to ceiling and through it was a view of a hundred buildings. In the hazy morning sun, the closest tower was indigo, the rest of the edifices faded to sapphire in the distance.

"Michael," he said, as he stood and stepped toward me, "good to see you."

Mr. Cedar was ten years older, an inch shorter, but sturdier. His hair, which stood up in front, was black, but lately, from different angles and in various lights, I'd seen flecks of grey. He was one of those men whose looks often go unnoticed. He was not stunningly handsome, and still had a faint scar down the middle of his face, but once the eye found the details beyond the basic color, texture, and silhouette, it could appreciate both his graceful features and the complexity of his steel eyes.

Today he wore what I assumed were his work clothes—an unconstructed charcoal jacket and matching pants, a soft-looking, off-white shirt, and a silvery ascot.

"Your suit design saved my life," I told him. "Thank you."

From the center of his chin grew a single black hair three inches long. He twirled it between his index and thumb a few times. "You exaggerate."

Next, he gave me a tour of the studio, showed me his de-weaving equipment, the design systems, water looms, and demonstrated a new sonic, double-lock sewing machine.

"Impressive," I said.

"We're quite modest." He then escorted me toward his screens and sat. "I understand that you have another publicity date."

"I do," I said, instantly depressed. "At the MonoBeat Tower. She's a *Petunia Tune* girl." As I mentioned the magazine, I saw him wince. "I don't like it either, but I don't have a choice." All morning I had tried to call Nora, tried to see her on the channels, tried to send messages, but everything was blocked by RiverGroup code. The same notice kept coming up: *You are disallowed from this communication, Michael. And your father has been informed.* After I had tried several dozen times, Father and the gold visor satin had come. Gold Visor picked me up by one ankle and we got as far as the garage, when I promised I wouldn't try to send Nora a message again. The satin summarily dropped me onto the floor, and I bruised my head.

Sitting up, I realized that I had slipped into a daydream and not finished my thought to my tailor. With a futile shrug, I added, "All I would like to do is share a single cream-coffee with Nora." I exhaled a shaky breath and tried to gather myself.

Twisting his beard hair a few more times, Mr. Cedar spun around, picked a brush from a jar, and began working. I watched the sable flip and dash over the glowing surface, and then glanced up at the overhead display where the drawing appeared.

On a terracotta oval, the figure assumed a pose like the models in *Pure H*. The left leg was forward, the foot, straight. The head was turned far to the left so that the face was in profile. The left arm rest on the hip, the right hung straight. As he worked, he added a tiny dot of red between the thumb and the index, as if a drop of her blood remained. While the suit was lean and elegant like always, it was boxier and darker. The lapels were higher. The white shirt looked stiff like paper, and the patterned ash tie gave an iridescent glow.

"There," he said, and touched a button labeled CUT AND SEW.

"It's superb!" I said, not actually sure that I loved it. The truth was it looked stiff and awkward, but I felt I didn't want to complain until I saw it in three dimensions. "What is the fiber content?"

"Moon wool and steel." He swiveled on his chair and pointed toward the back of the room. "Here we are."

Assistant Pheff came with a dark charcoal suit draped over

his arm. "Fresh from the Fuji-Merrow cut-and-sew automaton," he said, handing it to Mr. Cedar.

My tailor checked the seams, the lining, and the buttons. "Excellent. Bring Mr. Rivers' form," he instructed. Pheff did so, and Mr. Cedar dressed it.

In fabric and in three dimensions, I saw just how different the suit was. While all his previous garments had radiated an uplifting elegance, this one was heavy, anxious, and hard. The fabric had a ghostly metallic sheen and reminded me more of armor than the usual soft, satellite wools. To emphasize that harder feel, the buttons were cut roughly from slate, the collar hugged the neck as if the wearer were cold or frightened, and the shoulders slumped as if carrying a burden. With a sad laugh of recognition, I said, "Now I understand."

Mr. Cedar nodded as if that was what he had expected to hear. In a low drawer, he rooted through a dozen large brushes, scissors, rulers, tape measures, and spools of thread. "Ah!" he said, as he pulled out what looked like a green glass rod with a small orb at one end.

Stepping before the suit, he studied it as an artist might gaze at a canvas and then began drawing on the right shoulder with the rod. I flinched, fearing that he was going to color my suit green, but soon saw that the glass rod made no mark. I had no idea what he was doing. Glancing at Pheff, he seemed as baffled as I. So, the two of us waited for him to finish and explain.

But when he finished, he stepped back, gazed for a moment, and then told Pheff, "Turn off the lights. Close the blinds, and switch off all the screens."

The three of us were swallowed in darkness. Holding tightly onto the scooter handlebars so I felt like I wasn't drifting in space, I waited for my tailor to speak, or turn on a light, or do something. I heard nothing, but my own breathing.

Once my eyes adjusted to the tiny hint of light that came around the door, I could see my tailor standing absolutely still before the suit. While I couldn't fathom what this was about, I knew he had a reason and resolved to wait patiently.

Every few minutes Pheff cleared his throat, shifted his weight, or crossed or uncrossed his arms. Mr. Cedar was perfectly still. His arms hung at his sides. I couldn't see if his eyes were open, but guessed they were closed. He was meditating or making a silent offering of some sort. Maybe he always did this when he finished a suit.

I closed my eyes and tried to think of nothing, but images of Father screaming and dancing, and the abrasive hues from the color therapy screen, kept invading my consciousness like pollution. The more I tried to push them away, the more elastic they became. Finally, I imagined Nora's gloved hands, the texture of the material, the precise cut of the fabric, and the way it stretched over her knuckles. Gradually, the storm receded.

My body jerked, as if I was falling asleep, and I opened my eyes. The room was still black, and I feared I had dozed off for a few minutes. But there … on the right shoulder of the suit was a ghostly glowing grey circle six inches wide. It was like a large round, clockwise brushstroke, exactly like the logo of the SunEcho coffee shop.

Mr. Cedar said, "Lights."

As the studio floods flicked on. I clenched my eyes. Before I had a chance to ask what I'd seen, he told Pheff to turn them off again, and we were plunged back into darkness. The eerie logo was gone.

"Back on," he said. As the lights returned, he turned toward me. "Bright light bleaches visual purple in the eye."

"I thought I saw the SunEcho logo for a moment."

"You did," he said, "but I painted it on with a dye *almost* out of human perception." He took the jacket from the form and put it on a Chanel-Royce hanger. "You wanted to meet Nora for a cream coffee," he continued. "My idea is that she'll see the logo and go to meet you. But we want the message to be seen only by her, if possible."

"Right," I agreed. "My communication has been cut off."

"So," he said, "only those few people with a grey eye will have the ability to see it. Of that group, only those who have a muted décor, such that they would be watching your date in relative dim, will have enough visual purple in their grey eye to perceive it. And from that very small group, only those who are familiar with the logo of the *Pure H* coffee shop will comprehend."

As a cold shiver worked its way up my spine, I said, "You mean ... *her.*"

Later that afternoon, Joelene and I were traveling across the Pacificum Floating Bridge on our way to the city of Kong. While Joelene worked on her screen, I began to worry that Nora wouldn't see the message. What if the rods in her grey eye weren't working for some unfathomable reason? Or what if her father came in and switched on a bright light? Or what if she didn't watch the promotion date at all? She could be mad at me. Maybe she would hate me for going out with Elle, even though she had to know that I was being coerced.

"The itinerary for the date has just been finalized," said Joelene. With a sigh, she added, "I tried my best." Bringing over a screen, she sat beside me.

I looked over the date itinerary. We were to eat at a restaurant at the top of the MonoBeat Tower. That was good. I made my appearance first and drank one of the sponsor's beverages. That wasn't too bad—Nora and I had had sponsors. Elle then sampled another of the beverages. Then we described how delicious and refreshing they were. That was crass, but tolerable. For the next ten minutes she and I were to flirt. I stopped reading for a moment and felt a kind of dread that I hadn't before. Maybe I was in denial, but I had assumed we would just meet and talk. Reading ahead, I saw that we were to gaze in each other's eyes and pledge to get our parents to work together as an expression of our newfound love. Love?

I glanced at Joelene, who pursed her mouth as if to say that she knew how awful it was. After we ate dinner, one of Elle's favorite bands was to play, and we were to dance. I stared at the word. This was the worst, and yet, the next thing was unacceptable. During the dance, we were supposed to kiss, and the date was to end with one of my hands slipping between her legs.

Tossing the screen at the floor, I said, "That's disgusting!"

She retrieved the screen and sat for a moment. "I'll go back and say we can't do it from the kiss on. Your father's not going to like it."

I felt like laughing and crying at the same time. "I don't want to do any of it! Can't we go back to MKG? Do I have to forget Nora?"

"No," she said, gently, "of course not."

"I'm going to see her!" I whispered. Joelene looked confused, if curious, so I told her about the visual purple invitation to the SunEcho in my suit.

Taking a small, powered magnifying glass from a pocket, she stood and checked the jacket. "Interesting," she said. Since she did not have a grey eye, I didn't know what she was seeing. Once she had snapped the glass into its case, she said, "I applaud your courage and initiative." Her smile slowly faded, and she asked, "But how were you planning to get to the SunEcho?"

"By car?" I asked, fearing it wasn't the right answer.

"Our new driver is surely not going anywhere but straight to the promo-date wrap-party in Kobehaba where we are to meet with your father." An alarm sounded on one of her screens, she glanced toward it, then said, "I'm afraid getting to your meeting will not be easy, nor without substantial risks."

"Please?" I asked. "I have to see her and tell her that this thing with Ribo-Kool is nothing … that it doesn't mean anything to me. I have to tell her."

After nodding, as if she'd had an idea, she said, "I'll look into our options."

"Thank you!" I said. "I have to see her."

As she sat before her screens, she said, "Your father is on channel five thousand." She pushed a button and the monitor before me came on.

I recognized the garish nautical set of the interview show *Celebrity Research Yacht*. Across from the red-haired host, Milo Holly, who was dressed in his whites and captain's hat, sat Father in a green paisley jacket with large holes cut so that his black-painted nipples showed through like cartoon eyes. On his head he wore what looked like a rubber tire tread of a hat, and from both ears hung miniature crystal chandeliers. Usually his costumes were copies of his latest favorite Ültra band.

"It's all about love," said Father, the chandeliers jingled like wind chimes when he moved. "We make a product we love for clients we love. We do it to help all the families we love. It's in everything RiverGroup does. Love is our basic thing."

"It's all hate," I complained, with a roll of my eyes.

"But with the RiverGroup security stuff in everything, shouldn't we be worried about freeboots jumping out all over the place?" Milo Holly laughed as though it was supposed to be a joke, but he looked anxious.

"No!" said Father, smiling as though it were absurd. "Nothing to worry about. Everything's right back to our normal super-secure and super-protected ... you know ... normal." He smiled again. Harder. "Really. Everything's perfect."

"Maybe not *perfect*," said Milo. "I mean Michael was shot. The merger-marriage between you guys and MKG was cancelled. And your stock is sinking fast."

"RiverGroup has had a rough couple of days, but we're stronger than ever."

Milo eyed the camera, coyly. "And I saw a report that you got an implausibly big pimple on your ass!"

"Oh yeah," said Father playing along, as the audience howled. "Mount Fuji! Snow-capped and everything!" As the laugher died away, Father said, "Back to the freeboot shit for a second ... remember kids, bad shits come along. But the lesson is even if RiverGroup—the code bastards of system security—can be hit, just think how much worse it would have been if you'd been using the flimsy crap MKG sells!"

Milo smiled stiffly. "It was implausibly tragic," he said, as if afraid to insult a potential sponsor.

"It was much worse that that! It was *Fifty Layers of Bitch*." Father leaned forward and popped Milo's shoulder with a friendly punch. "That's my new favorite song."

"We could tell," said Milo, rubbing his arm. "But you're right, that band, Sister Revölver's Tongüe, is completely implausible!" To the camera, he said, "Hey everybody, let's see a clip of their newest Ültra epic."

Three men, dressed like Father and wielding chrome guitars, tore down a city street, smashing car windshields, storefronts, women with strollers. One began singing and screeching as though he were being cut in half. A chrome guitar hit him in the face. Then the three men were bashing each other until they were covered with blood.

"That's so Ültra you have to puke over the poop deck!" gushed Milo. "Or poop over the puke deck! But, wow! Implausible. I love the Tongüe!" After he had caught his breath, he shrugged and added, "Too bad they're all busted up and in comas now."

Father's head was still bouncing to the rhythm. "When I was a kid," he said, apropos of nothing, "I used to whack off and keep my semen in a jar in the fridge."

I let my head fall back. Did he have to say bizarre and disgusting things like that to the world? Didn't he care what they thought?

"Wait, Mom!" shouted Milo as he whipped off his captain's hat. "Don't drink that! That's not the coconut milk!"

The audience roared.

Father, who seemed taken aback, as if he'd had other plans for his story, said, "Yeah … coconut milk … funny! Anyway," he flicked a hand at one of his chandeliers, "I'm here to plug our new promotion date. Tonight, eight o'clock, my son will be going out with Elle of Ribo-Kool. She's the hot granddaughter of Konrad Kez, that dead quadrillionaire. And she's blazing."

"I'll be watching," said Milo. "She's the one who sat on that camera yesterday at a press conference. Talk about a debutante *ball!*"

"And," continued Father, as the audience whooped and hollered, "our big, new product show will be the day after tomorrow. By then, I expect Michael and Elle will be fucking like a couple of dirty, rabid skunks, *if* you know what I mean!"

"Oh, yeah!" said Milo, as he stood and did a few hip thrusts, "I think I know what you mean!" Next he shook hands with Father, and read a list of some of the top channels covering the date.

"That's enough of that!" I said.

"I agree," said Joelene. "But let's see what the buzz is like."

"Do we have to?"

"It's background," she said, as she switched the channel to a show called *Intellectuals and Soup.* Two women and two men dressed as if they were at a mad tea party sat around a gold-leaf rococo table before steaming bowls.

A chubby woman, with warm brown eyes, covered in a mass of pink soap bubbles and a wide, crimson-feathered hat, said, "I feel for Nora. Her story is *the* modern tragedy. But I can't believe Michael is so fickle and shallow to be interested in Elle Kez."

"Indeed," said a man wearing an azure bowtie with the wingspan of a goose and a matching striped morning jacket, "I'd not heard of Elle Kez before, but she is simply dreadful. She can't act, sing, or keep on her God-awful clothes for more than three minutes." Grainy, obviously stolen pictures of her nude body flashed on screen. "She has none of the blood or breeding of Michael Rivers or any *real* members of the families. Granddaughter of the wealthy and admired, if dead, Konrad Kez or not, I say she's a degenerate prostitute with a dripping nose. And as for the firm she represents, Ribo-Kool is an absolute nothing from somewhere in the dregs of America-3. I can't find any references to them before a week ago. How RiverGroup could be planning to merge with them is completely beyond understanding."

"So," said Pink Hat, lifting a spoonful of shellfish bisque, "you think it's another of the ever-increasingly sad and bizarre schemes from his father, Hiro Rivers?"

"I do," said Bow Tie.

"My problem is," continued Pink Hat, "if Michael doesn't stand up against his father this time, I'm afraid I'm going to be quite disappointed. He is only nineteen, but it's time he asserted himself." She stuck the spoon in her mouth. "Mmm!" she said. "So creamy and divine! The salty shark semen is succulent, but it doesn't overpower the denatured rhubarb leaves either!"

"What is this?" I asked Joelene. "Who are they?"

"They're better spoken than most channel talents," she said.

A bearded man in a brown beret spoke slowly, as if each of his words were bubbling up from the center of the Earth. "If RiverGroup can't protect Michael, no merger of any sort will help them win back customers. I am switching away from RiverGroup products. I believe the death knell has rung."

"If Ribo-Kool," said Bow Tie, "has a real solution, which I greatly doubt, it might stave off a complete collapse." He tasted a dab of his soup and said, "Oh! Such an incredible, rich yet pungent mouth-feel! Like swallowing used velvet panties."

I asked Joelene, "Do you know Ribo-Kool?"

"No," she said. "It was quite a surprise. Your father … and others … are difficult to predict."

"I feel for poor Michael," said another woman. She wore what looked like an iron bra and an intricately carved glass bowl over her head. "I was so sure he would finally lose his virginity with Nora. And I was *so* looking forward to it, I'm embarrassed to admit it." She laughed and fogged the glass in front of her face.

Bow Tie dabbed the corners of his mouth with a matching striped napkin and turned toward the glass bowl woman. "Must we always," he said, with a chuckle that made the wings of his bow tie quiver, "lower ourselves with this sensational tripe?"

"I would love to lower myself!" said Pink Hat, angrily, as a creamy drip undulated down her three chins. "I understand that Michael has got a beautiful penis, as proud, strong, and pure as a wild Arabian!"

"Indeed," said Iron Bra from behind her fogged glass, "I have studied his dancing outfits from the rages, and he's definitely bombastic down there."

I covered my face in embarrassment. They had to be talking about some other Michael Rivers. Maybe the real Michael Rivers—someone who I didn't even want to know. "Please," I said, "I can't watch this!"

"Just one more," said Joelene, as she turned the channel. Now two blondes stood nose-deep in a field of purple, violet, orange, and canary-colored sunflowers. "Another backgrounder," explained my advisor. "A *Petunia Tune* channel."

"Elle Kez," said one, in an airy singsong voice as though she were reading poetry, "is the luckiest girl in the whole, big, wide world!"

"I gabbed with her all this morning," gushed the other. "She's in the capital city of Petunialand right in the petunia center of everything." Holding her hands above her head, she did an awkward pirouette. "She's going to be marrying the *bestest* of the best family blood, and they'll have dozens of babies! I just know it!"

"What about her fashions for the date?" asked the first.

"You're going to '*gasm* when you see it! She's been working with her staff day and night."

I laughed, and asked, "Who are they?"

She snapped off the screen. "Yes, it's all dreadful, but the point is, tens of thousands of channels are going on and on." She massaged the bridge of her nose. "Elle is getting a lot of attention."

The news did not surprise me, but it did confirm my fears. Leaning forward, I touched the cool fabric of Mr. Cedar's suit jacket and hoped that Nora would see the hidden message. It was the only positive in this unfurling disaster.

Father's face flashed on the screen before me, and I jumped back.

"That's what you're going to wear?" he asked, making a sour face. "I thought you were going to get an actual color." To Joelene, he said, "Didn't we discuss blood red and chartreuse, or was I on slub drugs?"

"The silhouette is new," said Joelene, her voice congenial.

"*He tears her skin from her face!*" he sang, stretching his mouth wide as though impersonating a bullfrog.

Once he had finished, I said, "*This whisper of footsteps …*"

For just a second he stared blankly, then he pretended to be happy. "Thank you! Wow! More *Pure Hog,* right?" After a snort of a laugh, he said, "The world is actually in color. Like the sun is orange. The sky is blue." He inhaled and then bellowed, "And snot is green!"

"The soul," I said, "is colorless."

"The soul?" He looked off camera. "Like he knows the soul!" After fluttering a hand in the air as if to dispel what I had said, he continued, "Anyway, thanks to me and my magnificent acting skills on that stupid *Celebrity Research* show our stock is up fifteen points. And I'm calling to say that we need every up-tick we can get. So, I was thinking, when Elle's girly band plays, I want some old Michael Rivers dance moves! Let's see you—"

"No!" I interrupted. "I don't do that."

"Sheeeit!" he said, throwing up his hands. "Do you understand the pressure here? This afternoon we had to sell off the last of the RiverGroup real estate at shit prices just to finance this stupid promo-date. We don't own enough land to build an outhouse anymore. We're borrowing against everything we've got left. If this show doesn't work, we're in fuck-water up to our eyeballs. So, we have to pull out the stops!"

"I don't dance," I told him.

He rubbed his face hard. "You need an immediate brain transplant! You really do!" He turned as if complaining to Ken. "Stupid, fucking, wimpy-fashion, colorless, hairless ball-sack, teenage bullshit!" With that the screen went blank.

"He's a monster," I said to Joelene. "I hate him!"

The screen turned back on. "I heard that!" snarled Father. "I'm sitting right here, you dumb slubber butt!"

"Intense feelings are good," said Joelene, before I could react. "They play quite well in the media."

Father froze for a second, as if he had not been expecting that. "Good then. Let's see some intensity tonight. If he won't dance, we've got to have more than the boring crap from the dates with the grey-snot girl. I know," he said, his eyes glowing, "rub some dick vomit on her spoon so we can watch her eat it!"

The screen went black again. I tried to kick it, but missed and smacked my shin on a metal support bar. Momentarily, the pain obscured my revulsion and fury.

Six

I had been to the top of the three-hundred-story MonoBeat Tower before. Joelene and I had toured with channel reporters when it first opened. They showed us all the amenities, the mud and diamond lobby, the hay and crystal elevators, the light-emitting OLEDS that covered the surface and beamed advertisements, slogans, and channel shows on all sides. They also made a big deal about how the interior walls were made of a new kind of hard liquid that could be reconfigured in milliseconds. I was asked to touch some button that opened a wall as if it were a camera iris. They asked me what I thought and I tried to sound positive and interested. My attendance had been required as RiverGroup had a partnership with the company that built it, but honestly, the only appealing part of our visit was the meal at the restaurant on top, SpecificMotor 505.

Not only had my clothes-iron-scorched acorn salad and steamed elephant steak been sumptuous, but the décor had a definite *Pure H* flair. The dining room floor was black, toxic osmium tetroxide. The walls were tiled with human baby teeth, and the room was lit with a glass enclosure of glowing-orange molten lava behind.

Once Joelene and I had exited my car, we took the elevator to the three-hundredth floor and we were ushered to a green room. On the screens were a dozen channel feeds. One show was interviewing the SpecificMotor 505 chef. Another channel discussed the restaurant's design. Many were speculating on Elle's fashions for the evening. Another discussed and dissected the stolen nude photos of her. Still another reviewed RiverGroup's stock collapse, products, and chances for recovery.

I stood before it all for several minutes and felt discouraged.

Joelene turned them off and then handed me several screens. "I've written up some conversation notes for you. Elle is quite loquacious, so you probably don't have to say much but memorize this. And," she said, handing me another, "this is a list of the bands she likes and might mention. Below that are the channel shows she watches. And I included a run-down of the fashion magazines she reads. Mostly it's *Petunia Tune*, but she also likes *CuteKill*, *Ball Description*, and *Puffy Fluffer*."

"Those are terrible!"

"Regardless," she said, "look over the info. I'll see if I can work out a way for us to get to the SunEcho."

"Do you think we can?"

She took a breath. "Sneaking out of the MonoBeat, with all the security designed to seal us in, is quite problematic."

While she returned to her work at her screens, I looked over the dialogue, but it was all just silly references to Elle's awful fashion magazines. Mostly, I worried that Joelene wouldn't find a way to get to the SunEcho and Nora.

Soon, my makeup and hair artist, Petra, arrived. She was in her fifties, with bright red hair, wide, luminous sapphire eyes, a tiny blip of a nose, and pouting burgandy lips. As she lay out her tools she said, "I will do his hair, but under protest. This isn't the sort of thing he should be doing." Petra glared at Joelene.

"I agree," she said, "but we have no choice."

Petra stared coolly at me. "You poor boy. I have been so proud of you." Her lips trembled. "I remember when you danced. You were so good. I watched you all the time. And I remember when the whole world was glued to the channels when you suffered so." With one of her long black fingernails, she collected a tiny droplet from her left eye. "Unlike so many who were sorry that you didn't dance again, I loved your transformation. You were becoming a man—your own man." After shaking her head, her voice got quiet, "But this is a step backward. And it's heartbreaking. You and Nora looked so perfect together."

I said, "Thank you."

Petra picked up her glowing isotope shears. "And I don't believe that breach for a moment. That freeboot thing is crazy. It makes no sense!" She waved the blades in my face and I could smell their heat. "There has never been a breach of RiverGroup before, and it happens now? Someone was behind it. Believe me, someone was responsible!"

"Who do you think?" I asked, pulling back from her glowing scissors.

"It has to be the other families. They're jealous of you and RiverGroup."

"The report established that it was freeboot retaliation," said my advisor. "But we thank you for your opinion."

"I'm not allowed to speak my mind?" asked my hairdresser. "Is that what you mean? Are you censoring me? Is that what you're doing?"

"I didn't say that or mean to imply that."

Petra turned to me. "This whole thing makes me sick! Now your father has you sniffing the foul and over-exposed rump of this polka-dog! I didn't know Konrad Kez had grandchildren. I have never heard of Elle before, and I wasn't happy when I did."

"We are not exactly pleased either," said Joelene, "but we are trying to cope. Could we please …" She mimed cutting scissors, but Petra didn't get the hint.

"I should have gone after your father when I was young," she said, turning to me again. "I could have seduced him, when I had my full powers." She shook her abundant chest at me—it sloshed back and forth like warm gelatin. "I would have grabbed him by the ears, and gotten his attention. You know what Hiro Bruce's problem is?" asked Petra. "He's so fixed on success, he has managed to screw it up completely. Someone needs to throw him over their knee and make that ass of his glow in the dark."

"I agree with you, Petra," I said. "I agree with you completely."

Her face bloomed. "Thank you, sweet Michael! You're a darling." With that, she worked my hair in record time, applied a tanning solution to my face, did my eyes with a natural shade, and colored my lips. Once she was finished, she kissed me on the cheek, and told me she adored me.

My dresser, Stefano, helped me with my clothes, as he had done my whole life. His eyes were dark and small, his hands were as dry and rough as cigars, and he always called me Master Rivers. As I stood before the iMirrors, he sewed on my underwear, put socks on my feet; then helped me into my pants. On top, he put on an undershirt, then a gen-cotton shirt with an attached collar. Once he had gotten it tucked in and secured, he held out the jacket, and I slipped it on.

Mr. Cedar's suit looked even better now. And it didn't appear as downtrodden as I had originally thought. There was a power inside of it, as if instead of my body, it cloaked some sort of potent machine. Once Stefano had knotted my tie, he said, "You look excellent, Master Rivers." Once he had gone, Joelene looked me over.

"It's one of his best," she said. Then she got down on the tiles, and scratched at the floor. I watched dumbfounded. It was like she was imitating a cat. She found a trapdoor a foot square and lifted the lid.

I asked, "What are you doing?"

Sticking her hands inside, I heard what sounded like typing. "This building is all about liquid crystal," she said, pointing her chin toward the back of the room. The light green wall popped as if it were an enormous soap bubble—exactly as I had seen demonstrated when we toured the MonoBeat on opening day.

Behind the wall was a utility space filled with pipes, machines, and bundles of wires. In the center was a tube four feet wide with a giant toilet-bowl-shaped opening and a cut-off valve above.

"Is something wrong?" I asked, afraid a freeboot was trying to sneak up on us.

"No." I heard her type again. The wall was restored like a closing camera shutter.

A second later, we heard a knock on the door. "We're ready for Mr. Rivers."

My knees felt jittery as I walked down the entrance platform toward the table in the spotlight at the center of the restaurant. It wasn't because of the spectators in the stands, or the billions of viewers on the channels, or the sad prospect of this ridiculous promotion date, it was that I feared I wouldn't see Nora because it was too difficult. Joelene had opened the wall behind the green room, but only found pipes, tubes, and wires, not a way out. I hated to imagine that Nora would see the message on the suit, go to the SunEcho, but that I would have no way of joining her.

A deep and booming voice said, "And here he is, girls ... the greatest dancer the world has ever known, nineteen-year-old Michael Rivers of RiverGroup, looking very handsome in a sexy and scorching black suit!"

It's not black, I thought to myself. It's charcoal.

A waiter, in a military-cut navy jacket, pulled back my chair. Once I sat, he scooted me toward the carved, bituminous coal table. A moment later, a woman in a three-piece, coffee-colored bikini, took a bottle of Frix's Krill Kola Thirst Crusher from a golden tray and placed it before me with efficient moves. When I picked it up, a blast of music played and the girl did a dance and sang, "The renewable kola, with the outlaw taste! Yeah, Frix!" She smiled a toothy grin, and then dashed off.

Then I sat there before fifty channel cameras, holding the bottle and feeling like a performing seal in a circus. For a second, I considered throwing it down and leaving. The problem was, Father would probably take me back to the Loop and toss me over, and I could see the body of the dead bellybutton prostitute and the black flies that had crawled over her.

So, careful not to obscure the smiling monkey logo with an ill-placed thumb, I took a tiny sip. The stuff was salty and fishy, but not too terrible that I couldn't eke out a simulacrum of pleasure.

"He likes it," said the house voice. "Who wouldn't, with the taste and power of krill? And now, look who's joining him! It's the sexy and scintillating Elle Kez, of Ribo-Kool, granddaughter of that powerhouse of a capitalist, Konrad Kez!" After a fun-filled and faked laugh, the voice added, "Don't they look blistering?"

I saw her shoes first. They were furry pink pumps with tiny silky flowers around the sole. Her white socks had smiling pink cat faces. Her skirt was a ruffled and partly shredded carnation and plum polka-dot thing that looked like it might have belonged to a run-over flamenco dancer.

So far, it was basic *Petunia Tune* stuff, but when I looked up, I was taken aback. First of all, while her tailored grey jacket was clearly a nod to *Pure H*, the silhouette, material, and notions were all wrong. It looked more like concrete than a warm or lush fabric, and it was so pinched in the middle, I doubted she could breathe. Stranger yet, around her wasp waist, on a metal belt, ran a flock of tiny motorized hens that chased a red rooster. They orbited her every ten seconds, and while I guessed this was some reference to my fame, and maybe her and others' pursuit of me, I had no idea why it was there.

Beneath the jacket, she didn't wear a blouse. Instead, her chest was covered with pink fur that matched her pumps. On her neck the fur gradually disappeared, and from there up, she had been made-up like a cat, complete with a triangular black nose, white whiskers, and a few freckle-spots. Orange eye shadow over-emphasized her blue eyes.

On top of her head sat a massive, curly, golden wig with the texture of sea foam, three feet high and five across, shaped like an enormous bloated banana. Coming from the top were two three-foot-tall, pink rabbit ears. Between the ears were three small dioramas. One was the black, Pantheon-shaped PartyHaus. Another was a curve of Loop road with what was probably supposed to be my blue and orange car. Beside that were two naked dolls locked in an oral-genital embrace.

Once she saw that I had taken her in, she turned around, and from somewhere in the folds of the back of her skirt hung a wide, quilted beaver tail, the size of a swollen tennis racket. When she had spun all the way around, she began to sing to me in an off-key falsetto. "My heart is a daffodil! Oh, daffodil affection … daffodil affliction. Quivering daffodil of my love!" She then laughed and asked, "You know that? It's *so* petunia. Don't you think? It's by The Pipsqueak Beaver-boys. I just love them. You like my tail?"

"Your tail …" I repeated, unable to conjure anything positive. "Um … well … it's … um … "

"My heart is a daffodil!" she sang again louder and farther from key, as if she didn't know what else to do. "Daffodil affection! Daffodil affliction!"

"Hi!" I said, standing, hoping to make her stop singing. "Hello! How do you do? Yes, I saw your tail!" I made myself smile. "Please, sit down."

"Okay!" she said, relieved. "I know I sang that already!" She grit her teeth as if she felt bad. "Sorry! I guess I'm a little nervous."

From the left shoulder a teeny puff of green smoke caught my eye. Could it be her clothes had caught fire? I was saved! Our date would have to be cancelled! I was about to mention it, but then, a smoky red dot came from her other shoulder. Then more rose into the air. Her jacket was making smoky polka dots! After all the other atrocities of her costume, I don't know why that one—which actually struck me as half-clever—discouraged me most of all.

Two assistants of hers, with the same makeup, dressed in tight and shocking-pink jumpsuits, ran in, plucked the miniature hens and cock from her belt, then supported her wig and ears as she eased herself into her chair. A hulky man in blue short-shorts placed a can of Frix's Cinnamon Monkey Thirst Bomb beside her elbow. Elle didn't notice.

"You probably thought I was just a *Petunia Tune* girl, but really, I'm so much more. I'm into *Ball Description*, and I'm really into *CuteKill* and a bunch of other of the *bestest* magazines." She struck a pose, with one hand on her wig and another highlighting her cat face. "So I wanted to show everyone how mature I am. And I know *Pure H,* too!"

"Yes," I said. "I see. So, it's ... um ... good to meet you."

"Thank you!" she said, batting her eyelashes. "I don't have to tell you, but you're every girl's dream. I mean, *everyone* I know wants to keep you in her petunia dungeon!" As she laughed, she leaned forward, but then craned her neck backward to keep her wig and ears from tipping. "Listen," she whispered, "if this thing falls get out of the way."

As I gazed up at the mountain of hair, I pictured it tipping over and flattening me like something from a cartoon.

"Awe!" she cooed. "Your smile is so cute!" After a squeaky giggle, she said, "Let me tell you all about myself because I am so fascinating. Okay first, I had my big coming-out party yesterday. It was the biggest and *bestest* party ever. I had so many cute bands; I could have died. I even had The Pipsqueak Beaver-boys!" A second later she frowned. "You listen to them, don't you?"

"Pig Squeak Believer Boys," I confirmed. "Sorry, I'm not familiar with them."

"No!" she laughed, as if I had made a joke, "The Pipsqueak Beaver-boys! They're those adorable guys who dress like beavers, and ... you know ... have their little buns hanging out." She giggled in falsetto. "They're so hot and precious! I can't wait for them to sing tonight. They're music is the *bestest* ever. They played at my party and it was the *bestest* ever. You had to see it on the channels!"

"I must have missed it."

"Well," she pouted, "I'm into whatever you're into." She leaned forward an inch, so that her jacket revealed more of her furry cleavage. "You like hair?"

Glancing down at my hands, I felt like I was the one exposed, and it reminded me of the feeling I had when I woke from my heart attack and found myself before thousands of fans screaming to know if I had a catheter, bed sores, or brain damage.

"Oh, I'm sorry! Please, don't worry!" she said, seemingly distraught. "It comes off with a solution. I can be hairless if you like that. Or I could eat anything you want. I've eaten all sorts of weird things for boys who like that."

The cooling fans in my jacket came on, as I felt embarrassed for both of us. "No," I mumbled, "… um … no, thank you."

As if panicked, her eyes darted toward her assistants off camera. When she focused on me, she said, "So, my family's company—Ribo-Kool—is just the best ever! I know the critics are down on us, but the critics are stinky anus stupids! When we get together, we're going to show those critics, aren't we?"

The flirting was over, I presumed. Now we were supposed to suggest that our family companies merge. "Yes," I said, following along because that seemed the easiest thing to do, "our families could work together."

"That's a pink petunia idea!" she gushed. "I'm so excited! And I think RiverGroup is just the *bestest* ever. I mean, you guys were number one, once. Right?" After clearing her throat, she sat up, and said, "I just have to thank all my *bestest* of fashion friends." She began naming all her designers, stylists, sewers, shoppers, trainers, dieticians, cooks, and doctors.

Finally, the waiter saved me from hearing who breastfed her. She ordered Frix Corporation dried marine turtle parts stuffed in moon-dried raisins—a polka-dot dish. I requested the Frix Corporation satellite lamb roasted over butternut, redwood, and the seamed silk stockings of one hundred depressed housewives.

After the waiter left, the house voice said, "Stay tuned for the hot and naughty conclusion to this historic date between the two most powerful companies in the security system market, RiverGroup and Ribo-Kool."

"And we're clear," said the director, the same one making Father's documentary. He had long silvery hair and wide, feverish eyes. He must have known how fast he talked for he reiterated everything. "Guys," he began, "you're beautiful. Beautiful. But help me out here, okay? Help me out! Please, stay on the script! You remember the script? We're flirting. Flirting! We're in love. We're loving and fun."

Elle's two pink assistants, like a pit crew, ran to her side, fixed her hair, repositioned her ears, and repainted her nose. As they worked she complained to the director, "I thought I was totally petunia!"

"Oh, you're beautiful," he said. "Beautiful! Don't forget the script. Stay on the script. That's all I was saying. All right, honey?"

"I was speaking from my heart. My heart is a daffodil!" she tried to sing.

Joelene put her hand on my shoulder and whispered, "You look wounded." She sounded more amused than upset.

"I feel like I punctured a lung."

"Try to have fun," was her only advice.

"Remember the script!" shouted the director. "Let's clear. Clear everyone!" Joelene left, and after they applied another puff of the pink foundation to her forehead, Elle's people ran off. "Aaaaand … we're back!"

"I met that Nora at a fashion convention," said Elle, without missing a beat. "She didn't look at me, and she was just so full of herself. I'm not against her, but everyone on the channels was talking about how dull and ugly she is. What I don't get is her natural hair! *Hello?* She looks like a nasty slub girl." Although she tried to smile prettily, as if to temper what she'd said, I saw a droplet of undiluted malice in her eyes. "Everyone on the channels has been gushing gallons of nectar about me. And I wouldn't be surprised if I get twenty times her measly ratings."

That was definitely not on the itinerary, and until that point, I had tried to imagine that at some level, she was much like myself—a soft creature forced into a hard role. But once she had insulted Nora, I couldn't pretend to sympathize or even care. And as she continued on how to improve RiverGroup, I closed my right eye for several beats, and as if I were killing her, or at least neutralizing her style, bleached the pink from her face, the purple from her cat nose, and the gold from her wig.

Our meal was served, and at least the food was wonderful. My satellite lamb was perfectly roasted, savory, beautifully plated, and I could taste a hint of sensual despair.

Once the dishes were cleared, the PA said, "And now, let's watch these two love-dogs dance while the super fabulous Pipsqueak Beaver-boys sing their number one hit, *Palpitations 4 U, My Kitty-Cake Pussy-Willow Girl.*"

Six men in furry brown outfits, with huge buckteeth, quilted tails, and their aforementioned backsides exposed, took turns singing to us. Each had a shtick. One cried. Another beat his chest adamantly. The short one played with his hair. The last massaged his buttocks as a cook might knead dough. Their accompanying music was nothing more than an ocean of syrupy strings and an unflinching beat that sounded more like dynamite than a drum.

Fortunately, Elle had so much trouble balancing her wig that our proposed dance didn't happen. We wound up standing side by side, her assistants holding up her hair.

Fireworks filled the air with smoke, and as the Beavers ended their song with big bucktoothed smiles, the swimwear Frix soda man and woman returned, each cradling plastic baby monkeys in their arms. The crowd had been quiet until then, but must have been prompted to stand and cheer. And, as the silver-haired director called to us to smile and wave into the cameras, the house voice said, "There it was, folks … the greatest, most magical and romantic evening in the history of corporate mergers!"

Chapter 7

During the post-date interviews, the reporters were supposed to just ask about us and our feelings, but kept questioning my experience in the slubs, RiverGroup's troubles, the stock collapse, the exodus of customers, and the like. When someone finally asked Elle what she thought of me, she threw her arms around my chest and applied her tongue to my ear. The director thought that the place to end and yelled, "Cut!"

Minutes later, Joelene and I were back in the green room. Slumping in a chair, I swabbed the furrows of my ear with a sanitizing towelette. "Did you hear how vicious she was?"

Joelene got onto her stomach on the floor, opened the trapdoor, and stuck her hands in. After she had entered a code, the back wall disappeared. Standing, she picked up a bag, stepped before the wires and tubes, and ran her finger over a shiny metal label on the biggest pipe.

"Joelene," I said, worried she had lost her mind, "what are you doing?"

Pulling a handful of folded material from the bag, she tossed it to me and said, "Put that on."

When I shook the velvety thing open, it was an ugly dark maroon jumpsuit with a gathered waist, a hood, feet, and attached mittens. Worst of all were the closures down the front. "Snaps? What is this? I don't want to wear this."

As she began to slip into a matching outfit, she said, "Protection from the cold. Come on, we don't have much time. Put it on!"

"What are we doing? Are we going to see Nora?"

"Yes." She pulled the hood of her outfit over her head, and then she grasped the large, metal sprocket—like a steering wheel—and with great effort began turning it. The wide toilet-bowl-shaped opening began to fill with a clear, viscous liquid that reminded me of corn syrup.

Glancing at the maroon jumpsuit and the pipe and back, I said, "I am not getting in the sewer!"

"This is the building's cooling system."

"Whatever it is," I said with a nervous laugh, "I'm not getting in. Besides, I don't know how to swim."

She turned to me. "The elevators are on the system. The stairs—which would take us a couple of hours to climb down—are on the system. Even jumping off the side—as foolish and difficult as that would be—would be on the system. If you want to see Nora, this is it." Since I hadn't moved, she took the jumpsuit from my hand, tore open the front so that the dozen snaps sounded like a drum roll, and then held open one of the pant legs. "And don't worry," she added, "we won't be swimming. We'll be falling."

I didn't like her joke, but stepped into the first leg. "I'm not going to die, am I?"

"What kind of a question is that?" She eyed me. "No! The SunEcho isn't far. I've charted a course that will get us within one block. We just don't have much time." After I stepped into the other pant leg, she pulled the velvety material up and over my suit and began snapping the front closed. Then she dug into her bag and handed me what looked like a yellow diving mask. "Put it over your head," she said, showing me how it worked.

I gazed at the open pipe and the strange, convex bubble of thick liquid that looked like a clear pillow. "You sure about this?"

She grasped the metal wheel above, pulled herself up onto the rim, and straddled the opening. "It's just bulk metallic water." The phrase meant nothing to me. From a pocket, she produced a small spray bottle, and spritzed the surface, which turned dull like beach glass. Then she began stamping on the stuff with the force one might use to try and kill a steel cockroach.

Because she looked ridiculous, I laughed, but obviously the stuff was tough skinned, like a tomato. After several kicks, her foot finally punched through with a heavy *glop*. Clamping her teeth around the air-supply mask, she lowered herself in and as she did, the liquid made wet gurgles and burps. Holding onto the rim of the pipe with one mitten-covered hand, she turned, and reached her other toward me. She spoke, but with the air supply in her mouth, the only word I thought I understood sounded like *Ora*.

"I don't like this," I said, backing up.

"*Ora!*" she said louder. "*Ome ere!*" Pushing herself up a foot, she shot her hand toward me, and grasped the front of my jumpsuit.

"No!" I cried, as she began to pull me toward her. "Joelene, stop!" Although I tried to twist away, her mitten-covered grip was as strong as iron. I got my hands on either side of the pipe and, as though I were doing a push-up, tried to keep her from dragging me in. The jumpsuit stretched over my neck and shoulders. My arms began to vibrate and I could feel my muscles lose power. The stuff stunk like gasoline and bleach. "Okay!" I said, giving up. "Stop! Let me put the mask on!" When she let go, I slipped the mask over my face and bit the mouthpiece. For a second, I wasn't sure if I could breathe with it on. The plastic tasted sour and the goggles made everything distant and hazy. Peering at the thick fluid, I wasn't sure I really wanted to get in. There had to be another way!

Joelene, as if impatient, grasped the front of my jumpsuit again and dragged me in. Next, I was falling head first in complete darkness. I screamed into my air supply, but the stuff absorbed all sounds. I hated to be going head first, but there wasn't room to turn. It was like I was a human bullet in some strange slime-filled gun barrel.

A tiny green light shot by and for a split second illuminated the shiny walls and my mitten-covered hands. Two beats later another flew past at a hundred miles per hour. Craning my neck, I saw Joelene ahead in the next green strobe. She was two feet farther down and was covered in a slipstream of elongated bubbles like jade scimitars. Her head was down as if trying to see where we were going. In the next flash, she gazed up, as if checking on me.

How long were we going to fall? And what would happen when we hit bottom? Would we be squashed? Would they find us days later flat and frozen?

We were never going to get to the SunEcho. Nora would wait and wait. Finally, when the news of my death came, she would throw herself to the floor, devastated.

Trying to wave at Joelene, I wanted to signal her to stop this and get us out of here, but in the next several green flashes, she was gazing down. Then she extended her arms above her as though she were going to catch me.

Next, I smashed into her. Only, somehow we didn't quite touch, and when I flipped over backward, and fell onto my back, I was dizzy and shocked, but not hurt. Maybe the liquid had insulated the impact.

We weren't in the pipe anymore, but in a large tank, fifteen feet wide, illuminated with a grid of tiny blue lights like a geometric sky. The liquid was thicker, heavier, and colder down here, and it took all my strength just to suck air through the mouthpiece.

Joelene stood and put her masked face before mine. First she nodded, as if to confirm that I was alive, then she pointed left.

I shook my head. She pointed adamantly, but I shook my head harder.

Grasping my arms, she hoisted me up and carried me over her shoulder. I hit her back because I hated her and wanted her to get us out of this. After a few steps, she pushed me into another smaller pipe, and that's when I panicked because I didn't want to fall again.

Trashing, I tried to kick her and get her away from me and then I don't know if my air ran out, or if I just didn't have the strength to inhale. I got one hand to my face and yanked the air mask off so I could scream, but the thick goo filled my mouth and tasted sour and acidic like an uncoated aspirin. I began to gag and then instinctively inhaled and sucked in more of the cold lava.

I was dying. My chest was beginning to spasm. An adrenaline terror started in my heart and shot toward my hands. Flailing my arms and feet, I felt like I had milliseconds left.

Meanwhile, Joelene put one hand on my right shoulder, the other atop my head, and pushed me down. She was killing me! My body began to cry for air. I was frantic. My throat and lungs burned.

Below, my feet touched a distorted glowing yellow circle. She shoved me again. I squeezed through an opening and all around was blinding light. For a second, I was inside a blob, like a solid balloon. With a rubbery snap, the gunk tore itself from my throat and chest and all around, and dropped me onto a hard surface. I retched, and then sucked in air.

The warm, perfumed air smelled like fresh apples. I inhaled deeply, coughed, but could breathe. Then I sobbed a few times, because for a moment I had been sure I was I going to die.

Above, I heard wind and gently bubbling water and decided it was on a sound system. A couple of feet away, sat a glowing pink commode, and on a shelf was a vase of violet dahlias. This was a woman's bathroom.

Above was a hole torn in the white ceiling tiles. Inside the open end of a three-foot-wide pipe was the shine of the gunk and a few distorted blue lights. A dark shape appeared in the liquid and then a foot encased in clear goo emerged. I rolled away as Joelene was first lowered in an elongated orb of gel. When it snapped away, she fell to the floor.

Pulling off her mask, she laughed as if relieved. "We made it."

"I hate you!" I told her. "That was terrible! I couldn't breathe."

Scanning me up and down, as if afraid, she asked, "Are you all right?"

"No! You almost killed me."

"Can you move?"

"Yes," I said, sorry that I hadn't broken my skull.

"Come," she said, giving me a hand up. "We must hurry. Put your goggles on."

"I'm not going back in!"

"No," she said, "now it's your disguise."

I hesitated for a second, then pulled the mask over my face, but didn't breath through the tube. We stepped from the bathroom into a long dark hallway. At the end of it was a twelve-foot-tall wooden door. Joelene pushed it open.

Then we were on the street in boiling hot air filled with meat smoke from street vendors, hundreds of intense perfumes, and a note of rotting trash. Hundreds of people passed in all directions—salarymen in cheap cherry, peach, and lavender suits, shoppers with bags and boxes, tourists in night swimwear and headpieces, partiers in sheer garb, and dating couples holding hands, kissing, or leaning against the walls feeling each other. I saw two *Box 4* readers all in white with artificial tears dripping from metal tubes next to their eyes. I saw an *Om Om* girl in a brown suit with her lips cut open. Two *Ball Description* girls were dressed as cats in big pastel gowns. A group of Ültra boys, in all manner of fur, kelp, high-heeled boots, and scraggly black wigs, skipped by. And all up and down the street hung glaring speakers singing about rewoven fabrics, buttons, beads, lace, ric-rac, and other notions. Others promised recreational surgery, vegetable alcohols, and iambic psychodramas.

"'Is way," said Joelene, enunciating her words like someone might while holding a cigar between their teeth. As we wove our way through the masses, we must have looked like two service men on their way to a biohazard and no one recognized me. A block down, we crossed the street, ducked into an alley, and soon came to the unmarked side entrance to the SunEcho.

Joelene said, "We only have a minute."

I paid no attention as I started to unsnap the jumpsuit.

"No!" she said. "We're back on the system. Don't take if off."

"I can't see her in this!"

"You have to."

I hated to have come this far only to look this bad. Grasping the metal bar, I yanked the door open and marched inside.

The SunEcho had been in existence as long as I had been alive. The story goes that not one customer came in for a decade. Then, one day, a tall, lean man entered. He wore a long, dark grey jacket and had his face covered with charcoal net. After he drank a cream coffee, he sat and scribbled in a notebook for several hours. He then paid and never returned. Exactly a year later, a new magazine, called *Pure H*, appeared on the newsstands. The magazine soon sold out as fashion devotees discovered the brilliant writing and imagery. And in that issue was a story about a disfigured but disguised man, who visited the SunEcho, worked in his notebooks and went on to publish a copy magazine. Since then, the waiting list for the SunEcho was more than six thousand days.

Although Nora and I didn't need reservations, we were not going into the main sitting room. As was the custom, when one suggested to meet at the SunEcho that meant the auxiliary room.

It was a square room thirty by thirty feet at the back of the shop. Why it was there, or what purpose it served wasn't clear, except to the owner, one assumed. The walls were covered with a warm, double-warp wool broadcloth. Underfoot was a mosaic made of scrap metal from 100 Loop accidents. Besides the two doors, one leading out into an alley, and the other into the concierge's area, the only other feature was a single small, straight-backed wooden chair that sat in the middle.

The room was packed and warm. As my eyes adjusted to the dim, I saw Nora two feet from me. She wore a long grey coat buttoned to the neck. Her hair looked darker, her nose flatter, and something was odd about her eyes. For an instant, I worried that her father had hurt her—beaten her or given her some terrible and disfiguring drug. A second later, I realized it wasn't Nora.

The two women on either side of her resembled Nora, too. The one on the left had her eyes, but her lips were too thin. The other had her chin and neck, but her eyes were the wrong shade of mahogany. The three of them looked me up and down and sneered.

As my eyes continued to adjust to the dim, I saw that the room was filled with young women all Nora's height, with dark hair, and olive complexions. Each was similar to her, but wrong.

My heart sank. Nora wasn't here! She hadn't come because she had hated the date. And she hated me. She didn't want to see me after I had even pretended to flirt with that cat-bunny-beaver girl. And now instead of her, I was in a room filled with *Pure H* imposters and *Pure H* pretenders. I felt heartbroken and angry, and was about to tear off my goggles and throw them to the floor, when I noticed someone on the chair.

She too wore a long grey coat, but its material was smoother and more refined than all the others. And her loosely hanging hair had been brushed not combed and was at once perfectly ordered and yet free and unfussy. Most of all though, she was the only one not glaring at us, not trying to guess who we were, or trying to decide if we belonged. She alone waited patiently and calmly.

Eight

When I stepped before her and saw her face, I chided myself for thinking that any of the others even slightly resembled her. And it wasn't just that her skin was softer and smoother, her features perfectly symmetrical, her eyes a deeper achromatic black, but that she seemed at once stronger and more vulnerable than all of them put together.

She had been gazing forward, with her smoky-colored eyelids half closed, as if meditating. When I stepped beside her, first she looked up with fright, but then as she peered into my eyes through the mask, warmth filled her. Standing, she put her arms around me, nestled her mouth close to my ear, and said, *"A week of green rain."*

Her words completed the full quote from our first date. And she was right, we had become that dead couple in *Pure H*, who lay side by side, their hands an inch apart. Only it wasn't rigor mortis or chance that had separated our hands, it was the world … it was our families.

I held her to me for the first time and discovered how our bodies matched, how her eyes met the height of my lips, how my arms surrounded her and exactly fit the curve of her back. Squeezing her to me, I inhaled the sweet sandalwood of her hair.

Then she removed the goggles and air supply from my face. I felt silly for having left it on and was about to say so, when she tilted her head to the right then touched her mouth to mine.

Like an enormous bubble, the universe collapsed, and the only thing that remained was the two-dimensional plane where our lips met. Hers felt warm and creamy, like butter frosting. Then, I don't know which of us began moving first, we were circling our lips against each other. A tension like the winding of a miniature watch spring begin to build. We rubbed our lips together, and then we were pressing our bodies firmly against each other. We opened our mouths, and just as I felt like I wanted to kiss her hard, or bite her, she pulled back.

Her nostrils were flared, her lips, swollen. She was breathing through her mouth. And several errant hairs fluttered in front of her eyes. One stuck to her moist forehead. With a husky breath, she said, "Stop."

I wanted the opposite like I have never wanted anything and moved toward her, but she pushed me away. The world returned. I had completely forgotten, but we were in public—in the SunEcho auxiliary room. Fifty fake Noras were glaring at us, several were muttering to themselves, and all of their cheap perfumes filled the air with a saccharine and impatient musk. A shameful heat covered me. And as I let my arms fall to my sides, I could feel the ventilation system in my suit struggle to circulate air beneath the velvet jumpsuit.

"Michael," she said, as she stroked the side of my face with one of her dove-grey gloved hands. "Another time." She looked down shyly.

"Excuse me," said Joelene leaning in, "ten more seconds."

"Already?" I asked, dismayed.

Leaning in, Nora put her mouth beside my ear. I thought she was going to kiss me goodbye, but she said, "Someone is trying to keep us apart."

Her words surprised me. "Who?"

"Someone close."

Her words caused a shiver to pass through me. "Could someone close be keeping us apart?" I asked my advisor.

"We can't stay on the system," she said, glancing toward the camera in the corner of the room. "We must go."

Nora said, "Be careful, Michael."

I wanted to grasp her, maybe even pick her up and run. I wanted to take us somewhere where we would never be found.

"It's time," said Joelene.

Nora hugged me again. She said, "*Light is falling.*"

All the way to Kobehaba, where we were to meet Father for the wrap-party, I sat slumped in my Loop car seat. As much as I had been alive when with her, now I felt dead apart.

"It was Father," I said, not looking up. "He's trying to keep us apart. He hates what I've become, and he hates her."

"As yet," Joelene said, while monitoring her screen, "there's no evidence to support that theory." Her eyes met mine. "However, I do not mean that it can be completely ruled out either."

"He did it!" I said, sure. "This is his revenge for when I quit dancing. He made it so I couldn't be with Nora. He did this!"

Joelene didn't reply. A moment later, her eyes latched onto something on one of her screens. She turned it toward me and increased the volume. *Intellectuals and Soup* was on again.

"Unequivocally," said Bow Tie, "it was Michael Rivers."

They played a system video of Nora hugging me in my goggles and jumpsuit from the SunEcho from only minutes before.

"They found us?" I asked, surprised.

"Impossible!" scoffed Iron Bra from behind her glass bowl. "I've just checked the history from the channel cameras in the elevators and the stairs of the MonoBeat. He wasn't there. He could not have gotten from SpecificMotor to the SunEcho in time. What we're seeing is some sort of theater."

"I don't believe so," said Pink Hat thoughtfully, stirring a new bowl of soup. "It is Michael. And that's Nora. Just look at the sensuality of their kiss. It's palpable and pungent. The kind of kiss that connects the spheres, the spirits, and the glands.

They are sharing a final moment together. I feel sorry for them and their companies. Certainly with that power, the union of RiverGroup and MKG would have been strong, authoritative, and commanding."

"When she took your goggles off," said Joelene, as she snapped off the screen, "your disguise was compromised. I'm not surprised we were discovered, but I thought it wouldn't be for a day or two." She shook her head slowly. "We should have found a place off the system." Leaning back on her chair, she touched her fingertips together, and said, "This is trouble."

A moment later, the car entered the garage of the building where the wrap-party was, and as we headed up in the turbofan-powered elevator, operated by a woman in a violet hoop skirt and bonnet, I asked, "Does Father watch that *Soup* show?"

"Doubtful. But other channels will surely be speculating soon, so I suggest we make this as short a visit as possible."

"I'm telling him that I know what he did," I said. "He let the freeboot shoot me because he hates me."

"Michael," she said, quietly, "we don't have evidence to prove his involvement. I appreciate your ambition to confront him, but don't advise it now."

When the bonnet woman pulled a huge iron lever and the doors opened, I had to squint and cover my ears. Screeching music played and patterns of light flashed in all directions. The floor vibrated an agitated violet. All over the place, screens played over-saturated snippets of Ültra epics. Screaming men … knives cutting through flesh … stone clubs bashing stuffed animals, fruit, and medical specimens.

A hostess with heavy dark eye makeup, white lips, and a tube in her right nostril led us in. All the swirling colors, signs, and screens were giving me a headache. I closed my colored eye, but still the place blinked and vibrated like a hundred electrical storms.

Partiers, in all manner of Ültra costume, waved and remarked as we passed.

– She's hotrod!
– Loved her furry tits!
– Bereave her tail!
– Billion times better!
– *Subtract her and abstract her. Turn her and burn her!*

Keeping my eyes straight ahead, I ignored them and their words and ridiculous lyrics. Meanwhile, I wondered if Joelene was right. If I did accuse him, all he would do was deny it and scream louder than I ever could.

We came before a large, round table made out of a fresh redwood stump with the RiverGroup logo carved on top. Father sat with his back against the window that looked out onto the sparkling lights of the port city. His chocolate cake Afro was fluffier than ever. Around his neck he wore a green ruff, and his enormous jacket was covered with wet hunter-green paint. Stuffed in the breast pocket was what looked like a cut of raw pork and a black rubber glove.

His girls sat on either side. A blonde wore blue foil. A redhead was covered with tar. One wore blinking sequins and nothing else. A brunette looked like the Frix bikini girl from the date. The last was decorated with yellow icing like a birthday cake. The word *unhappy* was written across her chest with blue.

"There's our cunt Romeo!" said Father. As he stood and started around the table, he pointed left to right. "These are my girls: Conni, Penni, Hunni, and Benni." He stopped, pretended to suck a thumb, and spoke like a lisping baby, "All the *wittle* spaceships of cunt!" He guffawed so hard I feared he might cough up his spleen.

As he finished coming around, I noticed that whatever his jacket touched got smeared with green paint. "Close-up!" he said to his film crew, then proceeded to throw his arms around me.

"Get off!" I said, pushing him away. His jacket left stains on my hands, but not on my suit.

"The stock is up!" he said, pumping his fist. "You were still dull, but she was great, right girls?" The women rang in with approvals.

"If you don't mind," said Joelene, "we would like to retire. We're both very—"

"What's the matter?" interrupted Father. "You just got here! Come on! Have a drink! We've got some very lard car-*rot* juice." He then put his face before mine and breathily sang, "*Welcome to my fermented intestinal garden!*"

His breath was like compost. "You smell!" I said, leaning back.

Father thought that hilarious. Whipping around he said, "Ken-baby! O keeper of digits ... what were the magical and astounding ratings?"

Ken, who sat beside the birthday cake girl, glanced at a small glowing screen and answered, "The magical and astounding ratings were twenty-one point seven, sir!"

"Twenty-*fucking*-one-point-*fucking*-seven!" howled Father. "Is that a number!"

"That's a number!" said Ken.

"It's exceptional," said Xavid, who I hadn't noticed before. He was dressed in his usual black seal pelts, his huge, amber glasses, and a peak of white hair on top of his head.

"Five times higher than any of your dates with Nora," added Ken.

"There are mitigating factors," said Joelene. "The shooting caused a spike in—"

"And look here," continued Father, ignoring her. He pointed to a man who sat on the near side of the table between a woman with some sort of chrome medical-looking device that held her mouth open to expose her teeth and gums, and a nude man covered head to foot with what looked like olive oil and broken insect legs. "Let me introduce a real glazed ham: President, CEO, and Chief of Long Dickness at the distinguished company of Ribo-Kool, Chesterfield Kez." Father laughed and shook his shoulders like he was doing an odd, little dance. "He's Elle's uncle. Chester, this is my super famous son, Michael … in person and completely alive!"

Chesterfield had a hard, bony face that looked like little more than a skin-covered skull. His nostrils large, his lips, blue. Over his bright beetle-green suit, he wore a pile of carved wooden necklaces just like the devoted businessman's *LardLik* reader he obviously was. He stood, extended a hand, and said, "Very large pleasure, indeed."

Without shaking his hand, I said to Father, "I refuse to see Elle again."

"Hold on!" bellowed Father, with a laugh. "Family meeting. Be right back!" Grabbing my arm, he dragged me across the aisle in front of a row of flashing and whirring gambling and sex machines. "Shut your hole!" he snarled. "We're cooking with lard. Chesterfield likes the numbers so much we're going ahead full force. We're going to marry you two at the product show. That'll blow those MKG semen suckers away!"

It was a joke. It was insane. "No," I said, "I can't! I won't!"

"You're going to!" he said, stretching the "o" in *to* and covering my face with his vile breath. "You're marrying the spank skank and that's it!"

I wanted to smash his face. "You had me shot!" I fired back.

"Did not!" said Father, sounding exactly like a five-year-old.

"I know for sure."

"You do not!" He laughed. "That would be massive stupid—even for me!"

"You had the freeboot shoot me because you hate me. It was someone close."

Father glared at me as though I were crazy. When Joelene came to my side, he asked her, "What lies are you telling him?"

"I have not told him any lies, sir." She tried to smile, but I could see she was annoyed at me. "Understandably, given your histories, he assumes that you were somehow behind his misfortune."

"I would never do that. It doesn't make any business sense!"

"Sir," continued Joelene, "I'll take Michael home now. He

needs rest. We're very excited about the ratings, but we—"

"Ass missile!" he growled at her. "We have to keep moving!" Lowering his voice he said, "They're all against us! MKG is trying to take us down. Now, this date saved our holes tonight, but we've got to use this momentum for the product show." He kept having to unstick the armpits of his paint-covered jacket as he moved and gestured. "You know what we heard just ten minutes ago? MKG is planning to announce their new product the same time as our product show!" He jabbed a finger in my chest. "Don't accuse me or RiverGroup. It was them! That grey-sucking Nora and her shit-faced dad. They shot you! *That* makes sense."

"There's no evidence of that, sir," said Joelene.

"I'd find evidence if I had time to look for it. That whole thing is a joke. How did that fucking freeboot get out of there? And how did he shoot Michael in the hands and feet from where he was supposed to be? Answer me that?"

"Again," said my advisor, obviously keeping her exasperation in check, "I'm not saying that I have all the answers, but the family commission has stated that a single freeboot did the shooting. And no evidence was found that MKG was involved."

"Commission *com-fiction*!" he spat at her. "MKG is on the commission! Besides, all the families hate us because we have them by the balls. They've been waiting to fuck with us for years."

"That's all conjecture," said Joelene.

"No, it's butt-tastic truth!" he declared. "MKG planned it, did it, and now they think they're going to be number one!"

"That's not true," I said.

"It was them!" screamed Father. "They're a thick layer of butt snot on toast!" He shook his head solemnly. "They think they're going to win, but they're not! We're gonna screw them right back." He threw his arms out. "We're gonna have our big merger news, and an even bigger merger wedding."

"I'm not marrying her!" I said. "I will only marry Nora."

"Did I ask you a question?" he snarled. "No! So don't fucking talk. And besides, I banned *her* name. So don't even think it!"

"Nora!" I said into his face.

The tendons in his neck tightened. He stepped an inch before me. "Dare you to repeat it."

Into the rancid fog of his breath, I said, "Nora." I stood my ground even as my eyes began to water from both the rotten carrot stink and my own fear.

Red blotches appeared across his face and neck. His right shoulder rose and I was sure he was about to backhand me. At the last moment, though, he turned to his film crew and screamed. "Stop! I can't have my boy talking back like this! Turn it off, and get outta my face!" As the two men backed away, Father stepped before Joelene. "Doesn't he understand his duty to RiverGroup?" Before she answered, he asked me, "Why do you think I worked so hard to have a son?"

I said, "I wish you hadn't."

"Well, I did!" he scoffed. "And believe me, I'm *real* sorry now." He paused, and then his lower lip began to vibrate. Jamming his fist onto his lips he tried to control himself, but he was crying. "Fucker pies!" he said, his voice shaky.

While the threat of violence before had been scary, this really frightened me. I hated his screaming and ranting, but the idea that he was going to break down was worse. I stared down at my shoes, ashamed.

"I tried so hard," he said. "So hard. All I want is your help with the company. We're in real bad shit—the squishy kind of shit with whole corn kernels." He took a deep breath and swallowed as if to down his unhappiness. "I gave you life."

"But now you're taking it away."

"If there's no RiverGroup, there *is* no life. Don't you understand?"

I shook my head. "Without her, I have nothing."

He smacked his face with his hand, clenched his eyes, and said, "Get outta here! I can't take this. I can feel my hemorrhoids acting up!" Pointing at Joelene, he said, "Take the idiot home and teach him something!"

"Sir, let me reassure you that—"

"Excuse me!" interrupted Ken, who had run from the table. "Sorry, Mr. Rivers. Bad news!" After glancing at Joelene and me, he said, "Just heard it on the channels."

"What now?" asked Father, as if he wanted to collapse.

Gritting his teeth, his blue eyebrows practically knotted together over his nose, Ken said, "Please don't be mad at me."

Father rolled his eyes. "You raccoon rectum! Just tell me!"

Ken cupped his hands over Father's ear and whispered. As he did, Father's eyes got large. "No!" He stood back and glared at us. For a second, I thought he was going to laugh. "They didn't!" he said, shaking his head. "No. It's impossible! They couldn't have. I completely forbid it!"

Ken shrugged as if he couldn't explain it and backed away a step.

Father's face turned the color of salmon. The veins on his forehead throbbed. "Fucktastic bombastic!" he finally bellowed. "You saw *her!* You met our enemy!"

"Sir," said Joelene, shielding me with an arm, "please! Listen to the facts. What happened was that we—"

Father's right fist shot forward in a karate chop of a punch that slammed her breastbone. A loud and horrible *puhh* came from her as she fell backward, crashed into a vending machine, and crumpled onto the floor. "I should kill you!" screamed Father. "I should have them give you an ant enema. We're facing the biggest crisis of all time and you help him do this!"

When he turned to me, I saw a ripple of fury like I had never seen before pass through his face. It was like a tectonic shift beneath his skin. "I'm killing someone today," he said to me, his voice raw.

Crouching beside my advisor, but keeping an eye on him so he didn't try and bash me over the head, I asked her, "Are you all right?"

As she huffed to try and get air back into her lungs, I think she said, "Yeah."

"First we pull a super twenty-two rating!" said Father, tugging at his Afro like he wanted to rip it from his skull. "We're hard lard and now another disaster!" Pointing at Ken, he said, "Get back to the table and tell Chesterfield something. Say whatever he wants to hear. Beg him. Cry for him! Anything!"

"Anything!" said Ken. He ran back to the table.

Joelene was breathing easier now, but her eyes shined with tears, her mouth was scrunched into a frown, and her teeth were tightly clenched. She was glaring at Father as if she were going to burn a hole through his chest.

"You are officially fired from RiverGroup," said Father to her. "I'll get you kicked out of the families and sent to slubberland where they'll eat your guts alive."

"It was my plan!" I told him. "I did it."

"Dick-tastic!" he sneered as he rubbed his hand, as if now he felt the impact of his punch. "You're like the worse son in the history of the universe."

"Just leave her alone!"

"Hiro!" said Xavid as he approached, "look what you've done to your 'fro!" With three long, hornbeam chopsticks, he began to fluff Father's Afro back into shape.

"They saw Nora!" Father whined. "It's a betrayal of everything RiverGroup. Most of all it's a big fat slap in my face."

"You need to control this," said his hairdresser, quietly yet sternly, as he chopsticked Father's Afro.

"I won't do anything if you fire Joelene," I threatened.

With his hands on his hips, Father glared at me. "You're no help anyway!"

"Hiro," said Xavid, "remember what I said. We need him. You need to *use* him."

"He just mocks me or makes me look like an idiot!"

"Joelene didn't do any of this. It was my plan," I said, ignoring his ridiculous hairdresser.

"Michael," Joelene said, "maybe it's time that I should—"

"No!" I told her, hating even the suggestion that she should quit. The thing was, she didn't look so much angry or hurt, but resolute.

"She can't leave me!" I said to both Father and her. Looking her in the eye, I said, "I need her. She's like my real family."

Joelene suppressed a smile, and then patted the back of my hand.

"Butt vomit!" said Father. "What is the matter with you? She's your damn tutor! Not your *family*. Don't you know anything?"

"Well," I asked, thumbing toward Xavid, "who is *he?*"

"A damn good and loyal RiverGroup officer!" A drop of sweat rolled down Father's forehead. When he wiped it with the sleeve of his jacket, it left a green smear.

"Now look what you did!" said Xavid, scolding him like a little boy. As he got out a silky cloth and wiped Father's forehead, he leaned in and said, "I think you need to make it very clear to them what you expect."

"Yeah!" agreed Father. A beat later, he asked, "How do you think?"

"What about your friend in Europa-13?"

Father narrowed his eyes at his hairdresser. "Great idea. A threat!"

"Exactly!"

"Let us go back to the compound," I told Father.

"Don't think so! We're taking a drive." With a wink toward Xavid, he added, "I've got a rotten, horrible, stinking, evil bastard I'd like you to meet."

Nine

From the outside, our Loop cars were identical orange-and-blue-painted teardrops, with a tilted glass all around. Inside, his was not surprisingly a design catastrophe.

Every surface was upholstered with a different material so it looked like a cheap fabric sampler. Unlike the muted, indirect lighting in my car, here a hundred blue and orange pinpoint lasers scribbled Ültra lyrics everywhere at high speed. While it covered everything in a senseless, vibrating surface, occasionally a phrase lingered in the eye. *Unite our diseases ... Engage booster fuck ... My tender gender fatality.*

When I stepped in, I found that the floor was covered with an unpleasant super-shag rug that crunched like dried leaves. Scattered among the yarns was a vast assortment of garbage, including empty carrot liquor bottles, star-shaped pills, phallus-shaped pills, fist-shaped pills, skull-shaped pills, red and black dildos, some of which were twitching like dying insects, and several bits of what looked like bloody fur. I figured it was the debris of a debauched car-party while he watched the promotion date.

My car had only four seats with consoles; his had a dozen chairs all the way around. He and Xavid sat on the far side, the film crew set up in back, and Joelene and I were closest to the side door.

Once we were on the Loop, Father opened a bottle and poured glasses of carrot.

"Some rotten garden juice?" he asked us.

"Thank you, no," said Joelene.

Once he and Xavid had made a toast, he turned his glass upside down over his mouth and let the goop slowly drop in. "Thick!" he said, once he had finally swallowed it. For a while he turned on some painfully loud Ültra song and sang along. Joelene and I covered our ears. The phrase *Snuff Your Mind* flashed onto my leg. Instinctively, I swatted my hand at it as though it were a mosquito.

Then the music was off. "We have to start having rages again," said Father. "Dance parties every night! That's what we did when we were number one." As quickly as he had been excited, he slumped, and said, "Our clients all hate me," and stared at the black residue in his glass.

"They don't hate you," said Xavid. "You're a tough businessman. They admire you and fear you."

Father laughed. "They hate me because I'm a terrible businessman. They think I'm so stupid they can take me down. But I'm not going to let them." One of the lasers etched *Behold … The Immaculate Bruise* across his face.

The car exited the Loop, and after we traveled down the deceleration ramp, we were on local roads passing low buildings and wide avenues. I wasn't sure where we were, but it had to be somewhere in Europa-12, where there wasn't much of anything good. The streets became more narrow and bumpy. I saw stretches of abandoned buildings and junk everywhere. We came to a checkpoint; Father stepped out into the stink of the night and negotiated our passage with blue slub satins.

"Joelene," I whispered urgently, "what's going on?"

She just said, "Shh."

"No, sir," intoned one of the blue satins outside. "Off-limits to the families."

A moment later, Father was giving them bottles of carrot liquor and patting them on the back; soon we continued into the slubs.

Outside it was mostly just black. Only the occasional reddish electric light or fire illuminated anything. Along one road, I thought I saw what looked like thousands of broken and bent bikes. Down another were piles of garbage, with women and children picking through it.

Father was going to leave me out here, I figured. My only chance was to keep away from the slubbers until morning and then try and find my way back to the cities. Before, my mistake had been talking to them. This time I'd hide. I'd stay quiet.

The truth was, I doubted I would survive the night, so I said goodbye to Mr. Cedar, to *Pure H,* Joelene, and most of all, to Nora. I hated that I'd never see her again, but at least she would know that I would rather die than surrender my love.

The car made another turn; I saw people huddling around a bonfire. In the orange light, a naked girl danced. Farther along, I saw men fighting. One was hit in the face with a rock or a bottle. It knocked his head back with such force that I was sure his neck was broken. He dropped to the ground.

For several minutes I could see nothing. We made three more turns and then the car came to a stop. The engines whirred as they slowed. The laser lights stopped scribbling their madness all over us and, for an instant, the world was still and peaceful. The side door slid open, and in the faint moonlight, I saw dilapidated two-story cinderblock buildings.

"We're off the map," said Father. "*Way* off the map. So don't make a wrong turn 'cause there's no security, or satins, or anything. There's nothing here but bad, bad shit."

"The odor is unbearable," said Xavid.

"I've smelled worse!" said Father, as though it were a joke.

We stepped out onto gravel. The humid air reeked of manure and rotting flesh.

"Sir," said Joelene, covering her mouth as if she were about to gag, "this is already a stern and frightening warning. I'll take Michael back to the compound, and we'll work on an apology press release."

"Shut your holes!" he barked. "Come on." In the distance I heard screams like someone was being torn in two. His film crew wheeled around to try and find its source. I didn't want to see, and pulled the lapels of my jacket up over my neck. Farther away glass broke, and I heard a crazy laugh.

Father stopped before a black door and knocked. While we waited, he said, "Creepy, huh?"

Three knocks came from the other side. Father adjusted his jacket on his neck, then his sleeve, like a hack magician about to perform, then knocked seven times.

The door opened an inch.

"I am Melina Gwendalarra," said Father.

"You mean Kristina Suggs?" asked a groaning voice from inside.

Father winked at his camera. "No, I'm Osmond Miditulip."

The door opened and we entered a pitch-black space.

"Follow me," said a dark shape.

Father started forward. I held onto Joelene's shoulder as we shuffled into oblivion with the film crew lagging behind. It was so dark inside, my eyes began producing spirals and checkerboards as if I were asleep or had been plunged into an ocean of ink. The floor turned sandy and wet. Then, we were walking through several inches of water and the sound of the splashes reverberated as though we were in a stadium-sized space. We made a turn to the right, the floor became firm and dry, and we began up an incline.

"Where are we going?" I asked.

"Shh!" hissed Father.

"The humidity," complained his hairdresser, "it's too much."

Father shushed him, too.

Finally, we turned a corner and entered a small room. A single fluttering candle illuminated the space. The walls glistened with condensation. The air smelled of wet dirt and algae. Across the floor were curled wood shavings and what looked like the bones of small birds. I saw a waterbug three inches long dart away.

And in the middle of the room on a wooden stool sat a man in a white loincloth.

He appeared to be a burn victim. His skin looked like poorly cast rubber cement and had the flat tone of flesh-colored paint. His mouth was little more than a lipless hole, and instead of a nose, he had only one oblong black nostril. His eyes were green, bloodshot, and angry. I glanced away in disgust.

This is what he wanted me to see—a victim of torture. I heard stories about employees who had been punished with needles, fire, and poisonous fruit. Is that what he was going to do to me? I hated to think so.

"He's got no name," said Father. "No house. No family. No job, no numbers, no papers. He doesn't even have a bellybutton. Nothing!" To his crew he said, "Get a shot of his belly. It's as smooth as his back."

As they did, Xavid leaned in and said, "I feel sorry for him."

"Don't!" said Father, sharply. "He's a freeboot. As free and as boot as they come. And he's pure evil." Father folded his arms and gazed at the man proudly. "Didn't think I knew any freeboots, did you? Officially, these things are the enemy. And they *really* are. We work against them every day. But, if you're selling a solution," he puffed out his chest and smiled at his camera, "you gotta make sure there's plenty of problems to go with it."

Although the freeboot scared me, this was about RiverGroup. It was about how Father made sure the families needed the security we sold. I asked, "Can we go now?"

"Go?" asked Father, unfolding his arms. "Fuck pudding! We just got here. Why don't you ask him a question?"

After glancing at the man's sorry, distorted face, I said, "I don't want to."

"You should." He grinned. "He's real important to you. He's your motivation."

I probably should have understood, but didn't. My advisor held her head down as if frightened. "Meaning what?"

"Look at him," said Father, all smiles. "He's just waiting for my order."

"To shoot me?"

"No!" said Father, rolling his eyes. "From now on, if you see Nora, if you talk to her, or even think about her, then I give the order, and he finds her, and he kills her!"

In the next instant, two things happened. I felt a cold, black hate pour over me like subzero tar, and then I lunged at Father with the idea of shoving his Adam's apple through the back of his neck. After I had started forward just a foot or two, the freeboot leapt in front of me and grabbed my throat with his moist, iron-strong hands.

"Careful," he whispered, in an oddly high-pitched voice. "Please do not do that."

Up close, I could see just how gnarled and distorted was his face. It was like he had been sliced into a hundred pieces, sewn back together, and then covered with a clear salve. I got a whiff of sweat and feces. And when he smiled, he exposed his tiny sharp teeth and the bloody bits of flesh and veins stuck between them.

"Get away from me!" I said. Recoiling, I fell backward and knocked into Joelene. We both toppled to the floor.

Father laughed and pointed at us like we were two silly children who had fallen from a seesaw. "Sorry," he said, dabbing the corner of his eyes, "but that was funny. You should have seen your look!"

Xavid smiled sadly and said, "Comedic!"

Joelene stood and gave me a hand.

"Did you see those reflexes?" Father asked Xavid. "Did you get that?" he asked the film crew. They confirmed that they had. "He's boiled," said Father. "He's boiled down to the real shit."

"You can't," I told him.

"Oh, yes I can." Father snapped his fingers. "Like that he could have her tied up and ready for torture." The candle flame danced in his pupils. "So, now do you get it? You marry Elle and everything's lard. If you don't, he goes after your little puss ball. And believe me, he gets her. No question about it."

"That would be awful!" exclaimed Xavid.

"Right!" said Father. "Because he's good. He's so good, he's like the black plague injected in your eye. This guy can crack systems. He can scale walls. And no medicated bullets. No medicated anything." Turning to the freeboot, Father said, "Right? No medicated shit."

The freeboot, who like a trained but diseased hawk was perched back on his stool, said, "You are correct." His voice was soft and quiet, as if counterpoint to the grisly fury of his being. "The lovely Miss Nora Gonzalez-Matsu will feel every terrible, painful thing I do to her."

A hateful raging fire. That's what I felt as I sat in the car while we headed back to civilization. Joelene sat beside me, patting me, and whispered soothing words, but I felt alone and broken. Somehow, I was going to kill Father.

Back in Kobehaba, before we parted, Father said, "Listen, I don't want that hunk of gristle to tear Nora in half. The truth is, the guy scares me! Freeboots are usually pretty disgusting, but that one's completely evil. I'm telling you, you should see the fucker eat a jar of mayonnaise. It'll make you sick!" He snorted a laugh. Meanwhile, Xavid got out his chopsticks and began fluffing Father's hair again. "Nora's really nothing in the whole scheme of things. I know you like her and everything, but let's just do what we have to do and nothing bad will happen."

"You leave us little choice," said Joelene.

"That's the idea!" Father forced a laugh. Then to Xavid, he said, "Don't make it too perfect. I'd like to look like we went at it a little, you know?" Xavid pulled a corkscrew-looking thing and a spray bottle from a pocket and kept working.

"Look," continued Father, "the numbers from his date with Elle are just what we needed. We'll have the audience. We'll introduce our new partner, we'll demo their crap, and hopefully we'll be lard." He smiled and asked, "okay?"

I didn't answer.

"I know you don't like this, but every day, every hour, every minute, I do things I don't want to do. But I do them. I do them for the company."

Patting my shoulder, Joelene said, "He's very tired and upset, sir."

Father let out a big sigh. "Fine! Take him home. Wipe his ass with a silk doily, or whatever it is you do. Just get him ready for the show."

Ten

My sleep was distressed and filled with nightmare. At one point, I was on a rooftop in an unrecognizable city. In the distance, I saw a green and gold MKG train that I knew had only one passenger—her. I watched it slowly pull out of a station. When it came to a curve, it was like some strange momentum took over, and the train barreled forward, derailed, and crashed.

Frantic to get to her, I was climbing down an endless set of polished wooden stairs. At first, the stairs were normal and I could move fast, but as I continued, they got steeper, until I could no longer step up, but had to climb. Soon I was scaling a sheer wooden cliff. Then I was clinging with my fingernails onto tiny cracks.

I lost my grip and plunged down.

With a start, I woke sweaty and anxious, but determined to get a message to Nora about the freeboot.

"This isn't yours!" I heard Joelene say on the other side of the room. "I don't give a fuck about you. I repeat, just leave him the fuck alone!"

Peering toward my desk, I saw her profile in the blue light of her screens.

"Listen to me," she repeated, "stay away or I'll kill you!"

In all the years she had been with me, I think I had heard her swear once when she'd badly stubbed a toe. And she had never used this harsh tone, nor threatened anyone. Shutting my eyes, I put my head back onto my pillow, and pretended to be asleep. She spoke again, but not loud enough for me to hear.

Then the room was silent. I wanted to peek, as if to confirm that she was there—that I hadn't dreamed it, when I heard footsteps.

"Michael," she said, softly, "your father is coming."

Turning over, I saw that Joelene's eyes were puffy, and her cheeks were white. She had been up all night—talking to whom I didn't know. I asked, "What's going on?"

"I suspect he wants us to help plan the wedding."

It took me a moment to remember the product show and Elle. Pulling the chenille up over my face, I said, "Tell Father I died of head lice."

She sighed deeply and with obvious irritation. "They're here already!"

Sitting up, I saw the estimator clock count down … three … two … The front door was unlocked from the outside and Father and Xavid came in. Father wore a blue feather boa over a jacket so yellow it made my mouth pucker.

"We solved your shooting!" he announced. "Last night, our engineers found a worm in the code. I don't have to tell you how super-hideous and awful that is. Anyway that worm was responsible for the freeboot breach where you got shot."

The gold-visor-wearing orange satin stepped in carrying a naked man. Stooping, the satin then plopped him onto the middle of the floor. Dark purple and green bruises colored the man's arms, legs, and chest. A line of blood ran from one of his ears. In his mouth was a wad of blue cloth. I covered my chest with my blanket.

Pointing a finger at the man, Father declared, "This is the bastard who put the worm in our code and wanted you dead."

He writhed against the wires that tied his hands and feet. Scooting farther back in bed, I asked, "Who is he?"

"Ken Goh!"

I hadn't even recognized him without his blue and orange face paint. At once I felt furious at him, sympathetic for his present suffering, and confused. "Why would he do that?"

"We don't know!" said Father, as if I wasn't even supposed to ask. "But he did it. We caught him. End of story. And it was my hairdresser who figured out the evil plot."

"Simple deduction!" said Xavid, as he pushed up his glasses.

Father then snapped his fingers. "Take the prisoner to the dungeon beneath the PartyHaus." The gold visor satin picked up Ken and headed out. "You," he said to me, "get dressed. Chesterfield Kez is here, and he's brought Elle's brother to be your friend."

"Wait," I said, "if Ken was behind the shooting, that means it wasn't MKG!"

"Forget those puds! They're rancid lard! Besides, Elle's ratings killed Nora's. We need that hype to cover our asses."

I asked, "Why do we have to cover anything? I don't even understand why we have to merge with anyone in the first place."

That stopped Father. He stood staring at me for a long time.

"What?"

"All right!" he said, pretending to be happy. "So, what new product do you have? And what technology are you using? Frequencies? Anomaly theory? Or are you just hiding more shit in Brane-7, like your good ol' granddad?" He laughed because he knew I had no idea what he had just said. "Yeah!" he continued, "That's what I thought. And that's why it's your job to get out there and smile and wiggle your nut sack to the rhythm!" Before he stormed out, he added, "Get dressed! We'll be back in two minutes!" The door slammed shut.

I had heard of Brane-7 before. It was another dimension and had something to do with the RiverGroup system, but that was all I knew. As the sound of the door slamming repeated in my head, I felt contrite, even useless. And for the first time, I understood how much my ignorance trapped me.

On the tiles I saw several drops of blood. "Why would Ken want to kill me?" I asked Joelene.

She let out a breath. "It does seem odd."

"What's a code worm? And what's Brain-7 and those other things?"

"A code worm ..." she began, "is a very complicated type of leech that attaches itself to the host and can create a new entity that is formed ..." Her voice faded, as she seemed to sink into thought.

I waited for her to continue, but she turned, headed to her screens, and began working as if she had forgotten about me. Annoyed, I asked, "Were you talking to someone earlier?"

Her amethyst eyes darted toward me. "No." She smiled stiffly, and then said, "I need several minutes here. Why don't you get dressed."

"Before I woke, you were talking to someone."

"Please," she said, returning her eyes to her screen, "I have to work."

"You swore. And you said *leave him alone.* You were talking about me."

After a deep breath, she said, "Listen to me, I am trying to secure our future. Things have become extremely dangerous. Yes, I used strong language earlier, but I am working for exactly what you want." With that she continued to operate her screens.

I didn't know what to think. "What are you planning?" She didn't acknowledge me. "Hello? What is the plan?"

"Will you stop bothering me?"

Her tone was as harsh as I had heard before. Throwing off my blanket, I stood, and sped to my dressing room. After I rounded the corner, I waited for her to come after me, but heard no footsteps. I felt worse that I'd been forgotten.

My dressing room was as big as my living quarters, and was decorated with several shiny, charcoal-hematite chairs, an unfinished hemlock plank floor, adobe walls, and both color and black-and-white iMirrors. It was a simple, meditative space where I had spent hundreds of hours observing fabric in my loupe, admiring the evenness of stitches, and reading about the histories of various fibers. Today, I just wanted to break something.

To the left of my makeup chair was the tie rack, the underwear warmer, and shoe engine. Next sat my Mr. Renovation shirt machine, and filling most of the space were three rows of Stanley-Dior suit racks with my sixty Mr. Cedar suits. I couldn't touch them, so I grabbed a charcoal-and-burgundy-striped tie, reared back, and whipped it at the floor as though I were killing a snake.

I felt a stab of pain in my shoulder. The tie just lay there. The gesture had been pointless and I felt ridiculous. A moment later, the tie began to smoke, and then flames appeared. I had grabbed one of my favorite Mr. Cedar ties, *Love Alone,* which had nitrocellulose fibers. Using the dressing room fire extinguisher, I doused it with white powder. So much for my show of fury! I'd ruined a beautiful tie, covered my pajamas with sodium bicarbonate, tweaked my shoulder, and felt exactly the same sense of futility as before.

From the racks, I grabbed a suit at random, tore off my pajamas, got a pair of shorts and an ironed shirt from my machines, and dressed. Checking myself in the iMirror, I felt transformed. Without realizing it, I had gotten a suit titled *Constant Heart.* Mr. Cedar had designed it several months ago for a fashion show I hadn't attended. The fabric was a creamy moon-wool charcoal. The silhouette was slim and efficient.

"Joelene!" I called. "What tie should I wear?" Usually, my dresser, Stefano, would have come from his servant's entrance. I guessed he was sleeping. "Joelene," I said again, "Stefano's not here. Can you please help me?" I thought I heard a bump in the main room and headed out to check.

Xavid, Father, and his film crew were coming in. I didn't see Joelene.

"Come here!" said Father, waving urgently. "Let's do the big RiverGroup introduction together." Smiling, he added, "It'll be fun!"

"I'm not dressed. Where's Stefano?"

"We let that old fart go," he said. "Cost-cutting." He looked me up and down. "You're fine. Come here." Pointing at the closed door, he said, "They're waiting."

"I don't want to see anyone," I said, wishing Joelene could get me out of this.

"Get over here and be nice," he growled.

"Leave me alone."

"Why is everything a war with you?"

"Why are you threatening Nora?"

"I don't *want* to," he said as if it were self-evident.

"But you are!"

"I have to because you're such a disaster of a son."

"I hate you," I told him. "I hate the family, I hate the company. All I want is Nora and all you do is keep me from her."

His face turned purple. He looked angry and hurt, but mostly hurt. "Fuck-tastic!" he spat. "Things were going so lard six seconds ago. We caught Ken and his code worm. What do you think? That shows you I'm trying." Propping his hands on his hips, he said, "Thanks for ruining the whole day!"

"You've ruined my life."

He threw his hands up. "I can't believe you. I just can't deal with …" He kicked the air, then turned away, and while muttering, shook his head.

"Should I introduce our visitor?" asked Xavid.

Father said, "Whatever," with a flick of his wrist. He looked at me as if he had never been more disappointed with anything.

"I want my own life," I told him.

"You're not going to have anything if RiverGroup crashes and burns. And we've already crashed, and we are on fire!"

I asked, "Why did you hire Ken?"

For a second, I didn't think he was going to answer. His lips slowly tightened and it looked like he was going to have another outburst. "He passed all the tests! Okay?"

"What are your tests?"

He rolled his eyes and said, "Just shut up. All right?"

I could only guess how ridiculous they must have been. Could Ken dance Bäng? Did he like Father's newest favorite band, like the Palladiüm Pinheads or whatever? Or maybe the tests were whether Ken would wear the company colors, and agree with everything and anything Father said.

"They're still waiting," prompted Xavid.

"Go ahead," muttered Father.

Opening the door, Xavid poked his head out, and said, "Listen for your name, then come on in." Returning to our side, he held a hand beside his mouth as if shouting to a crowd of a hundred. "Introducing a new friend and brother to the RiverGroup way of life. A fantastic human being with billions of healthy red blood cells …"

As he continued his useless introduction, I glanced toward the bathroom door. Was Joelene in there? Usually, she took no more than a minute. I hoped she wasn't sick.

"… So," concluded Xavid, "let's bloody our shorts for one of RiverGroup's new friends. That's right! It's our new pal, the stylish and very intelligent Walter Kez!"

A second later, a young man peered in. His baby-fat cheeks were as pale as cake flour. His watery, blue, manga eyes were ringed with red as if he hadn't slept for three days. He wore a long, slender, dust-grey suit that was short in sleeve and trouser as if he had grown or it shrunk. It looked like one of the lesser tailors—Me-Yaki, SEEM, or Mix-a-Fibré. On his head he wore a wide-brim straw hat with a blue ribbon. The hat made him look like a *CubeEye* reader, albeit a pudgy, somewhat malformed one. He stood for a moment, adjusting the Windsor of his matching blue tie, and smiled a fidgety, nervous smile. Even from ten feet away, I could smell baby power.

"Welcome!" said Father, now trying to crank up the

enthusiasm. "Come in! Meet my son, the famous and amazing Michael Rivers. He's going to marry your sister at the big product show. That's really exciting!"

Chesterfield Kez, his uncle, the skull-faced man whose hand I had not shaken last night at the club, strode in past his nephew. Chesterfield wore the same sort of iridescent suit and a pile of mahogany-and-teak-beaded necklaces that covered his neck, chin, and half his lower lip.

"Hold on, Ches," cried Father, "Xavid will give you a big, fun intro!"

"Is that a camera?" whined Walter.

"They're filming my big, dopy, butt-tastic life!" said Father, shooting a quick evil eye my way. "'Seven hundred hours! You're welcome to start watching anytime."

"Thank you!" said Walter, his eyes tearing. "I just can't be around cameras."

"Kid's got allergies," explained Chesterfield. "Polyester, iron, dairy, trees, plastic, vegetables, chicken, cardboard, and ..." Chesterfield nodded toward the documentary crew, "...cameras."

"Butt rockets!" yelped Father. "Go on!" he told his crew. "Get out!" As they ran out the back door, Father said, "Xavid, grab the two security cameras!"

Xavid yanked the little cameras from the walls, but even so Walter was scratching feverishly at his neck, making the skin red and raw.

For the next hour—although it felt like a dozen—I sat polite prisoner before pale, powdery, straw-hat-wearing Walter Kez, as he showed me his magazine collection. His voice was whiny, nasal, and he had a habit of inflecting the end of his sentences.

"This is a rare *CubeEye* issue twenty-three?" He opened it and flipped through all the pages—past dozens of photos of men in felt and straw hats. "This," he said, picking up another, "is the first issue of *118 Tones*? It's very, very valuable? Oh, and this is *Blot* issue forty. There's a printing error on page five? So, it's worth billions?"

Blot was actually not bad. It dealt with reproduction fibers. I asked for it and browsed while he continued to show copies of *SKD, Re-Ax, Salon 17, École, Inhab*, and *Turncoat*. Meanwhile, I kept looking for Joelene. I worried that I upset her before. I shouldn't have stormed off to my dressing room like I had. She was probably mad at me.

"I really, really like *118 Tones*, don't you?" asked Walter, holding another issue.

It was a cheap imitation of *Pure H*, but I said, "Sure."

Walter narrowed his eyes at me and I felt defenseless, as though he could see how isolated and unhappy I was. Leaning toward me, he whispered, "My sister's mad at you 'cause you saw Nora."

The strange thing was, I had forgotten they were related. "Oh," I said, "I'm sorry to hear that."

He burst out laughing. "Don't worry! I don't like my sister." Bending farther toward me, he added, "I've seen her eat her own snot balls."

Unfortunately, I could easily conjure the image of Elle, dressed as a cat-beaver-bunny gnawing on a dark, waxy little bit stuck under a fingernail.

"I like Nora better," he said. "She's very alluring and enchanting."

"Thank you," I said, not sure I appreciated his admiration.

Reaching into an inside pocket of his jacket, he held out his hand. In his sweaty palm were two black cockroaches. "Want one?"

"No!" I said, recoiling.

"They're pills!" he said with a giggle. "They're ARU!" His eyes were glowing. "They're illegal, but so soothing! I get them in the slubs!"

The bug-shaped pills were hideously realistic with little eyes and painted-on legs. They were the ones Joelene had mentioned. Mother took them, and the freeboot who shot me had had something to do with them.

"They make *all* bad feelings go away," he said, as he first glanced toward his nannies, then placed one of the things onto his pink tongue, reared his head back, and swallowed. "Go on," he said, holding the other toward me.

"No," I said, "thank you."

After he pouted for a second, he returned the pill to his pocket.

"You go to the slubs?" I asked, since it was not just illegal and frowned upon but dangerous.

"Some places are very fascinating." He stuck out his lower lip. "Not the bad place where you were."

I was still shocked he went, let alone survived. "Doesn't your uncle watch you?"

"He can't," he whispered, with a sly smile. "I have such a bad camera allergy."

A beeping little alarm sounded in his jacket. I watched him check inside his left lapel. "Oh, gosh!" he said, all excited. "Nora is on the channels!" Turning to his nannies, he said, "Nora is on! May my friend Michael and I watch, please?"

We had not been left alone. Before Father, Xavid, and Chesterfield headed to one of the meeting theaters, two of Walter's nannies had come in to watch us. They were older, matronly woman who wore black suits and straw hats that matched his.

"I suppose that would be all right," said one, as she fiddled with the control Father had given her. Finally, she switched on the main screen. Against a raging forest fire were the words *Heavy Profit Camp* in black outlined with glittering gold.

The titles faded and sitting before a faux campfire was Nora's father, Mr. Gonzalez-Matsu. She had inherited his fierce eyes, but little else. While her features had an uplifting feel, his were the opposite. His mouth resembled the beak of a flesh-eating bird.

The bottom edge of his nose was tilted upward so that his nostrils formed a curvy lowercase m. But his two most distinctive features were the puffy bags under his eyes, which made him look like he hadn't slept in five years, and his oily, black hair, with its shiny, pointed locks that resembled crow feathers.

As for clothes, he wore a striped green jacket over a patterned gold shirt. The top four buttons were undone to expose a green and gold undershirt. His pants looked like a combination of woven yellow leather and maybe some sort of green vines with leaves and odd little persimmon flowers here and there. His shoes were thick soled and the leather was as so dull it looked more like pressed dryer-lint.

As he held a stick before him where a burnt wiener dangled on the end, he said, "Our product offers a dramatic choice and much less operating costs. Super non-symmetry takes a lot of power. We don't." He tried to laugh a friendly laugh, but all the lines in his face pulled the other way.

"Were you insulted by Mr. Rivers' assertion that MKG was at fault for the freeboot?" asked the interviewer, a man dressed in aquamarine and pink flannel who was toasting several marshmallows on a long fork.

"Idiots!" shouted Nora's father with such energy that his wiener did a summersault on his branch. "I don't have any comment. Except they're idiots and grubs!"

Beside Mr. Gonzalez-Matsu sat what were obviously his versions of Ken Goh and Xavid, two men in wooden suits with big hairdos, who chimed in with *Idiots* and *Grubs*, respectively.

To the right of the yes men, sat Nora. Her face was so serene, so perfectly at ease, and her clothes so minimal and colorless—that she looked like she was a photo of a woman from a different world pasted into the picture.

She wore a brilliant white shirt that looked at once downy-soft and as smart as folded high-silica paper. Her tailored jacket was a deep charcoal and the fabric had flecks of what looked like black quasar dust. The shoulders and arms so perfectly fit her body, in a strange way, it was indecent because it so perfectly reflected her nude body beneath. Her eyelids were a smoky brown; her eyelashes resembled the sable of a fine paintbrush lightly dusted with crushed black iron, and her hair had been trimmed and brushed so that it resembled finely grained mahogany.

She would breathe in, hold her air for an instant, and then exhale. Her blinking was the same. Each time her lids closed, they held as if she were resting, sleeping, or escaping for a single instant. When open, she focused on her father's profile in such an intense way that I got the idea that she had been required to be on the show, as if it were punishment for her meeting me at the SunEcho.

Her father tried to talk about their new product, and something he called integrity-cloak, but the interviewer kept asking about RiverGroup and me. After a minute or two of the back and forth, Nora's father began screaming. "RiverGroup is a foul and constipated old lady!" After he spoke, he wrenched his face into a smile.

Nora's eyes turned to mine. While I had been concentrating on her before, now I was transfixed. And I swore she could see me through the electromagnetic fields between us. As I looked back into her eyes, the blush in her face deepened, and the corners of her mouth quivered toward a smile. I wanted to reach through and pull her through to my side.

Her right hand, in one of her grey chenille gloves, moved from her lap and then her index finger touched one of the black chrome buttons on her jacket. Her hand held for an instant, and then fell back to her lap as if it had never moved. A moment later, her eyes returned to her father.

"We are a prestigious family of true blood!" he continued. "We will persevere and work hard for our clients. And as for that other so-called company, council has advised me not to mention that Ribo-Kool is nothing but an assemblage of snot-dripping vagrants!"

The screen went black. One of Walter's nannies had snapped it off. She then came to Walter's side and began stroking him. "There … there! Never mind him! He's nothing but an angry old snuffly-guffly."

I stared at the blank screen. Of course Nora could not see me—there was no possible way. And yet, I knew she had. Moreover, she had sent me a message, but what it meant, I wasn't sure. Did it reference a *Pure H* story in issue nine where a woman touches a shirt button on her blouse to signal her former husband that she has returned from an affair with machines? If I remembered, though, the reader knows that her heart stops the same instant she touches the button. Perhaps she was referencing a photo[R6] in issue nineteen. Amid a mass of black threads is one silvery button. The copy read *A single cast iron snowflake*. At least, that wasn't negative.

The front door opened. I expected Joelene, but in came a man in a four-foot-tall orange chef's hat and matching jacket, wheeling in a tray.

"Good morning!" he said, with a big smile. "I've brought a special breakfast especially chosen by Mr. Rivers Senior, himself. And this exciting, fast-breaking meal has graciously been provided by Frix Food Product Corporation—Making Your Life Something You Can Snarf." His broad smile faded as he glanced about, as if trying to find the cameras.

"They're gone," said one of the nannies.

"Oh," he said, disappointed, as if this was supposed to be his big moment.

As Walter's nannies seated him at the table, I said I'd be right back, and hurried to my bathroom, but she wasn't there. In the dressing room I knelt and looked under the hangers. "Hello?" I asked, as I opened the servant's door. Surprisingly, inside was a dark stairwell, and just ten feet ahead, a heavy locked gate.

She must have gone out the back door. I headed out of my dressing room and straight toward it. As I did, I heard Walter's feet across the iron tiles.

"Wait! Where're you going?" he asked, as if afraid I was leaving.

I pushed open the iron door and stepped outside. To the far left was the black PartyHaus, covered in shadows. Straight ahead were several technology buildings, and to the right, were the garages and storage buildings. I didn't see Joelene anywhere.

What would she be doing somewhere else in the compound? Or had she left me? Had she gotten so frustrated and angry she had quit? It didn't seem like Joelene, but maybe the past few days had been too much. And Father's punch last night couldn't have helped.

"What is it?" asked Walter.

"Nothing," I replied, discouraged.

"Look it!" he said, pointing at the PartyHaus. "The place you danced!"

"Yeah. Come on. Let's eat."

Back at the breakfast table, I told myself Joelene was doing as she had said—working to get me what I wanted. Maybe she was in a secret place sending Nora a message. She would be back soon; she would have good news. I had to be patient.

Meanwhile, the chef held a large covered dish before us, and then lifted the cover. A steam cloud rose and revealed two long cakes shaped like scantily clad women. I recognized Frix's slut cakes, as Father ate them all the time. The skin was a sweet, rubbery fondant. Inside was a layer of soft cake, around a candy skeleton, which, when fresh, bent at the major joints. The one nearer me was a brunette in bright green shorts, red platforms, and pasties. The other had red hair, a tiny blue skirt, boots, and big, dark nipples. The cook served them.

Walter clapped his pudgy hands as his was placed before him. "She's beautiful!"

I stared at the doll's tiny bump of a nose; her full, fuchsia lips, her large, dark-circled eyes, and her two sharp eyebrows and imagined Nora lying on an enormous plate in a sugary, suspended animation. Better yet, I saw the two of us, lying next to each other for a sweetened eternity.

Just then, I remembered that in *Pure H* seven was a photo[R4.5]: the front of a grey woolen jacket was wrapped over a fist, and over the middle knuckle a buttonhole was stretched taught. The image was violent and angry, and I hoped that wasn't what Nora was feeling. Then again, she had surely been coerced to appear with her father on that business show. Maybe she was expressing her frustration.

"How do you eat her?" asked Walter, turning his head from side to side, as if looking for instructions.

Father, Xavid, and Chesterfield returned after we'd eaten. Now Father and Xavid's hair was orange and braided into complicated shapes.

"We had the mother ass of all meetings!" said Father, spreading his arms as if to demonstrate. "The ScrotümKings sang their new hit to start us off. Then Xavid did our hair. And if all that wasn't lard enough, Chesterfield got up and jammed with the Kings." Father laughed an easy and joyful laugh that sounded so real compared to his usual forced guffaws and howls.

"Heard you enjoyed your slut cake!" Father said to Walter.

"Oh, I did, indeed!" he beamed, as he knit his hands together and then tried to pry them apart in a wiggly sort of excitement. "First I licked her boots, and then her bottom!"

"They're good that way! Take some home," said Father, as he presented him with a box. "You know, sometimes I bite off their feet first. Or other times, I start with their hair. I guess it's true what they say—there's no right way to eat a slut!"

"Thank you so much," said Walter, his face aglow. "We had a very enjoyable morning." He shot me an odd, rather mischievous smile.

Walter's nannies packed up his magazines, straightened his clothes and hat, and led him to me. Holding out his hand, he said, "It was my pleasure to meet you!" Without moving his lips, he whispered, "We can have a grand adventure in the slubs if you want."

"Thank you." I said, as I shook his moist hand.

He and his uncle then left and the second the door closed, Father turned to me. "Fucking disastrous destruction! Your Joelene is our second traitor of the day."

At first, I thought it a joke, but he wasn't laughing or making one of his stupid faces when he thought himself funny. "She is not!"

"We caught the bitch in the code workshop trying to send a message to MKG! So we tossed her in the dungeon next to Ken." By the end of his sentence he was screaming as loud as of one of his Ültra bands.

"Let her go!?" I said. "She's not a traitor!"

Father closed his eyes for a moment. "Anyway," he began, "here's the story. If I send the freeboot and he kills Nora now, then you're not going to be properly motivated for the product show. So, what we've come up with is that we send him to *harm* her, then she's still alive, and you're still in check." Father turned to Xavid. "Right?"

Xavid pushed up his glasses. "We'll just have him break off one of her little toes."

"Yeah ... that's good!" said Father. "So, I could send him to—"

I reared back but when I flung my fist at his face, he grabbed me and threw me to the iron tiles. A pinpoint of black pain burned at the back of my head. As I pushed myself up, I said, "Do not do send that beast!"

"God, you're weak!" said Father with a laugh. "I barely knocked you."

"Do not send the freeboot!"

He glanced at Xavid and rolled his eyes. "You're embarrassing me!" He started to head for the door then stopped. "Oh, and for the show ... none of your *Pure Haggis* clothes. Get some color."

Eleven

Once they left, I turned right around and raced to the back door. I was going to run to the garage, get in my car, and somehow make it to Nora's this time. Once I opened the door and stepped out, though, I nearly slammed into the orange satin with the gold visor.

"Out of my way!" I said.

He didn't reply, but grasped my shoulders and picked me up like a bag of groceries. After placing me back inside, he closed the door.

"Bastard!" I said, as I watched him through the peek-cam, hoping he'd go, but he just stood staring back through his visor. Turning, I sprinted to the front door, but an identical satin waited there.

I rushed to my desk and opened Joelene's screens. I turned every knob, but they had been wiped clean. Frantic, I grabbed the remote for the big screen, hoping to find the *Soup and Intellectual* show or something, but all the channels were blocked. Smacking the controller, I must have hit the history knob as it began playing a recording of *Heavy Profit Camp* that hadn't been erased.

Mr. Gonzalez-Matsu complained about RiverGroup again, and there was Nora.

"Hide," I told her. "Go somewhere safe." Stepping before the screen I leaned forward to kiss her gloved hand, and just before

131

I did, she lifted it, and touched the button. Up close, though, I saw something. Hitting the stop knob, I realized that she was pointing to a capital F that had been scratched into the shiny black surface of the button. The letter wasn't perfect and it looked as though Nora had done it with a needle or pin.

What did it mean? Father? Farther? Famous? Furious? I could think of a vulgar word, but surely Nora would never use it. Staring at it, I willed myself to understand, but without Joelene's help, I couldn't figure it out.

The estimator clock said Father wasn't due back for forty-seven minutes, but I had a bad feeling, so I erased the memory and switched off the screen.

At my desk, I pulled open the refrigerated drawer, took out several *Pure H* magazines, and began rifling through them, but nothing made sense. I felt a presence. Looking up, I saw Xavid with his head held high, his hands on his hips, as if he were posing. Once he saw that I'd seen him, he smiled, stepped closer, and said, "I crept up on you," as if pleased.

"What do you want?" I asked, irritated.

Combing his white-capped hair with a hand, he gazed around my place and said, "We are going to have to learn to work together, because you are also one of the extremely valuable assets here."

Assuming that was some sort of bizarre compliment, I just asked, "Can you help me with Joelene?"

He laughed at me. "You're fond of her, aren't you?"

"Yes."

"I'm not. There's something strange about her. I have a sense like that. I'm good with people." He pushed up his amber glasses. "Besides, her hair is awful. That color is wrong for her and it's ugly. I've never liked it."

Her natural curly hair was fine. I said, "I'd like to see her."

Frowning, he said, "She's gone."

I hoped he didn't mean dead. "I thought she was at the PartyHaus dungeon."

He whipped around as if someone was sneaking up on him. His eyes darted left and right behind his amber glasses. Finally, when he seemed satisfied that we were alone, he turned and asked, "What?" as if he had forgotten what we were talking about.

"Joelene …" I said, wondering what was wrong with him, "is she all right?"

As if it didn't matter, he said, "I suppose."

"I want to see her."

He started walking around my apartment, looking over my things. "I don't think so." He stopped before my couch, bent close enough to smell it, and asked, "Do you have any real skills or anything?"

For an instant, I felt depressed. The truth was I wasn't sure. "What do you want?"

He then headed to my small kitchen. "I think RiverGroup can make a comeback," he said, admiring the black gold cabinets. "Some don't, but I do. They don't know what *I* know." Turning, he smiled and asked, "Did I tell you that I'm very fucking smart?"

"I think you did." I knew I'd heard him say that before.

"If I can turn it around, there will be profits. Extraordinary profits, because it's one thing to build something, it is quite another to rebuild. That's a particular type of skill. It's not just creating, but destroying, too. Do you know what I mean?"

I said, "Yes," but didn't and didn't care.

Narrowing his eyes, he said, "You never answered. Do you have any skills? Are you smart at all?"

"I am smart," I said, and lamented how little conviction was in my voice.

"Well," he said, as though disappointed, "when the time comes … if it does … will you support me?"

I had no idea what he meant, but said, "Yes, if I can see Joelene."

"Excellent!" Pushing up his glasses again, he said, "I'll give you one minute."

"I want more than that!"

"I don't expect I'll actually need your approval. Your father has all the voting rights, but you never know ... you might become useful." He stared at me blankly. "At this point, that's all you may have. One minute."

Outside, while Xavid explained to Gold Visor that we were going to the PartyHaus for business, I watched Father's hairdresser. Obviously, he thought he was more important than he was, and while I had found talking with him demoralizing, Joelene was worth a million humiliations.

Soon, the three of us, Xavid, the satin, and I started along the path toward the access road. A buzz filled the compound like it had not in years. From a dozen delivery trucks, men hauled crates of carrot wine, food, fuel, and other equipment toward the black building. In the oxygen gardens and all along the access roads, a battalion of gardeners were clearing away weeds, pruning trees, planting flowers, and Fluffing father's prized dandelions.

Bamboo scaffolding covered half of the PartyHaus where workers were repainting it, or adding highlights of gold leaf. And as much as I hated the building, had hoped for years that it would collapse, I felt as if its restoration summoned the end of things, like it was the rearming of a bomb.

When we reached the base of the stairs, I paused and gazed up at the fifty-seven steps, not relishing the climb. After maybe twenty, I had to stop. My legs burned.

"Back when you danced," said Xavid, as he wiped his brow, "I bet you could have walked up on your hands."

"I suppose," I replied. Then, as if to show him, I climbed the rest without pause.

At the top, two workers stepped aside from the huge front doors. I had forgotten how intricate and demonic they were. Made out of black marble, they had been carved with hundreds of animals, but like a zoo gone sexually mad, tigers kissed hogs, ducks groped gophers, boa constrictors fellated elephants, and bison mounted giraffes.

Gold Visor took hold of one of the massive handles and pulled. It creaked open with a low, painful note, and we entered. Before my eyes adjusted, I couldn't see anything, but heard sounds all around. Straight ahead, metal banged against metal. From the right, I heard a high-pitched grinding. Several amplified voices wove together into a mishmash of feedback and reverb. Curiously, the air still smelled like it had years ago: a blend of sweat, sex, and desperation, like a pungent curry.

In the foyer, while Gold Visor and Xavid conferred with another satin, I peered toward the main dance hall. As my eyes became accustomed to the darkness I saw a hundred workers polishing the floors, cleaning the walls, washing the ceilings, the carvings, the mosaics, and the bronzes. All of them wore ugly blue and orange leotards and they reminded me of the velvety maroon thing I had worn when Joelene and I had descended the cooling system in the MonoBeat. And I felt nostalgic—not for that dreadful experience—but for all the times we shared. I knew she wasn't a traitor, and her profanity before, even her grumpiness was because she was hard at work on what sounded like our exit strategy. How I longed for exactly that.

The PartyHaus was laid out in the shape of a giant X. In the center were the circular dance floor and the balconies that surrounded it. In the four arms of the X were bars, restaurants, shops, and the guest rooms. When the rages were happening every night, thousands crowded every floor and every inch of the building. These days, Father said it housed ten times as many rats.

"This way," said Gold Visor. Xavid and I followed.

We headed across the old dance floor. When I did my routines, it had been covered with a springy black material. Today. It looked like they had put down uranium tiles. On the other side, a stage had been erected. At the back a forklift was placing a jet engine into some sort of pipe organ. Above the stage hung a fifteen-story screen. On it glowed a vivid test pattern of horizontal stripes. At stage-front were three actors and father's silver-haired director who had also worked the promo-date with Elle.

"You go to that side. That side," he said to a man who wore a sign that read *Super Distinguished RiverGroup CEO*. The other man wore a sign that said *Michael*. The girl's read *Interest*. "Yes," he continued, "and now the girl will come down the middle. She's the center. She's bringing not just the two families together, but this family as well." He spotted me and waved. "Oh, hello! Michael. How you doing? Look here, this is the wedding blocking! We're mapping out the big wedding!"

"I see."

"It starts out minimal then gets maximal. You know? Flow. Change. Difference." Smiling and combing back his chrome locks, he added, "You know, you can't have loud without quiet. You can't have big without small. So at first, it'll just be you and your dad, and then we'll add the girl. Then we've got the triangle. Next the square and then the pentagon. Shape follows meaning."

I nodded, if only to indicate that I'd heard, as we continued across the dance floor.

At the far side, we came to the stairs that led into the building's bowels. Most of the entrance was in the process of being covered over with a wall of vending machines. When I danced, streams of people were always going in and out but I had never set foot below. It was where the real freaks: the Wets, the Kate Wools, and the Bügs went. I'd heard rumors of the surgically and pharmaceutically enhanced who sometimes killed themselves for pleasure or fantastic dance moves. Supposedly, one woman hadn't come up for two years and lived on nothing but sweat and semen.

The farther down we went, the cool and heavier was the air. The odor was of mildew and rotting meat. And as the cacophony of construction from above dimmed, odd sounds, like the pings of electronics and the squelches of bats, began to echo and ricochet around us. Orange sodium bulbs had been placed here and there on stands as a few workers mopped the floor and patched, what I decided were, hundreds of rat holes.

"Where is she?" I asked.

"Lower level," said Gold Visor. His deep voice reverberated into the recesses.

We continued for several minutes then came to another set of stairs. The satin held out his arm for support as these stairs were wet and slippery. The light was dimmer here and I was afraid that if I lost my footing, I would tumble to the center of the Earth.

Gold Visor produced a flashlight. The walls looked wet, and all around water dripped from tiny stalactites that covered the ceiling. I saw a large black salamander with yellow eyes hold for a second, then dash off, its tail zigzagging in the liquid.

We reached the end of the stairs and continued forward. As the satin shone his light back and forth, I decided that the walls weren't as wet as I thought, but made of glass. Ten feet ahead, we came to a forest of sculptures like the carvings on the front doors only huge and more repulsive. A twelve-foot-tall teddy bear had an enormous, veined phallus so big, it rose five feet above its head.

After we had wound our way around a dozen ever more cartoony and debauched turtles, hamsters, and bunnies, we came to a clear area. Another orange satin, with long white hair, sat at a table covered with half a dozen screens. He stood and bowed.

Beyond him, on the black floor, lay Joelene, in nothing but her green bra and underwear. I crouched beside her. Her skin was mottled with a hundred small bruises, as if she'd been peppered with pool balls. Father had beaten her and left her to die.

Xavid stepped above us. He kicked at the thick metal cuff on her left wrist. Then he toed the chain that connected it to the floor. "Good," he said, peering down at her.

"Get away," I told him. After he sneered at me and stepped away, I knelt closer to her. "Joelene, can you hear me?" She didn't speak or move. I had been hoping she could help me with Nora's message, but clearly, I was the one who would be helping her. Touching her cheek, I found it warm and worried she had a fever. "It's me. Michael," I said. She moaned like she was dreaming. "I'm going to help you." Her eyes finally opened, and I was never happier to see those amethyst irises.

"Pain," she whispered, her dry lips sticking together. "Get me …" Her voice faded and her eyes closed.

"Get you what?"

Farther back, I heard Gold Visor say, "This prisoner's dead."

Beside the satin, I saw Ken Goh ten feet away. His mouth was wide open as if he had died screaming.

Xavid stepped over him. "Corporate selection," he said. "Only the smart survive."

I wanted him to shut up and go away and was about to tell him so, when Joelene mumbled something. Putting my ear close, I asked her to repeat it, but she just moaned. "Don't worry," I said, stroking her forehead, "I'm going to get you out of here."

"Are you …" she began.

"Am I what?" I asked. She didn't reply. "Am I marrying Elle? No! I'm not. I'm not going to."

"Are you …" she repeated.

"No, I'm not!"

"That's it!" said Xavid. "Your minute's up. Let's go."

"I'm staying here with her."

Xavid rolled his eyes far up in his glasses. "It's been more than a minute." Pointing a thumb at the satin, he said, "He will be happy to drag you back to your apartment."

"I want more time."

He stepped closer. "I used to watch you dance on the channels. I thought you were just wonderful. But now that I've gotten to know you, you're as selfish and stupid, as your father says." I could have hated him—I probably already did—but wasting more energy on him seemed futile.

Behind, I heard Joelene say, "Are you ..." again. An instant later, I understood.

Twelve

As I hurried through the long spiral to Mr. Cedar's showroom, I again remembered the times when I had stopped to admire his displays, contemplate the exhibits, and learn from his interactive experiments. Today, I even passed what looked like a fascinating exhibit on the history of pockets, but I had too much to accomplish before midnight. As I neared his sugar maple and hammered-palladium doors, though, I felt compelled to act civilized for at least one moment and stopped before a wood and glass display.

Inside was a large swatch of charcoal fabric held vertical and flat by several robotic arms. When I pushed the single red button on the front of the experiment, a mannequin's hand, representing the wearer, rose on the right side of the fabric and a metal rod lowered on the left. A fierce spark jumped from the rod toward the hand, but as indicated on a series of meters, the fabric's electronic network reflected the lethal shock.

I stood before the experiment for several beats as I thought of the *Miniature city flickers* quote and the woman in the alpaca-silk and platinum dress who was covered with a thin, vaporous layer of flame, the necktie from Mr. Cedar I had thrown at the floor that burned, and the wedding blocking I had just seen at the PartyHaus, where Father and I were to stand alone on the stage.

"Michael," said Mr. Cedar, his voice startling me, "do come in."

Last time I'd visited, the gallery was filled with posing mannequins. This time it was empty except for his sketching board and a large sports screen, tuned to the AppleBoard Shirt Ironing Invitational. I couldn't believe that I had forgotten about one of my favorite events. Last year, my tailor and I had attended in person.

"It's the last round," said Mr. Cedar. "Fanjor versus Isé–B again."

Competitive ironing was the oldest and most prestigious sport played among the fashionable. In my dressing room at my apartment, I had my own speed and sleeve boards and several competitive irons, but of course, I was nothing compared to the people who made it their life. For the past several years, one man, Fanjor, dominated the tournaments. In the beginning, I had admired his ironing, but gradually, as he kept winning, and got more and more arrogant, I got sick of him.

Now my favorite was Isé–B. He was a handsome, wiry man with short-cropped, dark hair, stern russet eyes, and always had a five-o'clock shadow. Unlike the rest of the ironers, who used modern, souped-up, Intel-Sunbeams, Greikos, or Jaun-Tees, he preferred a coal-powered Schiaparelli-Firemaster 77, with duel chimneys, and a customized Steam-Jet 188. It was incredible to watch him work that thirty-two pound-hunk of polished iron over crisp white shirts, as it spat clouds of steam and belched black smoke. And while he was truly a brilliant ironer who regularly won the smoothest-in-show and wrinkle creativity awards, he had yet to beat Fanjor head to head.

The channel was showing a replay from Masters Trophy last year, where Isé–B had lost by a twentieth of a second. After being awarded the coveted Golden Cuff, Fanjor, dressed in his signature yellow, pranced about the stage, chanting his own name.

"How's Isé–B doing today?" I asked, as Fanjor, now in slow motion, leapt into the crowd where his fans began licking him as though he were a lemon candy.

"He's two hundredths of a second behind."

That wasn't good. In this last speed round, Isé–B needed a lead to have a chance.

"So," said Mr. Cedar, turning his attention to me. "Another suit?"

"I suspect my last." He raised an eyebrow as if concerned I might be changing styles or tailors. "I have an idea," I began. "You see, yesterday, that neck tie you made for me, *Love Alone* … burned."

"The stolen silk was juxtaposed with a small amount of nitrocellulose." With a grimace, he eyed my neck and asked, "You weren't injured, were you?"

"Not at all," I said, contrite that I had thrown it at the floor in a fit.

"You need it replaced?" he guessed.

"Not that." After an exhale, I looked him in the eye and said, "Since Nora and I can't be together, we'll have to be apart." I swallowed and asked, "Can you make me a whole suit of nitrocellulose?"

He stopped twisting his beard. His eyes fell to his sketching board, and his expression turned somber. While I knew my request was extreme, now I feared I had overstepped the bounds of our relationship. How could I have asked my tailor, of all people, to help me kill my father and myself? Frantic, I tried to think of some plausible way to claim I was joking.

He asked, "Your situation is that dire?" and I saw the calm gravity I had been hoping for.

"It's worse," I answered, thinking of Father's freeboot.

He began rolling his beard hair again. "Yesterday … I saw something new by Pentagon-Straus in The Official Fabric Guide." After he manipulated something on his table, he nodded toward the screen. "It's quite dangerous and curiously comes in a single color—a luminescent orange licensed from the famous suits in the Bäng epic, *Adjoining Tissue*."

During a commercial for a vacuum-pressing table, he ran

highlights from the *Tissue* movie, which I hadn't seen in years. It opened in an eerie moonlight garden filled with long walkways, beautiful marble fountains, and dozens of perfectly trimmed geometric bushes. One by one, the forty band members of HammørHêds enter, sing, and begin having sex (simulated sex, I suppose) with the shrubs. As the drums fire and the organ plays, they sing of loneliness and desperation. Then the garden is lit on fire and the blue is burned away so that it becomes daytime. Now, wearing big, bright orange suits, they are happy, they punch each other and scream about the band's glorious future. In the last sequence, each member cuts off the ends of their pinkies. Doctors stitch all forty together—pinky stump to pinky stump. The epic ends as the camera spins above and they have become one big, human volvox.

"My old anthem," I said. The song I associated with my first death would also be connected to my second. "Perfect."

He switched off the video. The screen returned to the ironing competition and a buzzer sounded—the ironers were to report to their boards. I watched Isé–B step onto the stage. He added several more embers into his iron, primed it, rolled his shoulders and neck, and then stared at the heated vacuum table. What I loved about him was that he existed in his own perfect world, concerned with nothing but cotton, heat, and steam. I longed for such a purity, such a singularity of mind.

"He doesn't have a chance, does he?" I asked, trying to be lighthearted as if that might temper yet another second-place finish.

My tailor was busy at his drawing screen and had finished half a dozen quick sketches. The drawings disturbed me. And the way the material shimmered and smoldered made it look like fire. Worse, the silhouette was large, bold, and muscular like something a satin would wear.

Before I had time to figure out how to express my displeasure without insulting him, the commentator said, "They're off! This is the final heat for the gold!"

Fanjor and Isé–B stood beside two parallel ironing boards arranging their white cotton shirts. Fanjor started on the cuffs, Isé–B, the back.

"Fanjor is off to another fast start," said the announcer.

"He's been in a zone all week," enthused the color man.

"Go Isé," said Mr. Cedar.

"Isé–B has finished the back," said the commentator. "But Fanjor and his incredible quickness are already in evidence!"

Isé–B got out his sleeve board and began the left. Fanjor didn't bother and just crushed the material flat, leaving two creases on the sleeve.

"Why isn't he penalized for that?" I asked. "That's not right!"

"Indeed," agreed Mr. Cedar.

"He just guts it out with that speed," added Color, as if he'd heard my complaint. "Fanjor wills his victories. They're not subtle or graceful, but they're fast."

"They're brutal!" I complained. "And they're ugly!"

"Isé–B is close," said Mr. Cedar. "He's got a chance."

"I just want him to beat Fanjor!"

A close-up showed Fanjor leaning in as he started the collar. While picking up his iron, he hit the steam and a blast filled the air. His goggles fogged so badly, he had to stop, and wipe them off.

"Uh oh!" cried the announcer. "That could be a costly error!"

"Yes!" I screamed. "Go! Isé–B. Go!"

"Three years ago, a steam-up just like that cost Fanjor the Northern Invitational," explained Color. "That was the last major won by the veteran Matús before he retired, leaving Fanjor to dominate. Today of course, Fanjor is the veteran, and Isé–B, the upstart."

I couldn't believe it, but I was about to see Isé–B finally beat him! "Go!" I shouted, as Isé–B ran his Schiaparelli across the shoulder yoke. Then he flipped his shirt around and worked the collar.

"Faster! Come on! Hurry!"

"It's neck and neck!" said the announcer.

"I'd say it's completely up for grabs!" added Color.

"No!" I screamed. "Isé–B's ahead! He's winning!"

As Isé–B finished the collar; Fanjor flew his Intel across the front. In another flash, he grabbed a hanger and slapped it onto the finishing rod. The horn sounded. An instant later Isé–B, hung his.

"Incredible!" said Color. "Just incredible!"

"Fanjor pulled it out again!"

"He's unbeatable," declared Color. "And you could see it in his eyes. Right at the end, he just wanted it more."

I felt teased, then crushed again. And it wasn't so much that I wanted Isé–B to win, but Fanjor to be beaten, as if I wanted some proof that good things happened, if not for me, for someone somewhere. But it was just like the Tournament of Ironing Champions, The Weave, and Fiber-Con. It was always the same. It was unfair, just like everything.

"We're going to go down to the boards," said the announcer. "Our own very attractive Lindsay Beech is down on the stage with Fanjor, who —"

Mr. Cedar snapped off the screen. He worked on his sketching board for several moments "Watch," he said.

On the screen played a rendered movie of myself in a radiant orange suit. I stood in a generic-looking coffee shop of polished iron, black cement, and silver furniture. In my right hand, I held a black glass of what I assumed was cream coffee.

"It's boxy," I noted, unhappily.

"It's the bastard child of early Ültra and *Pure H*."

"Indeed."

Holding up a finger, he said, "Observe." He touched a few things on his board. Another figure, wearing black, entered the frame. He tossed what looked like a fist-sized rock. When the rock hit the orange suit, it exploded in a white flash, sending the head and arms flying. An instant later, nothing but a few glowing embers and a black spot remained on the floor.

"I'll deliver it this evening," said my tailor.

Thirteen

During the first few minutes of my trip back to the family compound, a feeling of regret began to swell in my stomach like a hastily eaten meal. I wanted to tell my driver to turn around, so I could go back to Mr. Cedar, ask him to design a normal suit, and devise some other way to stop Father. When I had thrown *Love Alone* to the floor, it had burned like a piece of paper, not a stick of dynamite. I didn't want to end up as a fireball with my limbs flying across the stage in different directions.

Each time I was about to press the intercom button I came up with a reason why the suit made sense. First, instead of a smoldering fire like the tie, when the suit detonated, I probably wouldn't feel much. I'd see a flash of yellow, sense a flare of pain, but then I'd be dead. Second, the power assured Father's elimination.

Then I worried about the color of the suit. While the *Adjoining Tissue* orange was symmetrical and fatalistic, did I really want to end my life in an Ültra disaster? And more importantly, what would Nora think? My death would devastate her, but would the color of the suit and the ferociousness of the explosion contaminate my sacrifice and ruin our grey perfection? Or did the color separate my death from our love and protect our colorlessness?

Gazing straight ahead at the red emergency brake button with its big white E, I took several deep breaths, and tried to clear my head. I thought of how desperate Father was. I thought of Elle and the ridiculous marriage that was supposed to happen tonight. And most of all, I thought of my beautiful Nora and the freeboot and Father's threats of violence. No, the orange was good. Father had asked for color and he would get it.

Then I felt the car slowing. We weren't stopping again, were we? Pressing the intercom, I asked, "What's going on?"

"A car is approaching from behind."

Spinning around, I saw a shiny gleam on the horizon. "Is it Father?" He had discovered my plan!

"They have not identified themselves, but are nearing our safety zone."

"Is the car blue and orange?"

A beat later, the driver said, "Negative. Green and gold … MKG colors."

I raced to the back of my car and peered out the window. Was it Mr. Gonzalez-Matsu coming to get me? Was it he all along? Or was it Nora? And if it was, what was she doing?

"They're gaining on us," said my driver. "I have orders to take evasive action." After he spoke, I could hear a harsh whine from below as the engines began to overdrive. When they engaged, we would be shot out of range, and I would never know who it was.

Then a peculiar feeling filled me, as if I had just seen something. I searched the inside of the car, hoping the answer was close by. When I looked at the red emergency button up at the front of the cabin, my skin went cold. When Nora had touched the button on her jacket during *Heavy Profit Camp*, her finger had covered the bottom edge of both the button and the letter she had scratched on the surface. It wasn't an F. It was an E!

The vacuum motors had just about reached their final velocity. As fast as I could, I ran forward, leaped, and hit the red button. The brakes engaged instantly. Baffles and airbrakes shot out from the sides of the car, and a large parachute was released behind. The force slammed me into the upholstered partition.

When I came to, I sat up and felt a spasm of pain shoot through my head and neck, like a long skewer had been plunged through me. I heard nothing. The motors were all off. Everything was still except for a flickering emergency light in the center of the cabin roof. The air was sour with the tang of burnt electronics and rubber. Then from the car speakers came the message, "Emergency stop engaged. Rate: zero. Systems: go."

Holding my head with my right hand, as if that eased the pain, I stood, and looked out back. The road was clear. I rubbed my eyes, but they weren't deceiving me. Striding to the back of the car, I was sure I was missing something. Nothing but sunlight reflected off the white tiles for a thousand miles.

Nora's car was gone. It had disappeared, or had been a mirage. It probably hadn't been her at all, but some MKG official, a muskrat of a man dressed in stripes and plaid, who cared for nothing but statistics, investments, and earnings. He didn't stop. He didn't slow, but raced past to a board meeting in Kong. Moreover, the letter scratched onto her button had been an F, not a partially covered up E as I had thought. And what it meant, I was just too dumb to figure out.

I felt desolate, and for several moments just stood there staring out at the Loop.

When I turned around to glare at the emergency button as though it were to blame, I saw a green and gold Loop car twenty feet ahead. It was in our lane, but sat at a slight angle, as though it swerved at the last second to avoid a crash. Several steamy wisps of smoke came from beneath, but it was intact.

Wrenching the side door open, I jumped down to the tiles, stumbled, but kept my balance, and ran. The sun was scorching, the air stunk, but I didn't care. She was here.

A hatch on the back of her car was partly open, and several gears were recoiling the last of a green and gold parachute. She must have been watching and hit her emergency button a split second after me. Beside her car was the orange tarp where I had fallen off the Loop. I couldn't believe I had returned to the same spot. But maybe it was perfect because I knew we were off the system here.

"Nora!" I called. The windows on her car were tinted a dark green and it was impossible to see in. "Can you hear me?" I banged on the door with my fist and worried she was unconscious. "You all right?" A second later, I heard a tap from the inside. The lock disengaged. The seal broke and a small whoosh of cool air escaped. The door rolled back.

And there she stood. For each of our four promotion dates, she had worn her signature satellite suits and jackets. This time she wore an evening dress and her hair was up. I was so surprised how elegant, formal, and beautiful she looked that I inhaled a gulp of air and almost choked.

Her dress was made of hundreds of layers of the sheerest fabric I had ever seen—probably the incredibly rare nano-wool that only came from the soft underbelly of a single, faultless, genetic-T angora goat from Asia-1. The outer edge resembled vapor, but as the layers built up and created ever-shifting moiré patterns, the tone deepened to where the center was the absolute black of outer space. The fabric hung beautifully from her hips like a spray of gradient mist and was four feet wide at the floor. On her feet, she wore shiny black pumps made of what looked like unnilseptium-coated deerskin. The waist was small, and the charcoal bodice, covered with an intricate pattern that reminded me of ginkgo leaves scattered on pond water, fit her like paint. Her hands and arms were covered with long, chenille opera gloves that matched her dress. The scoop neck showed her graceful neck, around which hung a single string of the rare, double-heterojunction, light-emitting diamonds.

Her lips were painted a soft, moist watermelon. Her eyes looked luminous and pure black. Her lashes were thick, and her eyelids, the color of ironwood smoke. Woven into her hair were glistening strands of silvery-white rhodium isotope.

With an impish smile, she said, "I'm no longer a Gonzalez-Matsu," as though she had become a nameless outlaw. Then her expression turned serious and sultry. "What I am … is yours."

Grasping the doorframe, I pulled myself up. "I'm not Michael Rivers," I said, as I inhaled her redolent mixture of exotic woods and ambergris. We stood inches apart, and for several seconds her eyes darted from my left to right eye before finally settling on my grey left.

In that moment, we left ourselves, and as we closed our colored eyes, we shed our names, our families, and even the hues of our being.

Softly, I touched my lips to hers, but a moment later, I felt like my being was falling into her mouth. As we kissed, I gathered a handful of the gossamer of her skirt and squeezed it hard enough to press my fingerprints into the fibers. She in turn, put her chenille-covered hands around my neck and began to press on my Adam's apple as if to heighten my senses.

We lay side by side in the near silence of her car. It was only after we had become one that I heard what was playing on the sound system. It was Love Emitting Diode's *Down for Pianoforte*, where a ton of goose feathers were slowly dropped puff-by-puff onto a vintage Steinway Grand.

Across Nora's upper lip and forehead were droplets of perspiration. While listening to the chromatic silence, I watched the light refract in them, like so many tiny magnifying glasses. The rhythm of her breathing was just now returning to normal.

Sitting up on an elbow, I closed my eyes for a moment as if to gather strength. "Father is trying to harm you. He has a freeboot looking for you."

With a sad and mocking laugh, she said, "I heard my father hired satins to hurt you."

Her news confirmed my plan in a way I hadn't even thought of before, but the fighting between MKG and RiverGroup was sure to escalate unless it was stopped. "After tonight," I said, "there won't be anything to find."

Her eyes flit right and left as if trying to decide what I meant.

"I've just come from my tailor," I explained, "with my last suit."

Her expression turned to concern. "You mean ..."

"Nitrocellulose," I confirmed.

"Michael," she said, frowning, "not that."

"The fabric is orange ... Ültra orange." She flinched as if she knew that color was a precursor of worse things. "My plan is to eliminate Father." The corners of her mouth darkened, and I could tell she was about to tell me that was unacceptable, but before she spoke, I added, "Unless he is destroyed, you're never going to be safe. And I can't kill him to be with you. Everything must end."

The quarrelsome spark in her eyes faded, and slowly, like a turtle retreating into its shell, she sunk into her self. "I feared this," she said quietly, as tears rolled down her face. "We are not for this world."

With my fingertips, I gathered the drops on her cheeks, and touched them to my lips. "We aren't," I agreed.

She looked into my eyes as if for possibilities, options, or alternatives. Then, as if she couldn't find any either, her gaze fell. "I'll say goodbye to my Michael now. Later, I'll know you're someone else. Someone who is sacrificing himself for us."

That was it! I could see myself as a young boy—in the very beginning when I had loved the music and the crowd's adulation. This would be his final appearance.

"And afterward," she said, her lips trembling, "I'll join you."

"No!" I sat up and grasped her hands. "Please, Nora. Hide. Go somewhere where you won't be found ... somewhere far off the system. Stay there and you'll be safe."

"Without you?" As if defeated, as if our time was over, she smoothed the silky chenille on her forearms and hands.

I could have argued. I could have insisted that she go on, live her life, find someone else, but I knew I wouldn't convince her. Knowing we would both be dead tonight, I felt wretched and hallowed at the same time.

When we were both gone, the world would know how we were meant for each other and how much we were willing to sacrifice.

Reaching toward her, I grasped her cool, smooth chenille-covered hands, after squeezing, I let go, and pulled back an inch. We looked at each other, and I could tell she was thinking the same: we *were* the beautiful but dead couple in the plutonium button ad with our yearning hands outstretched but unconnected.

Fourteen

Without another word, I stood, straightened my pants and jacket, opened the door, and stepped out into the putrid, hot air. I walked quickly, hoisted myself up into my car and sat. I knew if I looked back I wouldn't have been able to leave.

As I buckled myself into my seat, I could hear the vacuum-arc engines in Nora's car rev. A part of me couldn't believe that we had just made love. I wished it could happen forever. And even now I could feel my memories shrink and darken like a fall leaf.

"Close the side door, please," I said into the intercom.

Her car began to roll slowly. I fought back tears, but willed myself not to cry. After taxiing fifty feet, the engines engaged and her car shot forward. Goodbye, I thought after her. Goodbye, Nora.

Once I had wiped my face and blown my nose, I repeated, "Side door, please." No reply came. Nora's car soon shrank to a watery-looking dot on the horizon. "Driver? Hello?" I pressed the intercom switch firmly. "Please acknowledge!"

Since we had stopped, I hadn't heard from him. Undoing my seatbelt, I worried that something had happened. I lowered myself to the tiles again and headed to the front. The round pilot door was ajar. Wedging my fingernails under the edge, I coaxed it open. "The intercom isn't working," I said. "Could you close the door?"

Inside, it was pitch-black and silent. A second later, a pinkish light flickered from what I assumed was some control panel low on the dash. I hadn't ever been inside a pilot's cabin. They were barely four feet tall and the seat was designed for someone who weighed less than seventy-five pounds. On the silvery dashboard were two steering sticks, several switches, and knobs. In the sculpted black seat, the driver looked young—my age perhaps. All of my previous drivers had been older. He looked like a bug boy, and I wondered why someone so inexperienced was driving.

"Are you all right?" I asked. When my eyes adjusted to the dim, I saw that his helmet was off kilter and half of his face was dark. I was about to ask what was the matter, when I realized it wasn't face-paint, but blood flowing from a gash on his forehead. His eyes were three-quarters closed. Touching his neck, I was glad to find him at least warm.

This was my fault! I had pressed the emergency button without any warning. As soon as I had thought that, I saw that his seat belts were hanging at his sides and a corresponding splat of blood was on the inside of the windshield.

Reaching in, I got one hand under his legs and the other behind his shoulders, but the space was so cramped, and he so heavy, I couldn't budge him. Then I worried he had a neck injury, and left him in the chair.

Glancing up and down the Loop, I saw nothing either way. I could wait and hope help came or try to drive myself. I didn't want to do either, but I decided to see if I could get in and at least move the car to the side of the road.

I barely fit through the pilot door, but I was able to squeeze my way in. The best I could do was to lay sideways, propped up on one elbow with my feet dangling out the open door. That way, at least I could operate the controls, see out the windshield, and watch the three screens below.

The leftmost was on. A woman with frizzy hair in a white plastic jacket placed an enormous blue and white capsule on a man's tongue. After he wiped his nose, he struggled and swallowed it. Then he returned the favor with a pill the size of a baby's fist. He shoved it into her mouth and while she gagged and her eyes watered, he continued to push it farther down her throat with his thumbs. Snapping off the screen, I felt repulsed by whatever smut or torture that was supposed to be.

Then I had a bad feeling. Pushing myself off the driver's lap, I glanced down at his crotch; his uniform was unsnapped and there, lay a flaccid, ruby-colored organ.

"Gross!" I said.

Fetching a handkerchief from my pocket, I spread it over him and returned my attention to the controls. On bits of white tape someone had labeled the six switches. From left to right they read: *Warm up, Full, Tuning, Cruise, Decay*, and *Off*. I flipped the first to see what would happen and heard the familiar gradual rising whine of the motors. After thirty seconds, I hit the second, but the motor's pitch continued to rise and red lights blinked on a dial. I switched off *Full*, but the motors kept going faster and faster. I smelled an acidic smoke. Switching off *Warm up*, they finally began to slow. Once they returned to what sounded like their normal speed, I flipped *Full* and they held. One switch at a time, I told myself.

Now, how did the car actually move? As I looked over the controls, the middle screen blinked on. I saw Xavid's big glasses and his snow-capped hair. As he squinted into the dark, I quickly covered my face with my arm. "Turn on the lights!" he said. "Where are you? You hear me, you slubber butt? You're late! Get that fucking shit-ball dancing-boy back here. I need him for my show."

I didn't move or breathe.

"You pill freak, where are you?" A blast of static came from the screen as if Xavid had huffed at it. "Fucking useless Goddamned cousin!" he muttered. A second later, it shut off.

While Xavid's Ültra bombast and complete hatred of me weren't surprising, what was his obviously incompetent cousin doing driving my car? And why was Father's hairdresser hiring key personnel?

Grasping the left steering stick, I turned off *Full* and flipped *Cruise*. The car didn't move.

"How do you make this thing go?" I asked. My unconscious driver had no advice. The middle screen came on again. Only this time it wasn't Xavid, but a diagram. At the bottom was a teardrop, which I guessed represented my car, and at the top was a blinking light. Looking through the windshield, I saw nothing. A moment later, though, I saw the familiar shine of a Loop car on the horizon.

Was it Nora, returning to help? Or was it Father and his orange satin coming to get me? Or was it just some other car? And what would happen when it blasted past me? When I had been on the road, the winds from the passing cars pummeled me. I knew that the vibrating skin on Loop cars had something to do with their stability, but if we weren't moving, I didn't think it worked.

Bending my head until I was against the driver's shins, I saw three more knobs below labeled *Tempo*, *Track*, and *Mode*. I gave Tempo a twist and the car barreled forward into the other lane. Grabbing the left steering stick, I leaned it hard the other way, but not before we slammed into the wall, and a horrible twisting metal sound reverberated all the way down the side.

The center screen blinked the word *collision* as if I had no idea. The right showed a diagram with several red arrows, presumably where I had just caused damage. I maneuvered the car back into the right lane and just as I did, the on-coming car blasted past us and knocked us against the other wall. The screens lit up again.

Seconds later, I had centered the car and we were moving fast. Soon, I saw an exit sign to America-3 and made the wide turn. I was no longer on the Loop proper, but a tributary heading north.

"Find Walter Kez," I said to the screens. The center one

displayed a map, and it didn't look far. Less then fifteen minutes later, I switched from *Full* to *Decay* and then *Off*. The car came to an easy stop. I had made it!

Once I had extricated myself from the pilot's cabin, I turned to get a look at the Kez residence and the surroundings.

The house was just two stories made of a blush-colored brick. The windows on the second story were covered over with red-painted wood. Fifteen feet from me was the matching red front door centered on a dilapidated front porch. For about half a mile in all directions were browned fields of corn. Beyond that were thousands of the yellow and red square houses that dominated the slubs.

The front door opened. Walter stepped out. He wore a silver jacket over an undershirt. His hair was a mess, and he looked sleepy. "Elle's not here!" he shouted, as if reluctant to come closer.

"My driver's injured," I said. "Can you help him?"

He turned and darted back in.

While I waited, I told myself that this was the slubs—not a terrible area obviously, but the slubs anyway. Had Father come to look at their place? Did he have any idea who he was trying to merge with? Sure, they could have some amazing new technology behind those covered-over windows on the second story, something that might even save RiverGroup, but I doubted it.

Walter came back out, pulling on the same light-grey suit jacket as he had worn before, and I figured it was the only one he owned. Behind him was the other nanny.

"Where is the patient?" she asked, with a modicum of medical authority. I motioned to the pilot door and while she stuck her head in, Walter dug a toe into the dirt.

"You probably shouldn't be here."

"I know, but do you have any more of that ARU?"

"Oh," he said, pouting, "sorry. I ate the last one."

"Can we get more?"

"My sister has the car. She's in Yooku getting ready for the show." Peering up, he asked, "Aren't you going to marry her at midnight?"

Glancing out at the dusty cornfields, I felt far away from everything. I said, "I don't know."

His nanny had managed to pull out the injured driver. She held him in her arms as a mother might cradle a baby.

"He's bloody!" said Walter, stepping back.

I asked, "Will he be all right?"

She nodded once then took him back to the house.

"Do you have someone who can drive my car?"

He said he did and he directed us around the main building to a small slubber shed of a house ten feet square. As he knocked on the black door, he said, "She's very nice. And very helpful."

A young girl, in loose beige pants and a long, ugly unwoven undershirt, answered the door. She didn't look especially pleased to see Walter, and her eyes were heavy as though his knock woke her.

"We're going to buy ARU. We need you to drive Michael Rivers' Loop car."

This child could drive a Loop car?

Leaning around Walter, she peered at me as if she were the one unsure. "*The* Michael Rivers?" she asked, as she wiped her wet nose.

"See!" he said, teasingly. "I told you I know him!"

Curling a lip, she asked, "What are *you* doing here?"

Once I had a better look, I decided she was probably in her twenties. "*Trying,*" I said, emphasizing the word because I was beginning to doubt my decision to come here, "to get ARU."

"For you?" she wanted to know.

"A friend."

She rolled her eyes, as if she didn't believe. When I showed her my car, the first thing she did was walk all the way around it, dragging her finger over the surface.

"It's nice, but we'll probably barely get three point two." Turning and squinting accusingly at me, she added, "Someone scraped off a bunch of the fast fibers."

"Fine," I said, unhappy with her manner, but at least semi-confident she could drive. I asked Walter, "Where do we get the stuff?"

"Asia-12."

I wanted to collapse. After all I had gone through to get here, the place was on the other side of the globe, hours and hours away. We would never make it in time.

Wiping her nose again, the girl asked, "What about the Arctic pass?"

"What's that?"

She turned and spoke toward the north presumably. "Supposed to be part of the new Loop, but they never finished."

I asked, "Is it safe?"

Starting toward the pilot door, she said, "Nope," and crawled in.

Walter grunted and stepped on a waterbug almost as big as his foot. Gritting his teeth in disgust, he said, "Come on! She's good."

The Artic pass turned out to be a decrepit one-lane, floating metal bridge that stretched across the North Pole. It rose one hundred feet above the blood-red water and the thousands of brown and orange junks that covered the ocean like water birds. The bridge had no walls, no guardrails, and swayed back and forth in the currents. Gripping the upholstery of my seat, as if to hang on and help steer, it was like riding a wild bull, especially since the road wasn't surfaced, and it felt like we were thumping over railroad ties.

Walter threw up into his handkerchief half a dozen times. Several of the windows cracked, but held together. The main screen snapped and showered the floor with bits of glass and glowing goo. The overhead light blinked out and when the auxiliaries came on, two of them flicked off as well.

When we were finally off the bridge and back on real roads in Asia-12, I felt grateful, but wasn't sure if my bones were in the same order.

Meanwhile, night had descended and everything had gone black. Outside, I saw not a single spot of light, and except for the road ahead in the beams, we could have been in outer space.

Walter stood and freshened up in the bathroom. When he sat, I could see that he was at least his normal pale.

I wasn't attacking him, or accusing, but I just wanted to confirm what I suspected. "There is no Ribo-Kool, is there?"

Although he didn't look up, his fingers began worrying an errant thread on his jacket. "Sorry."

"What is there?"

"Nothing," he said, with a sob. "Don't turn me in, please! It wasn't my idea! I didn't want to change my name."

"Your name?" I asked surprised. "Who are you?"

"Noole. My grandfather made bricks in that building where I live."

Changing identity was not just illegal but impossible, especially from slubber to family member. RiverGroup, or one of the other security companies, protected all names and numbers. "How did your uncle do that?

Shaking his head, he said, "Xavid Xarry did."

"My father's hairdresser?" I asked, as if he were crazy.

Walter peered at me. "He's CFO and COO of RiverGroup."

I had forgotten about his titles. Maybe because when Father announced it, it seemed like a joke. "How do you know Xavid?" I asked. "Or how does he know you?"

"He's Chesterfield's brother." He smiled hopefully, but his grin was short lived. "Xavid is very smart?" he said, the questioning intonation returning to his speech. "I guess he just wants to become part of the families?"

I didn't care that they were slubbers, but I knew Father had no idea. I knew he hadn't even gone to their house to take a look. And I knew that once it was discovered, the other families would cry foul that RiverGroup was merging with the enemy. Grabbing the control, I tried to turn on the cracked screen to call Father and tell him what an idiot he was, but of course, it didn't work. I longed to see his face turn red as he learned that yet another of his magnificent plans had died an ugly death.

"Look it!" said Walter, pointing.

Outside, lights had appeared on the horizon. I thought of the *Pure H* copy, *Miniature city flickers*, and that was exactly what it looked like—a tiny metropolis gleaming white, blue, and orange.

I asked, "That the place?"

"No. I think it's Moscostan. I go there to see creepy things." Frowning, he added, "I have bad nightmares about it sometimes."

"Where do we get the ARU?"

"A little farther." Pointing to something approaching on the left, he asked, "What is that?"

Leaning over to get a better view from the windows, we were quickly approaching a tall, lit yellow and red sign. As we neared, I could read the ornate, script letters. It read, *Tanoshi No Wah*. Behind the sign was a large red-and-yellow-striped tent.On each of the six peaks, a red flag flapped in the breeze. Around the central tent were a dozen smaller ones and what looked like parked trucks and several lit rides with mechanical women, giant ducks, and golden blimps. To one side was a makeshift parking lot with a few rusted but garishly decorated four-wheeled trucks.

I said, "It's my mother!"

Fifteen

Walter laughed as if I were insane. "Your mother?"

"I mean it's her carnival ... the one she travels with."

He looked horrified. "Way out here?"

"She left Father years ago. She joined this carnival. I don't know. It's like she does it to embarrass me."

"Why would she leave your dad?" he asked. "He's so nice!"

I was about to explain, but it did not seem worth it, or maybe it only confirmed his dreadfulness that he had charmed one odd and insignificant boy. Instead, I said, "We're stopping."

"Oh no!" he said. "It's too dangerous around here! Moscostan is not good."

"Driver," I said into the intercom. "Stop at this carnival." As I spoke, we zipped past it, but she began to slow immediately.

"You didn't tell me about this!" said Walter, panicked. "The places you go aren't good!"

"You don't have to get out. I'll go alone."

Frowning, he said, "No, I'll go with you." Then he sat pouting, as if he regretted our friendship.

Soon Walter's driver had turned the car around and parked it in the muddy lot.

"Look how big they are," he said, pointing to a group of slubbers in the same silver and white jackets and loose pants I had seen when I fell off the Loop. As the door slid open and the car was filled with hot smoky air, voices, I began to have second thoughts. I had just been so surprised to see the sign for Tanoshi No Wah, that I felt I had to stop, but really it made no sense. Worse, Mother would probably cry and plead with me to stay and when I refused, she would begin ranting and screaming.

Before I changed my mind, I grasped the side of the door and swung myself down. The ground squished underfoot.

From somewhere—maybe from the big tent—I heard an odd singing. The voice was at once lyrical and beautiful, but also oddly stinging, as though it was the combination of an accomplished opera soprano and a giant mosquito.

"I need a step." Walter still stood in the car, his toes over the edge, looking down the three-foot drop.

"Come on," I said, holding up my arms, "I'll help you." He jumped right into me and almost knocked me backward. I grasped the shoulders of his jacket, though, held him and kept myself up, too.

Straightening his jacket and hat, he frowned and said, "I don't want to die."

"We'll be fine," I said, hoping that was true. From here, I could see that the smoke was coming from one of the smaller tents where a vendor was roasting meats.

As Walter and I walked across the muddy field, slubbers who had been milling about stopped to watch. A few pointed at us, some gestured at my Loop car. Most looked unhappy that we were there. Several children laughed at us. They pulled their loose, nonwoven shirts taut as if to mock our tailored jackets. A tall, heavy man in a silver jacket had purple blotches all over his face. From his left nostril a clear viscous drip began to lower itself. I thought of the goo at the MonoBeat Tower, but tried not to show my disgust. Sniffing violently, he sucked the mucus back into his nose, and then turned away.

Walter tugged on my sleeve as if he wanted to run back to the car.

"He was just trying to frighten us," I said, not sure that's what he'd really meant.

As we continued, I saw a makeshift fence surrounding the tents, and next to the opening stood a small red booth. On top of the booth was a sign that read TICKETS. Inside was a man in a shiny gold shirt. He had a small face, a heavy brow, and what seemed like a permanent scowl.

"Good evening handsome and distinguished guests," he said, louder that I expected. "It seems you have come from afar in a very fancy car! I am so very sorry to say that the Tanoshi No Wah has already performed tonight." His glowering expression was gone. Now he beamed at me with a manic look. "I can offer you both the very best seats for tomorrow's performance," he said. "Only one hundred thousand apiece, gentlemen."

Exiting slubbers slowed to gawk at us. Two women in white plastic pointed at us. A man in silver and the same bunny shirt as I had seen before, scowled.

"Thank you," I said, leaning in so the others might not hear. "Actually, I'm Michael Rivers. I believe my mother works here." I wasn't sure if *work* was the right word. "I'd like to see her if I could."

He leaned slowly back as his eyes circled my face. For an instant, I thought he was going to tell me to go away. "Forgive me! I should have recognized you! Please, forgive me." He then fumbled with the things on the little desktop—a roll of tickets, pieces of blue and green paper, a grey metal box. After he had jammed everything in the container, he jumped down from his chair and disappeared. A second later, he emerged from a small door on the right side of the booth. He was just three feet tall.

"I'll tell her! I should have recognized you. I'll go tell her right now! Forgive me, please." In his right hand, he held the metal box. "I'll run and tell her right now!" He hadn't yet moved.

"Yes," I said. "Thank you."

"No, *thank you!*" He laughed. "Thank you, Mr. Rivers!" Next, he threw his arms around my right leg, as if hugging me. Walter must have thought I was being attacked. He yelped, stumbled backward, and fell to the ground with a splat.

The golden man let go. "Forgive me! Is this … another of our brothers?"

"No, he's a friend," I said, as I stepped to Walter's side to help him up. The golden man got on the other side and together we righted Walter. Several of the circled slubbers laughed. Walter frowned at them. His back was covered with mud and bits of trampled grass.

"I'll go tell her now!" said the golden man. He ran ten feet away, then stopped, and came back. "Forgive me," he said. "Please come in! You and your friend. Please, come with me! Come inside! I don't know what's the matter with me!"

At the entrance stood a woman in a frilly, dusty mauve dress, wearing a matching cone-shaped hat with a green feathery puffball at the top. Her exposed shoulders were bony and sad. The way she moved, she didn't appear able to turn her neck, head, or eyes. She strained to smile, and said, "Welcome to Tanoshi No Wah," in such a hush of a voice I barely heard.

Meanwhile, the golden man was running around shouting. "Michael Rivers is here! Everyone, he's really here!"

From the open door in the tent and from the trucks and smaller tents strange creatures began toward us. I felt Walter's hand on my sleeve again. "Freaks," he said with what sounded like both curiosity and dread.

A man, who looked my age, had no arms but fingers like plumes of feathers on his shoulders, stepped forward and stared at me intently as if he wanted something. A young woman, dressed in a tight silver bodysuit, had a tongue so long it hung to her knees. A clear, steady stream of saliva dripped from it. A boy had huge eyeballs that bulged from his head like a koi. A shorter, stout young man had another smaller head growing upside down from the top of his. Two men were dressed in red costumes with pointed yellow hats. One was holding what looked to be the enormous, gold spandex-covered genitals of the other. A bare-chested boy of maybe sixteen had a metal and glass contraption attached to his chest. Inside were tubes filled with blood, a spinning motor, and odd, glowing blue lights.

They stood and stared. The man with the genitals reached out a hand, but I retreated a half step.

"Don't hurt us!" whimpered Walter.

From the tent came a young woman in a flowing black skirt and a black bra with three cups. She had sharp green eyes, long flowing brown hair, but no mouth. Instead her face ended an inch below her nose. As she came closer, I could see that the black thing in the center of her chest was not another bra cup, but a speaker cone affixed to her flesh.

"You've come," she said. I recognized her voice. She had been the one singing before. Her speaking voice was like a cross between a castrato and an electric shaver. "I hoped you would!"

I knew what was going on! Mother hadn't just hoped I would come to live with her, she'd told all of her strange friends. "Where's my mother?" I asked, wishing I hadn't stopped after all.

"I'll get her," said the speaker-girl.

"I will!" said the man in red, who set down the genitals of the other. "I'll get her." He turned and dashed off. "Judy! Come quick! Judy, your son's here!"

"Welcome!" said a man dressed in the same kind of ratskins that my mother had worn when I saw her last. "Welcome to our simple and true way of life!" He had long, greasy black hair, a gaunt face, but fierce, supernova eyes. "Welcome to the Tanoshi No Wah!" He spread his arms and his cane as if he were introducing a show.

"They're all so very peculiar," I heard Walter say.

"Michael! My darling!" It was my mother. Her hair was slicked back with what looked like mud. Her eyes were puffy and the ratskin robe she wore was open. On her belly was either a tattoo or paint. Below the word *Wah* was an arrow that pointed to her crotch. She closed her robe and put her arms around me and squeezed. I felt the cold mud on my face. "I knew it," she said, sobbing gently. "I knew you'd save us!"

The others, who seemed to have been waiting for her to say just that, started to cheer.

"We just happened by," I began. "We came to the slubs looking for ARU." I was going to continue, but she touched my face with her cold hands.

"Michael! I'm so sorry, but we weren't meant to live like this, with this guilt and remorse. I've got a few pills in my purse. Do you need one now?" She glanced toward the man in the skins and whispered, "Just don't tell Mason!"

I guessed Mason was the master of ceremonies, and the way Mother spoke I figured he didn't approve of her drugs. I also got the distinct and uncomfortable feeling they were having an affair.

"Not for me," I said, "I need it for Joelene. And I want to explain something."

"Maricell, sweetie," said Mother, addressing the speaker-girl, "this is Michael," she said, introducing us. "Michael ... Maricell."

She reached her right hand toward me slowly, as if afraid. I did the same and just as our palms touched, a titter of sound came from her and she jumped back.

"So shy," said Mother, touching her shoulder gently. "Could you do me a favor and get my bag? It's on the door of my trailer. Hurry! I have something for my son."

Maricell's eyes lit as though happy to do something for me. She turned and ran off.

"We'll drink a toast," said Mason, raising his cane. "We'll drink a grand toast. We'll drink to rebirth! To reincarnation. To resurrection. We're all saved by our brother, *the golden dancer.*" The way he said it, so large and dramatically, I imagined he wanted to put it on their sign.

"Who's your friend?" asked Mother.

I introduced Walter.

"Hello, Michael Rivers' mother," he said bowing and then glancing toward my Loop car as if afraid it had left.

"I'm so glad you came," she said, touching him on the cheek and making him flinch. "I'm glad my son has friends."

Walter giggled uncomfortably.

"Mother," I whispered, "I have something to tell you."

Maricell, the speaker-girl, returned. She was out of breath and her nostrils flared as she breathed in and out. The skin beneath her nose was scarred, and I wondered what sort of an accident it had been. Handing a ratskin purse to Mother, Maricell gazed at me and began singing again. The song was haunting and eerily familiar. And as she sang, she gazed at me with so much hope, I had to look away, pretend to scrape mud from my shoes, because I knew I was going soon and figured that would disappoint her terribly.

"These are my last three today," whispered Mother, as she rooted around in her bag. Meanwhile, others began singing with the speaker-girl. "I can get more. Don't worry. Does your friend need any?"

"No," I said.

Walter held out his hand. "Two for me, please!"

Mother eyed him and placed one in each of our palms. Walter tossed his into his mouth and crunched it with glee. I hid mine in a secret pocket inside my jacket.

A woman, with skin that looked like scrambled eggs, stepped toward me. She touched my face gently, and then ran away just as quickly.

"Ari," cried Mother. "Come and say hello." She stopped five feet away, but wouldn't return. "Don't mind them," said Mother. "They didn't believe that you'd come." Her eyes got watery. "I didn't even know if I really believed. But you're here! Sweet, Michael, you've found the truth."

"Yes," I said, swallowing hard. "The truth is, I have plans for tonight."

"We all have plans!" she said, as if this were what she had longed to hear. As tears began down her face, she said, "We can have our future together."

Behind, I saw several of them bringing out a long table and chairs as if we were going to have some sort of a feast right out in the open. Others brought trays of what looked like roasted rats piled on metal plates. Mason directed everyone with his cane.

Mother kissed me on the cheek. "You're home. I'm so glad you're with *your* family."

I owed it to her to tell her about my plans for the show, but the way she had stressed *your* and now gazed intently at me, I asked, "My family?"

Turning, she looked at the others, who were all laughing, joking, and smiling, I felt they might never have been happier. "Before you came along," she said, "your father had trouble producing healthy children. He had more than six thousand with all sorts of women. Most didn't survive." She hugged me to her. "You were the best and the prettiest boy," she continued. "Even so," she waved toward the others with her left hand, "you needed lots of pieces from your siblings."

Sixteen

They sat me in the middle of the worn wooden table as if I were the guest of honor. Above, they had strung dozens of LEDs that glowed like tiny red planets. The speaker-girl handed me a tall stemmed glass filled with a clear, yellowish drink.

"Corn wine," she said, her eyes filled with happy tears.

I put it to my lips but just pretended to drink as I watched them talk, laugh, and make a dozen hopeful toasts. "What do you mean *pieces?*"

"To fix what was wrong. You were deformed, like the rest."

"From now on," announced Mason, who had climbed atop his chair, "we'll be allowed inside the families' cities. We'll put on shows for them." He spun his cane in his hand and laughed as though he were drunk. "We can raise our ticket prices a hundred times. We'll get new tents. Better trucks. And new costumes for everyone."

After she poured for the others, the speaker-girl sat across from me. While they drank and celebrated, she stared at me as if she couldn't believe I existed. The man with the enormous genitals pointed at her.

"Sing, Maricell! Sing for our brother!"

She stood and did so. For the longest time, I couldn't place the song, and then I knew. It was her version of *Adjoining Tissue.* Only her odd, beautiful, and sad voice made the song poignant and serene in a way it never was before.

171

"You got your mouth from her," said Mother.

"My mouth?" I asked, afraid what this meant.

"Yours was too disfigured," she whispered. "You didn't have a working jawbone so, the doctors used Maricell's. It was just the right size."

I stared at the scar just below her nose and wondered if Mother could be right. Touching my face, I traced my lower jaw though my flesh as though I could tell if it were mine or not.

The young man without arms, only fingers, suggested that he and I dance together in their show. "I have ideas for us!" he said, his eyes wild and joyful.

"We'll have plenty of time to talk about that, Rex," said Mother. Whispering, she told me, I had gotten my arms from him.

"No," I said.

"Yes, tour father wanted you to have good, strong arms. Yours were thin, your bones, brittle."

As others made toasts and praised my arrival, I reached inside my jacket, under my shirt, and touched my shoulder as if searching for a seam or scar. I wasn't sure if I believed Mother or not, but as I scanned the faces around me, I began to see similarities to Father and me. One had a mouth the shape of his. Another had his nose. The speaker-girl's eyes resembled mine.

At the far end of the table, the boy with the mechanical heart stood and made a toast. Before Mother leaned toward me, I knew.

"After my heart attack," I guessed.

She nodded.

I didn't want any of it to be true, but I couldn't disbelieve it away either. It explained the way I felt sometimes. When I woke from the coma after my aneurysm I sensed that I was different, that I shouldn't be alive. Maybe I should have died. And maybe that was why I quit dancing, because I knew something was wrong. And was this what I had wanted to know all along? "Why?" I asked her. "Why them and why me?"

"Your father, Hiro Bruce Rivers." She gazed into my eyes with a wisdom and tenor I had never seen from her before. "He wanted to have a beautiful son. He did everything he could to make you perfect." Scanning their faces, she concluded, "Your brothers and sisters and your half brothers and half sisters were your spare parts."

"*Spare parts?*"

After a deep breath she said, "For years I've debated whether or not to tell you … whether it was fair or you were ready." She combed hair from my cheek and said, "I think you're ready now."

"What do you mean? What happened?"

Spinning her empty glass, she stared forward and said, "You should ask your father."

"You won't tell me?"

"It's really between you two." Frowning, she added, "I think that's best."

"Mother!" Her quiet resolve was more frustrating than her usual hysteria, but she was right. It was between Father and I. As I glanced around, I felt like I should thank them, or apologize, or better yet, somehow give all of their flesh and bones back. "What should I do?"

"Dance with us." Tilting her head to the left, she smiled and added, "Dance with Tanoshi No Wah."

I wished I hadn't asked. As responsible as I felt, I didn't want to dance—I had vowed not to ever again. Besides, I didn't fit in here. Not that I wasn't obviously a freak in my own right, but I was a city boy. A family boy. I should be with Nora, drinking cream coffees, appreciating silences and colorless interiors.

Of course, I wasn't going to be that either. I was going to destroy Father and myself. Then again, maybe that would be my brothers and sisters' salvation: once RiverGroup, Father, and I were gone, none of them would be used again.

Looking Mother in the eye, I said, "I can't."

"You don't have to dance," she replied. "There are other

possibilities. We're just glad that you found us and that you're here."

"I can't stay. I'm sorry, but I can't help. I have to destroy Father. I'm going to kill him, end RiverGroup, and save Nora." Now I expected Mother to have one of her fits. Instead, she gazed at me solemnly. "Because he is going to kill her," I explained. "There's no other way to stop him."

Her expression darkened. She bit her bottom lip and fixed her eyes on her empty glass. She said, "Not good," so quietly, it made me feel terrible.

"I know, but Tanoshi No Wah will be free," I said. "When Father and RiverGroup are gone, they won't be used anymore. That will be good, won't it?"

She touched her muddy hair, but still didn't look at me. "I don't think I told you, but I thought you would be a poet someday. I always hoped for a gentle and quiet life for you. Maybe because I knew it never would be." Smiling sadly, she shook her head once. "I didn't expect you to even visit me out here."

"Mother," I said, annoyed that she was now trying to guilt me. "I have to protect Nora. I love her. It's the only way."

She gazed at the others, the way a mother does, admiring not just the faces, but the spirits and souls.

I shouldn't have stopped, I told myself. Now, I felt hopeless and culpable. But what could I do? Staying was impossible, and I couldn't fathom anything else.

A voice in the distance screamed, *"Satins!"* Everyone at the table stood and started running as if for their lives. Several bumped into each other. The genitals-man fell to the ground.

"We must hide you," said Mother. "Wait here!" With that she dashed toward one of the metal trailers.

"Mother!" I cried. "What's wrong?" In the confusion and noise, she didn't hear. Maricell stopped before me. Her eyes were big and fearful. "You should go," she said in that buzzing voice of hers. Turning, she sprinted toward the tent as quickly as a fawn.

I felt a hand on my shoulder. It was Walter. "We had better go," he said.

"What's happening?"

"I don't know, but you shouldn't be here in the slubs." Turning, he started toward my car half-skipping, half-running. "Come on!" he said.

I didn't know where Mother had gone. Everyone else was in a mad dash back and forth, as if they didn't know what to do.

Maybe Walter was right. I had the ARU and I needed to get it to Joelene as soon as I could. Besides, my nitrocellulose suit would be arriving soon and I had my plans. I started after him. As we neared my car, the side door slid open. Walter tried to leap up into the opening, but only managed to get his torso into the car. His legs dangled over the edge. Once I shoved him in, I grabbed the side and swung myself up.

"RiverGroup compound," I said to the driver on the intercom.

Walter got himself seated. The side door slid closed. "What's going on?" she asked, as we began to taxi back to the road.

"I don't know," I said, as I fumbled with the safety belt.

The car slipped in the mud, for a moment, then we made a sharp turn onto the road.

"Look it!" said Walter.

Three very tall men, with crooked faces and beady eyes, were wearing shiny gold, military-cut uniforms. They stood beside the table where we had just sat. One of them, with heavy boots, knocked over the table with one tremendous kick. Trays of roasted rat and bottles of corn wine flew into the air and landed in the mud.

"What are they doing?" I asked.

"They're terrible," was all Walter said.

One of the golden satins chased after the genitals-man. The satin produced a black stick, pointed it at him, and a bolt of lightening shot from the end. The genitals-man flopped forward into the mud as if dead. The speaker-girl dashed toward the satin and pounded him on his lower back with her little fists. The giant turned around, and using the electronic stick as a club, whacked her across the head. She fell sideways and lay still.

"No!" I screamed as I tore off my seat belt. We were just taxiing past the tent, with the motors still revving, when I pressed the intercom. "Stop the car! Open the door!"

"No!" said Walter. "We have to go. They'll kill us! They don't care."

The car stopped and the side door slid open. When I started for it, Walter grasped my jacket. "Don't!" he said. "They're giants. They have killer sticks. They don't care who you are."

I tore myself from his grip.

"No!" he screamed, as I jumped.

I landed in a slick spot and fell onto my face. Pushing myself up, I began running toward the satin who had killed the speaker-girl. "Son of a bitch!" I yelled.

The seven-foot-tall satin turned to me. Its skin was pallid, its eyes, light green. The long pointed nose hooked over the lips like a beak. He bared his yellow teeth, as if he relished an attack.

As I ran, I knew this was suicide. I wasn't going to help Joelene, kill Father, destroy RiverGroup, and protect Nora. I was going to be killed in the slubs for the death of my half sister. It was all wrong, but I couldn't and didn't want to stop. "You're dead!" I said, although I couldn't imagine how I could even hurt the thing.

As I landed a punch on its stomach, he grasped my head, as one might an orange, and lifted me off the ground. My face and ears were crushed under his thick, ironlike fingers. My neck felt like it might break and let my body fall.

"Let go!" I swung my fists as hard as I could at the arm that held me, but my blows slipped off the slick fabric like drops of rain.

Pointing the electric rod at my chest, he said, "You die." A loud crack and a white explosion came from the end of the stick.

The ground came up, crashed into my legs. I fell forward.

The last thing I knew was the stench of burnt hair, and then I disappeared.

A fleshy gurgle, like wet flatulence, came from nearby. I heard breathing that was going a hundred miles a minute. My skull felt like it was being crushed. My ears felt like they'd been sheared off. I was alive, but couldn't move. And although I decided the fast breathing was mine, I didn't think any air was getting into my lungs. I tried to move my arms or legs but couldn't. Something was on top of me.

This was my death. I hadn't died when the electric rod had gone off. It must have knocked me out. Mother and the others thought I was dead and they buried me. Now, I woke buried underground only to die again. I made one last effort to move or make a sound, but I couldn't. The earth was too heavy.

"Pull!" I heard from a hundred miles away.

An instant later everything was quiet and I decided I was dreaming.

"Pull!" I heard again as the earth above me moved. "Pull harder!"

I knew the voice. It was Mason, the master of ceremonies.

"Again!" he said. "Pull!"

The earth slid from me. Light and air touched my face like divine hands. I could see. I could breathe. When I inhaled, I felt a searing pain in my lungs.

Now it was my mother's voice. "Michael, can you hear me? Speak to me."

"I'm alive," I said, choking.

Hands grasped my arms and I was turned face up, but it took several moments for a terrible dizziness to leave. My mother's face floated before me. Bright lipstick was smeared across her chin and nose. Some of it dripped onto my face as she came closer.

"Michael, you're so brave!"

The air tasted cool in my lungs. I asked, "What happened?"

"We all saw it. When the satin touched you with the rod, the spark jumped off of you, back to him. You killed that satin!" She wiped her face. It wasn't lipstick. Blood was flowing from her nose. Someone, Mason, I think, handed her a cloth.

"They killed Fenn," she said, as she mopped her nose, eyes, and forehead. I didn't know who Fenn was, but imagined it was the man with the genitals. "Becka is bleeding badly. They took her to a doctor. We don't know about her. Mason's hand was broken. But you scared the rest of those ghastly satins off before they did any more damage."

I lifted my right arm and inspected the fabric of my jacket. It was just like before. Clean, smooth, subtle, and perfect. I thought of the electricity impedance test—the display where I had pressed the button just yesterday before the doors to Mr. Cedar's workshop. My suit's subsystem channeled the electricity right back to the satin.

"But what about Maricell?" I asked as I began to cry. "She okay?"

Mother nodded. "She's hurt, but we think she's going to live."

Seventeen

As we raced back through Europa and across the Atlanticum bridge to America-1, and Walter sat slumped and silent, I tried to understand what had happened. That I had risked my life to try to revenge my half brothers and sisters, whom I had never met before—or even knew existed—perplexed and frightened me. But more troubling than my suicide run at the satin, was the depth of my feelings for them.

Did that mean that Mother was right all along? Was it where I belonged? Should I join Tanoshi No Wah and be in their shows? If I did, certainly my fame would change their lives. As Mason had said, they could tour the cities and charge a hundred times more. They wouldn't have to eat roasted rat, live in the mud, and be attacked by pillaging satins.

Or maybe it wasn't that simple. Maybe I wasn't what they needed at all. Maybe my fame would only do to them what it had done to me. The way they celebrated, toasted, and cheered me, I had been a deity and a promise I doubted I could ever fulfill. And what would it be like for me, traveling around the world, holding Mother's clothes as she stripped or even dancing with her? I couldn't fathom it. Worse, I could imagine tens of thousands of channel reporters chasing after us, trampling the grounds and ripping the tents to get the story and images of my new peculiar career.

What if what I really felt was guilt? What if that was why I had run at the satin? But the truth was I hadn't caused their misery. I hadn't taken Maricell's jaw, one brother's arms, another's heart, and whatever else. No, I decided, the best I could do for Tanoshi No Wah was stay with my plan and destroy the man who had made them suffer.

After exiting the Loop, we sped past the lights of Ros Begas, and up ahead, on the mountain, searchlights and lasers wove a fabric of light into the night sky. Halfway up the access road we had to stop, as the rest of the way was jammed with thousands of cars. A moment later, though, officials recognized us, and we were directed straight to the steps of the PartyHaus.

The area was flooded with people, smoke, bright screens, and sequined dancers. I saw *LardLik* men in big wooden necklaces; *Ball Description* girls dressed as mice and cats. Hundreds of *Petunia Tune* women wore elaborate gowns covered with spots and dots. But most were Ültra in super-saturated stripes, plaids, and florals, with feathers, metals, leathers, cardboards, necklaces, ruffs, lace, hats, ribbons, and lights. From the top step of the PartyHaus all the way down to the oxygen gardens, they formed a writhing mass of colors, textures, and shapes like the grotesque and oily guts of an enormous sausage made of every possible fashion catastrophe.

Even before the door slid back, I could hear an ominous Ültra beat in the distance. And when the door did open, a cascade of blue and orange fireworks exploded along the road sending sparks sizzling through the air. The gunpowder and smoke combined with an odd rubbery odor, and while it wasn't as bad as some of the smells in the slubs, the stench sat in the back of my mouth and burned like a splash of stomach acid. The sea of partiers before the car cheered, clapped, and screamed at us.

— They thought you were dead!

— I wanna see inside Elle!

— Michael, Nora was attacked!

— *Fist my heart muscle!*

— I love you, but I hate you!

I tried to locate the person who had mentioned Nora, but it was impossible in the mass of movement and sounds coming from every direction. Fighting their way through the crowd, two hospitality girls, like those of old—covered with food, soap, oils, paint, wax, vomit, and other bodily fluids—came to greet us.

"Welcome to the RiverGroup product show," said one, who had a big splat of what I assumed was pudding across her face and chest. "It promises to be the most fun show of all time, throughout the universe and perpetuity!"

"Was Nora attacked?" I asked her, as I stepped from the car.

Before she could answer, a man in a striped vest, checked pants, with blood-red eyes bellowed, "Should be! Hate that whore!" He began choking and then threw up black coagulated carrot juice onto his pink neon platforms.

Shoving him backward, toppling him and several others like bowling pins, Pudding snarled, "Back up, fuckers! Make room."

"Excuse me," I said to her, with instant respect, "could you please keep an eye on my friend." I thumbed toward Walter, who still stood in the car, his eyes wide and apprehensive. She said she would and then cleared a narrow path up the stairs.

Halfway up, I heard a familiar voice.

"Were you assaulted by MKG's satins?" The question came from the heavy woman from *Intellectuals and Soup*—the one I'd dubbed Pink Hat. She wore a simple, tasteful, long orange and red gown that looked like a TUNE-21, and her trademark feathered chapeau.

I stopped. I was surprised to see her here and asked, "MKG's satins?"

Her brown eyes grew wide as if she hadn't expected me to recognize her or respond. "Michael," she said, the same way she might have savored lobster bisque, "I saw a report." In person, her face reminded me of a young girl because she only wore cherry eye shadow, but otherwise her skin looked clean. "The report was about a dead satin in Asia-12 … an MGK satin."

Of course! The satins had been gold—one of the MKG colors, and Nora told me her father had sent them. The news was crushing because it meant that I had brought those satins to my brothers and sisters. I asked her, "Is Nora okay?"

Pink Hat's mouth tightened and her eyes—which looked larger, and a deeper shade of milk chocolate in person—watered. "It hasn't been confirmed," she said, in a voice that didn't seem to want to believe, "but I think she was injured."

"Who did it?" I asked, as if I couldn't fathom the answer.

"*Crush my ass in my head!*" screamed some Ültra goon behind her.

After she grimaced at the shouter, all she seemed able to say was, "I'm sorry."

"She's not dead, is she?"

"No!" She shook her head, and a tear skittered down her cheek and disappeared into the folds of her chin. "I just love you two," she added, as she pulled pink tissues from her tiny beaded handbag.

"RiverGroup," said Goatee in that slow, reflective way he had, "is barely viable." He stood beside Pink Hat, like her escort, but I hadn't even noticed him in his plain if handsome brown suit and a matching beret. His eyes focused on me with both intensity and feeling. "Despite tonight's histrionics," he continued, "my investigations suggest that RiverGroup is bankrupt. Monetarily and morally. There is one possibility now."

"*Rip it!*" screamed a woman with a green face. "*Break it blue!*"

After I nodded to the intellectuals, I continued up the stairs. Goatee was right; there was only one possibility, and I needed to find my nitrocellulose suit. At the top, the Ültra was loud and each drumbeat knocked a half-breath from my lungs.

"VIP area," shouted Pudding, "is level fifteen." She motioned at an elevator bank.

"I had a suit delivered. Know where it is?"

She shook her head and shrugged. I thanked her, and then

headed through the doors. The foyer had been turned into a lounge. Bars lined the walls. Behind it stood hulky men in see-through tuxedos. Partiers lined up in front of blinking carrot, beet, and radish lights. "Sir," said one of the bartenders, who was coming toward me with a long orange tube, "tap root enema?"

I continued right past him. Inside, every inch of the PartyHaus was clogged with Ültra addicts. Two men in white were bound like the three-legged race but with barbed wire. Their white clothes were soaked with blood. A brunette dressed in red rags that stunk of gasoline had several squirming, wet amphibians in her mouth.

Most recognized me. Danced at me. Shouted and sang at me.

– You're our only chance, Michael!

– *Crush my hope!*

"Excuse me," I said. "Pardon me." They wouldn't get out of my way, so I adopted the hospitality girl's strategy and pushed them back as best I could.

I touched the back of a man's lime suit, but found it coated with some sticky goo. Going around him, a woman covered in what looked like broken shards of glass tried to bite my face. I ducked and slipped by.

– *Golden boy must die!*

– Murder Elle! Murder her love!

"Get out of the way!" I told them again and again, as I continued across the floor.

When I finally got to the stairwell, I felt exhausted and sickened, but began down. Below, in the glare of the orange lights, I saw a couple in matching lavender outfits thrust needles into each other's throats. I assumed the black stuff in their hypodermics was carrot liquor, but the woman's face quickly turned so red, she looked like a hemorrhaging tomato. I turned afraid she would split open.

Another group in untanned hides and broken feathers were

smashing each other in their faces with tremendous kicks and elbow punches. A man on his back was knocked in his face several times by a larger man's knee. As the victim smeared his blood over his face, like a child might finger-paint, he giggled as though pain had become pleasure.

Many sang to the blasting Ültra, which ricocheted against the hard walls. Others, dressed in tight sequined outfits, did flips and tumbles in all directions. Farther along, I saw a man sitting on the floor gagging on a huge carrot that was stuffed halfway down his throat. A vaguely amused group stood watching.

The second stairwell led into the same inky darkness as before, but now among the giant sex sculptures were dozens of mostly naked people rolling, groping, and taking each other. A woman mounted a man and then slammed her fists into his face like a crazed jockey beating a horse. Soon he was unconscious, but still she rode him hard.

When I found my advisor, three people were dripping vegetable alcohols on her and laughing. "Get away!" I told them, as I shoved a man in a pink frock.

"Fuck shit idiot!" he bellowed. He could barely stand. "I'll kill you," he said, his eyes fierce but unfocused. "Eat your fuck brain!" he blathered, as he swung a wild fist. He missed by five feet, stumbled backward, and fell onto the hard floor. His laughing friends began to drip alcohol on him.

"Joelene!" I said, as I got down beside her. With my handkerchief, I wiped the black gunk from her chapped lips and swollen face. "You all right?" She didn't respond. "I have the ARU." Her forehead felt broiling hot. "It's me, Michael."

Barely opening her eyes, she murmured, "MKG."

That she mentioned Nora's company surprised me. "They sent satins to try to kill me," I told her. Her eyelids hovered halfway, like indicators of her consciousness. I gave up explaining and got out the roach-looking pill my mother gave me. "I have it."

I think she said, "Yes," so I touched the pill to her dry lips. She opened them and took it between her teeth. A second later,

I heard a crunch.

As I took off my jacket to drape over her, I inspected her left hand in the heavy metal cuff. I wasn't sure, but thought it might be infected. After I tucked my jacket around her for warmth, I said, "I'll be back. I promise."

When I stood, I saw Father's silver-haired director before me. "I *thought* it was you!" he said. He wore a blue suit with an orange shirt and shoes. "We had rehearsals earlier. Except you weren't there. We used a stand-in, but you were supposed to rehearse! Then I see you running down here. So, I chase after you. And here you are!"

"Can you unlock this?" I asked of the cuff on Joelene's wrist.

"No," he said with a frown. "The show's beginning! We have to go."

"I have to help her!"

Shrugging, he said, "The show! You must get ready."

"I had a suit made," I told him. "Is it here?"

"There's no time! You'll have to wear what you have on." As he spoke, he looked me up and down, then at my jacket on Joelene and grimaced. "God, you're not even dressed! I know your dad got some clothes for you. Let's go look."

"I had a suit made!" I said again. "Like the orange ones from *Adjoining Tissue*."

"HammørHêds? One of my favorites! Love them." Getting out a small screen, he checked with someone. "Michael's got a suit on the way. Did it get here? … Oh! Great! Level fifteen!" he said to me. "It's waiting on fifteen. Hurry. We have to hurry!"

We dashed past the sculptures and the people everywhere, up the stairs and past the violence in the orange lights, and back to the dance floor. Now the director was in charge of pushing the Ültras back and shouting, "Coming through!" We made a right and headed to the stage. Across the huge orange curtain a swarm of lights circled as though it were about to open.

"He's here!" he said, once we had gone through a black door

to the backstage. Hulking boxes of equipment sat everywhere. The floor was covered with lines of taped-down power cords. The workers were all dressed in blue leotards with words on their chests—pyrotechnics, lighting, fluffer, sound, security, continuity, costume, makeup, and so on. Several stopped before the director and me and cheered.

A woman with the word *food* on her chest said, "They're just serving slut cakes now. You've got a minute."

"Good!" he said. "Good, we'll be right back!"

He led me to a decrepit elevator—obviously the PartyHaus was just refurbished for the public—and we headed up to the fifteenth floor. When the door slid open, the director held the doors for me. "Here we go," he said, pointing to a sign. "This way."

Soon we came to a door with the number 15-T. He opened it and we entered.

At first I thought it was a huge bathroom. It was fifty feet wide and all surfaces were covered with some sort of cobalt tiles. Around the perimeter were thirty or so black metal toilets. The far wall was glass that looked out at the distant lights of Ros Begas, and in the middle sat several boxy pastel couches and chairs. On the center cushion of a lacy gold and pink sofa sat Mr. Cedar. He had one leg folded over the other, his hands in his lap. Even in the light, I could see how supple, smooth, and soft was the material of his jacket. After all the Ültra nonsense, it was like the beautiful and calm eye of a hurricane. Under his jacket, he wore a pure white cotton shirt that I suspected had been ironed by Isé–B, as it had that distinctive combination of formality and insouciance. As for neckwear, his tie was a deep shade of magnesium. On his feet, his thin-soled shoes were a midnight brown.

Standing, he bowed and said, "Greetings."

To his right, partially hidden in the darkness, stood his assistant Pheff, and behind him was a six-foot-tall black case covered with latches and several glowing dials. They had brought it!

"Thank you," I said.

"We have to hurry!" said the director. "Big hurry. Show's about to start."

Pheff began unlocking the box with both speed and care. Clearly, they had guarded the suit to make sure it didn't fall into the wrong hands. Once he had opened all the locks, he pulled a lever, broke a seal, which released a slow hiss of gas, then he swung open the door.

"Love it!" gushed the director, his eyes wide. "Incredible! I just love it!"

"Thank you," said my tailor, coolly.

Inside the box, on a top-of-the-line Silver-Dream Chanel-Royce hanger was a wide-shouldered, orange suit. Even as I could see Mr. Cedar's impeccable tailoring, the supple lines, and the gentle roll of the lapel, it was a fierce-looking thing. It shimmered as if with heat or some catastrophic potential energy.

For a long beat, I stood staring at it, mesmerized and afraid.

"Finally, color!" said a familiar voice. Turning, I saw Xavid. He wore a huge blue and orange color-blocked suit with bloody seal pelts hung here and there like hunting trophies. His face was covered with operatic-styled makeup and his hair was braided and looped into a complicated mess like the collapsed skeleton of a crashed blimp. "Your father," he said, stepping closer, "will be exceedingly proud." Then he spoke to everyone. "I need a minute with Michael. If you could all excuse us."

"He has to dress for the show!" said the director. "We're about to start."

"I have an extremely important message from his father." He waved his hands as if to urge them out. "Thank you so much! Just one minute. There you go."

As Mr. Cedar, Pheff, and the director headed out, I stood facing the box, and worried that Father had found out about the suit. What could I do? Could I grab it, run, and then just throw it at him? Or was this about Xavid and what I now knew about him and his identity thievery?

"I'm so glad you're back," said Xavid, stepping before me and smiling. "We have a big show after all." Now he narrowed his eyes. "I'm not sure what happened to you out there. Contradictory rumors are going around." He paused, as if I was going to explain anything to him. "In any case," he began again, "like I said, your father will be most pleased with your suit. We're all glad you're giving up that tedious grey shit."

"What do you want?" I asked, impatient.

"Listen to me," he said, his voice turning hard and angry, "from now on and for the rest of your life, you are forbidden from leaving the compound. You are forbidden from speaking to the press. You must ask me before you do anything! And you will do exactly as I say." He began to dig into a pocket. "If not, he'll go get the rest." He then tossed a small glass vial at me.

I caught the thing and held it up. Inside, floating in a clear fluid was a small human toe. The nail had been painted a metallic charcoal.

All the blood cells in my body seized. My muscles froze. Then a single synapse jumped from one nerve to another and eked out a single message: Nora.

The toe was hers. The freeboot beast had cut it off.

"I can't tell you what happened in the past," continued Xavid, his voice light and dreamy. "I don't even know, nor do I care to know all the mistakes your father made. That's the past and Xavid doesn't worry about the past. Now, what's expedient is to gain control of this enterprise. It's like a massive colony of algae that has choked itself and I know that I will do an extremely good—"

"Shut the hell up." I didn't say it loud, but he heard the boiling anger in me. His eyes, like two small, frightened fish in the aquariums of his lenses, darted toward me and held. Stepping past him, I stopped before the nitrocellulose suit. "Get out," I told him. "I have to dress."

Chapter 18

Nora was right—I wasn't her Michael anymore. I wasn't the dancer, or the crazed half brother I had been when I ran at the satin. Instead, as I stood before the suit, and the orange ebbed and throbbed like the surface of a violent and stormy planet, I felt that I was nearing a final point, one beyond anger and revenge, a place of only action.

I heard the door close. I had wanted to pummel Xavid's face as I had seen them do in the PartyHaus basement, but I knew he wasn't worth it.

"Let's get you ready!" said the director, as he rushed back in. "Dressed for the show." Behind him came Mr. Cedar and Pheff.

"The show," I repeated, thinking of the audience in the PartyHaus. When I'd thought about blowing up Father and me, I had not imagined an audience and wasn't sure I liked the idea. The problem was, this crowd would love the brutality, and I hated to imagine them standing and cheering our charred bodies. But I couldn't let it worry me. Whether they loved it, thought of me as a fool or a horrible and ungrateful son, and whether or not they came to understand what had happened, none of that mattered.

Stepping beside me, Mr. Cedar spoke quietly. "The original material was too volatile. I doubted you would last the evening, so I rewove it, created a twill with two layers and functions. The top is both photo-luminescent and protective. The lower layer is …" He paused and twisted his beard hair once. "… quite hazardous."

As he spoke, Pheff removed the suit from the box and took the pants from the hanger. I glanced from the fabric to my tailor. Maybe it was the glow from the suit, but the scar that ran down the middle of his face was more visible than usual, and I swore it looked like a nearly microscopic, flat-fell seam with two lines of stitches.

His steel-grey eyes met mine and held, and while I sensed the same serene I always did, I felt something else, something much darker. My tailor was originally from the slubs, and although we had never spoken about it, he must have struggled, and I began to think that he had suffered much more than I had ever imagined, and probably experienced far worse than I.

Turning, he pointed to the box and said, "The shirt and tie."

From a separate compartment, Pheff took out a beautifully ironed shirt and an exact copy of *Love Alone*. Mr. Cedar presented them to me. I wanted to thank him, not just for what he had done today, but for all he had done for me, but it was so much, I couldn't fathom how.

Pheff helped me slip on the pants, the jacket, and knotted the tie. The jacket felt wider and heavier, but much like any of my others. When I ran my hand over the slightly rough material, the orange turned russet as though my body heat, my presence, or maybe my intentions tarnished it.

"A firm impact," whispered my tailor, as he mimed a punch at my shoulder.

Then, bowing his head, he quoted, "*Texture of her overcoat.*"

His quote felt jarring—*Pure H*, grey satellite wools, coffee shops, and silence music seemed, like a distant and forgotten land. And the image that accompanied that copy was strange. A man and woman, both in elaborate clothes—a frock and vest suit for him, a high-necked ball gown for her—sit on a small, odd, two-horse carrousel. He faces right, she, left. From their somber, even perturbed expressions, they have been arguing. I assumed, and Joelene agreed, that they were no longer in love, but I couldn't imagine that was how Mr. Cedar saw it. Maybe he thought the couple on the carrousel was as doomed as Nora and I.

"We're ready!" said the director, into one of his screens. "He looks great! Yes … we're coming down. Get ready to start the show!"

The director and I rode down in a different elevator and he talked on his screens the whole time. "Tell Hiro we're ready. Check on the speaker power … they were running the line to the grid. … Are all the channel guests ready? Talk to Thomas and make sure he doesn't go over—"

"Can I ask you a favor?" I tried to interrupt.

"No! Don't look there. I put more vacuum bulbs behind the station … Clear out the backstage and …" He turned to me. "What?"

"My advisor." With the show about to begin, I worried that I wouldn't be able to see Joelene again. "She was the one on the floor in the dungeon where you found me. It's a mistake that she's there. Could you please get her released?"

His eyes searched my face, as if baffled. "I'll try."

"I'm counting on you," I said. "Please remember."

"Yes." He smiled for a moment but still looked confused.

When the elevator doors opened, we were beneath the balconies, opposite the stage. From here, I could see over the crowd. The curtains were straight ahead. The air was dense with a hundred perfumes, the sticky sweet of fermented vegetables, vomit, and that ever-present sweaty, PartyHaus desperation. Different parts of the crowd were chanting, as though they wanted things to begin.

"You'll walk out," said the director, pointing. "Straight down this aisle. Just go down and take a bow. Wave and smile. That's your father and the VIPs' table down front. You sit and watch the show. Just clap and cheer. We've got cameras on you, so no nose picking. Before it's time for the wedding, I'll come and get you, so don't worry." Into a screen, he said, "Cue the girls ... music ... lights ... announcer ... and go!"

"And now," said a tremendous, deep-throated house voice, as a distorted drum began pounding, "it is my super-amazing and spectacular honor to welcome you to the thirty-third annual RiverGroup product show and Ültra extravaganza. As you all know, recent events have tried to cloud our future, but tonight's show will obliterate those clouds, all doubts, and all eardrums within a seventy-five-mile radius!"

The audience howled. Nearby, I heard someone shout, "Execute my ears!"

Meanwhile, along either side of the aisle, hospitality girls all covered with sticky and shiny liquids and semisolids lined up on either side and saluted. A thousand colored spotlights fluttered over them, like glowing confetti. From high above, tendrils of violet smoke poured down like a million octopus legs. Four feet above the crowd, the phalanxes of smoke were chopped up by the frenzy of the crowd.

"Go!" said the director. "Go on!" He nudged me.

"Don't touch!" I said, afraid he would set off the suit. I stepped forward and a blinding light hit me in the face.

"There he is, Ültra children of pain, the famous, sexy, funny, exciting, clever, pliable, willing Michael Rivers. The greatest dancer in the history of the universe has on a fabulous suit that is just like the famous suits in HammørHêds' *Adjoining Tissue*. Let's scream our throats raw!"

The crowd rose and cheered, and with the light in my eyes, it was just like when I had danced. The energy spurred me on as I continued down the aisle.

"There's a rumor," continued the voice, "that he's going to get married tonight, but will he really end the drenched and debauched dreams of a billion insanely horny girls? You'll definitely want to sit through the exciting product upgrades and important business announcements to see if it all happens right here before your eyes!"

At the end of the aisle, stood Father, cheering. He wore a dark blue short-sleeve jacket, made of something that looked as stiff and luxurious as recycled cardboard. The orange shirt beneath it had huge, bloated sleeves that hung like semi-deflated pumpkins. At his wrists were enormous cuffs and a dozen black snaps. Around his neck was a wad of rhubarb-colored paisley fabric that wanted to be a collar, turtleneck, and tie. It spilled down his front in a floppy, unappetizing mess. As for pants, he wore iridescent blue bell-bottoms with too-tight dark orange shorts over top. The front zipper was open and what amounted to a large, white, codpiece hung out. So swollen and fat was it, he appeared to be giving birth to two honeydews and a plumber's wrench. His wig, a stringy, purple thing, was long and dangled around his ears and down his back. Scattered in his hair were white blobs—mushrooms or marshmallows, maybe. Whipping his arms at the crowd to spur them on, he looked like a flightless, technicolor pirate.

For a moment, I considered rushing him now and blowing us up. The problem was, too many innocent people were near, including Walter Kez—or whatever his name was. I wished I'd asked the director about the wedding! I hoped it was still supposed to be like the choreography I had seen before, where Father and I were alone on the stage. That would be *the moment.*

I stopped behind an empty chair. The crowd hadn't let up at all.

"Bombastic fantastic!" enthused Father, over the roar. "I got you a Poünd outfit like mine, but that's the greatest suit I've ever seen in the history of my life!" Turning to the others he said, "Look at him! It's like *Adjoining Tissue!* Remember that epic?"

"An all-time classic," screamed Jun.

"We're going all out!" said Father. "You have to hang with us now! You can't leave when he's getting Ültra again!"

Around the circular, shiny ultramarine table, where rest bowls of puffy snacks, bottles of wine, programs, and what looked like motorcycle helmets, sat twelve others. Starting on my left and going counterclockwise was an empty chair, presumably for Elle after the wedding, then Walter and his uncle in his beetle-green suit and necklaces.

The rest I recognized like I might have great aunts and uncles. Back when the rages were happening, I saw them every night, but now, it was just once a year at the product shows. Jun, the CEO from BrainBrain, who had become a soft, rounded little man, wore a black suit covered with little mirrors, green makeup, and vampire hair. He smiled at me and the flesh around his eyes turned wrinkled and dry. To his right were the LETTT brothers. Both had muskrat faces—all pointy noses, toothy mouths, and bushy blond eyebrows. Their matching articulated aluminum shirts made them look like robot clichés. Looped around their necks was a half a mile of orange string. Beside the aluminum twins was the president of iip-2. Instead of Ültra, she seemed to think she had become a teenager again and was dressed like an *Om Om* girl in a brown suit with her lips cut open. The next two wore striped jackets, plaid shirts, and awful nonwoven ties. They had on so much crusty purple makeup they looked more like two freshly dug-up beets. I didn't know who they were or what company they represented. Finally, the man in the paisley robe, neon shirt, and a frilly tie that looked like soap suds, was CEO of SLT. Ten years ago he had had an aneurysm at the PartyHaus and since then never missed an opportunity to tell me we were alike.

Beside the SLT man sat Father's woman. She had bright green hair and red-colored teeth. Through her transparent orange dress, I could see the phrase *gender fatality* scrawled across her breasts in what looked like dried blood.

By this time, the crowd had settled down. The people at the table said hello or sang lyrics at me, like the LETTT brothers did.

With their arms over their shoulders, they screamed,

"One crusty bruise to remember her by!" Then they laughed triumphantly and got compliments from the others.

The CEO of SLT man winked, and said, "You and I … we're heart attack twins!"

The *Om Om* woman got up, came around, and kissed me on the cheek. "I've christened him with my blood!" she exclaimed in her rasping voice. "Now, we're blood lovers." As if giving advice, she said, "You should cut Elle and suck her wound, like they do in *Crüsh Töne.*"

"No!" said Jun of BrainBrain, "*Perfect Infinity Dëath* by DïkCräkør! It's romantic how they poke each other with those splinters."

As they all began arguing which Ültra disaster my honeymoon should be like, I told myself this would all be over soon, and I wouldn't have to see these creatures again.

Walter glanced at me fearfully as though afraid I was going to tell the world about his identity crimes. Frowning, he said, "I think something bad is going to happen."

As I nodded at him, the house announcer began again. "Get in your last orders now. The show is about to start!" A moment later, the voice sped up. "Fine china, plumbing, and fireworks graciously provided by Oh!Teen. Slut cakes and taproot beverages and suppositories by Frix Corporation. Also, please take a moment to check your listening and viewing helmet—provided by Volvo-Sony LTD. We'll let you know when you need to put it on."

A waiter, with a RiverGroup logo scarred on his bare chest, stepped beside Father.

"More shrimp loops, love chips, and those salamander hotties," Father said. "Oh, and a dozen bottles of the Frix Carrot-Chablis for the table." Leaning toward me he said, "Watch this." To the table, he hollered, "Ültra is the greatest of all time!"

Like lemmings, they all cheered back. Jun stood, beat his chest, and bellowed, "Deadly Ültra calamity in my brain pan!"

Right, I thought, as I grabbed one of the programs and

began to flip through the shiny, unreadable ads, photos, and promises until I found a schedule. It read: 1. Hiro Bruce Rivers on Business. 2. Super-secret guests introduce new music from Alüminüm Anüs and Dark Cästle of Poünd. 3. Exciting super-upgrade announcements. 4. RiverGroup new product demonstration.

"When is the wedding?" I asked.

"Shush!" shout-whispered Father, as he leaned toward me. "It's a damn surprise!"

"Everyone knows!"

"Yes, but if we pretend it's a surprise, they can think they're smarter than us." He laughed and said, "That's the trick! People love to think they're smarter than you. And it worked," he smiled. "They're all here. Two days ago, they were threatening to give up on us, but the lousy, dumb bastards are here!"

Tan-colored foundation covered his skin. It had looked good from far away, but up close, it accentuated all the lines around his eyes and mouth, like a million, tiny, dry tributaries. Across his forehead were three deep valleys. The top two arched smoothly from side to side. The third dipped toward the bridge of his nose and came close to two vertical lines that rose asymmetrically between his brows. What occurred to me was that he looked more like a grandfather than a dad.

"But when is it?" I asked again.

"Can't wait to get into her salmon-skin panties?" As he laughed, I could see how the alcohol was slowing his motor skills and making his eyelids heavy.

"The greatest Ültra band is Töxic Tësticle Färm!" proclaimed green-faced Jun as he held up his arms as if in victory.

"No!" scoffed Father, whipping his sleeves at him. "Alüminüm Anüs is the greatest. They're big lard! They kill those tiny Tësticles in every way!"

"Tësticle's *Kiss the Axe Meät*," declared Jun, throwing up his hands again, "is the greatest God damned, total, super, fucking classic of all time—forever—no argument!"

"God, no!" cried Father. "It's butt garbage! Right, my spaceship?" He looked to his girl, but she just shrugged. "My dick can fart better than that song!"

While they swore and argued about bands, costumes, and lyrics, I watched Father. The problem was, after drinking carrot all afternoon, and now with his old rage buddies, he was happy—happier than I had seen him in a long time. I didn't like it. He had no idea what I was going through or felt, or why I was going to destroy the both of us.

"Can you feel it?" he asked them, gesturing around the PartyHaus. "A fearful anticipation is building like a pandemic! And we're in for real, clean-your-colon Ültra."

"We never miss Anüs," said one of the LETTT brothers.

"Not one single performance," agreed the other.

"I missed them only once," said Father. "And I was unconscious!" He laughed, and then added what he thought was the final punch, "Same result, though!"

As if to derail his evening, I told him, "I saw Mother."

Turning, he asked, "What are you talking about?"

"I saw her. I talked to her!"

"You better not!" he said, leaning in so we wouldn't be heard. "I forbid it! I let that whore see you after the shooting, but I don't want you talking to her or hearing any of her super-bullshit lies."

"And now!" boomed the house voice, as the curtains parted to reveal the enormous gold, silver, chrome, ice, and black-satin decorated stage. With its three sets of curved, light-blue stairs, angular crystalline walls, and strange, intricate dark blue foliation, it resembled the collision between a glacier and a lingerie factory. On the fifteen-story-tall screen in the back spun a thousand RiverGroup logos. "It's time to say hello to a man so visionary, he has his toilet paper laid out for next week … a man with so much brains, he has to keep most of them in his colon … a leader so strong, even his underwear stands at attention!"

As the crowd laughed and clapped, I told Father, "They're not lies!"

"I don't want to hear it!" He pointed one of his thick fingers in my face. "Shut up about that bitch freak of your God damned mother!" Grabbing one of the carrot bottles, he downed a thick gulp.

"She told me everything." My words were swallowed up in the announcer's.

"Join me in welcoming President, CEO, COO, CIO, CPO, Chief Programmer, and all-around Super Code Bastard, let's tear down the PartyHaus for the biggest, loudest, and the lardest rager of all time … Ültra lover, silence hater, the screaming, howling master of the pelvic thrust, party critter numero uno, Hiro … Bruce … Rivers!"

After glaring at me once more, Father jogged to the stage and tripped up the five steps. Once he'd regained his balance, he cried, "Children of pain! Let's rage on the stage! Let's crack our spine and drink wine! Let's grind our ass and make some gas." The audience's enthusiasm dimmed as if disappointed with what were the oldest and lamest Ültra shouts. Undaunted, he pumped his fists in the air and sent the floppy bags of his shirtsleeves in motion. "Be my Ültra baby of anguish!"

That got them going again.

"Come on up!" he said to his girl. "Before we begin, I'd like to introduce my newest cunt spaceship, Jenni Haska-Martin-Biochem, who used to work as a monkey trainer for Frix Corporation." As she came to his side, he walloped her plastic-covered ass. "She's great, but with this great crowd tonight, you never know, maybe I'll meet someone new!" Jenni puffed out her cheeks and made an angry face. Many laughed as if she were funny or cute.

"All joking aside," continued Father, "this has been a great year for us at RiverGroup. Yeah, we had a few days in fucktown, and hey, there are always critics." He curled a lip in my direction. "We're back, and let's fuck the critics. We don't make our

SymmetryMax products for critics! RiverGroup makes our stuff for love. And our love is stronger than ever!"

I wanted to scream at him, but told myself to be patient.

"Believe me," he continued, "we've got some secret and stunning surprises later, so stick around for the whole incredible show." On the huge screen behind him appeared a series of complicated neon pie charts that zoomed in and out, broke apart, and reassembled themselves like a mad geometric ballet. As he spoke, his girl, maybe thinking this was her moment, began licking her lips and caressing her chest. As people hooted and yelled, Father would smile and wink as if he thought it was for him. "Today," he said, "RiverGroup SymmetryMax Super-Secret-Pass 45.882 is used by forty-two percent of the market. Our SecretSuite is the standard with fifty point three percent. And our new SecretDuper Embedded CodeBitch Asymmetry-Regulator is *the* measure for critical applications with a whopping twenty-two percent!"

The screen was filled with numbers and graphics all flying around like gnats. I took the vial from my jacket and gazed at the flesh inside. My poor Nora. I couldn't believe what he had done to her.

"Yeah!" said Father, who had noticed Jenni now stroking her crotch. He started doing his pelvis thrusts at her. "It's about love, Ültra children! It's about love and love is all about forgiveness. We're still strong. We're still there for you! We love you!"

Clutching the vial, I shouted, "We hate you!" and felt like I'd been possessed, like the Ültra color of the suit was contaminating or infecting me. For a moment, I wondered if I should tear it off before I lost my mind.

Walter stared at me. Across the table, though, green-faced Jun pointed and said, "That's right!" With what looked like venom in his eyes, he added, "Sweet hate!" It was odd that Father's biggest client and one of his oldest friends had just agreed. Or maybe he was drunk on carrot and had no idea what he was saying.

Sirens began whirring. Blinking orange lights surrounded

the stage. Hospitality girls ran toward Father and Jenni with helmets.

"You know what this means!" said Father, apparently done with his boring business charts and his ridiculous dance. "Time to rage!"

The announcer said, "Attention! Attention! Please don your safety helmets and make sure they are securely over your ears and eyes." The voice sped up again. "By attending the RiverGroup product show, you wave all rights expressed or implied, includin—without limitation—the right to sue for optic nerve, ear drum, spinal cord, or any sensory damage, and you will not hold RiverGroup, its affiliates, or subsidiaries responsible. Safety helmets provided are not endorsed or guaranteed by RiverGroup, and should they fail, are not the liability of RiverGroup. In the event that a situation arises concerning injury, our hospitality girls will assist you, but they are not medically trained personnel and cannot and will not be held accountable for further injury or negligence." The voice returned to its normal speed. "To introduce our first song, please welcome the gigantic and super-celebrated epic star of *Blood Bile and Cum2*, Erik Heimlick!"

As Father and his girl took their seats, he turned away as if he were going to ignore me the rest of the show.

From stage right, Erik came rushing out covered in nothing but his own glistening sweat. "I will shatter your nuts!" he said, as that was the dreadful catchphrase that had made him famous. "Wow!" he continued, peering all around, "This is … I don't know … I mean … there aren't words to describe it … gosh … it's just so beyond words!"

"I saw Tanoshi No Wah," I told Father.

"Shut up! Shut up!" he roared, then glanced about as if afraid what everyone would think. In a shout-whisper he added, "Don't mention that shit. It's all fucking lies. All of it! God damned lies! Now shut your mouth, or I'll beat you right here."

"Go ahead!" I dared him. In that instant, I didn't care. I wanted him to blow us up with a stupid punch.

"Don't ruin this for me!" he said, through clenched teeth. "I've got this whole thing working *lardly*—don't fuck it up! Shit-face bastard licker, can't you just shut up?"

"Excuse me!" chimed a hospitality girl covered with melted lemon ice cream, "What volume would you like, sir?" She held out my helmet and smiled.

All around the others were putting on their safety helmets. The ones right in front were given clear plastic to cover themselves. I told her, "As low as possible."

She flicked rocker switches on the back of the helmet, handed it to me, and then moved on to Walter. Meanwhile, Father had slipped on his helmet, turned away again, and folded his arms over his chest.

As I slipped on mine, I felt my hands vibrating. But I was ready. I was just action now—a tiger, ready to make my leap.

On stage, Erik was back on script. "I've got something I know you're gonna love—Alüminüm Anüs. *The* Ültra band of all time!" The crowd roared. He made an angry face, and then, as if taunting the audience, and like he did in his horrible channel movies, shouted, "You stupid bum cums! You plastic cunts! You spoiled brain cakes! I don't think you're ready!" The crowd howled. "Are you? Are you really ready?" The seventy-three thousand shouted back *yes*. "No!" he waved a dismissive hand. "No, you're not ready for Ültra!" They answered again, louder. "I mean real Ültra! Not that fake crap, but real, genuine, certified Ültra. Alüminüm Anüs Ültra!" Now they were in a frenzy. Erik's carbonate plastic smile flashed brilliant white. "Okay then! Maybe you *are* ready! Maybe you're ready for a new song from their unreleased epic, *Pulverized Entrails*."

As if he had disappeared without a trace, Erik was gone. The spotlight that had illuminated him ebbed away until the PartyHaus was pitch-black. For several moments, everything was still. Then the crowd began shouting.

– Give it to us!

– Bloody our ears!

– Make me pee red!

– Hiro, you lousy bastard, flatten me!

Father stood, pumped a fist in the air and said, "I'm gonna try!" as if happy for any attention other than mine.

A naked man walked to the middle of the stage. Another, dressed in black, stepped beside him. The man in black was holding something, a stick maybe. In the darkness, I couldn't tell.

The first man's face slowly came into focus on the giant screen behind them, where before Father's pie charts had flown like giant insects. He was handsome with a proud nose, dark green eyes, and full lips. What struck me was how vacant, neutral, and nothing was his expression. It was the gaze of those perverted sculptures in the dungeon.

The two men just stood there, so I leaned toward Father again, and said, "I know what you did."

With his right hand, he tried to shush me away like a housefly.

On stage, the man in black spun around and wielded a ball-peen hammer at the head of the naked man. We saw the blow in close-up on the screen and with the impact of metal against skin, came the recognizable blast of the colossal Ültra drum. The beat was hard and powerful, like a solid smack in the face.

I held still for an instant, as if any additional force would set off the nitrocellulose. Then I moved into the chair for Elle, and scooted it behind Walter, hoping his body might shield me.

When another hammer blow hit the naked man, I could see how the force rocked his head and neck and sent him wobbling. A line of blood ran from the top of his scalp. Another blow brought another enormous thud of drum and a thick spill of blood flowed across his eyes, which made him blink, as it must have stung. Gradually the hammer's rate increased and with each hit came the same solid thud. Blood streamed over his eyes, nose, and mouth. I felt terrible for him.

Finally, a blow cracked his skull open and when it did, the head exploded and sent out a detonation of sound so loud, it made the floor bend and twist. It swatted the drinks from the table and blew the shrimp loops into the air like confetti. Had I not been behind Walter, I'm sure I would have gone up in flames.

In an instant, the stage was filled with more than a dozen drummers attacking the black and chrome munitions drums that sat before each like rocket launchers. The sound was a continuous roar, like a hurricane, a train, and a never-ending series of exploding bombs. Father and the LETT brothers grabbed our table to keep it from buzzing away. My chair began to rotate counterclockwise and Walter's started going in the opposite direction.

In the crowd behind us, people were standing, screaming, and waving their arms. Some were ripping off their clothes. Others began fighting—throwing punches and slamming their elbows into each other's ribs. Amid the chaos, the only words I could make out were *love*, *disgust*, *vomit*, and *agony*.

Hospitality girls, now in safety helmets, rescued Walter and me and locked our chairs to the floor. They cleaned the broken glass and wiped up the fallen snacks.

Beneath Father's silvery visor, I saw him mouthing along to the words as he pounded his fists on the table and thrust his hips. Jenni, beside him, held her arms in the air, where the percussive thuds shook them like twigs in a cyclone.

After a chorus of what sounded like *torture in your bowels*, the song crescendoed. As squealing feedback shattered lights and cracked several of the glacierlike structures on stage, I slipped off the chair and hid below the table. Around us, I saw several people grab at their ears as if in pain. Farther back, a man's helmet cracked open and his exposed head lasted just two seconds before it imploded into a bloody mass and his limp body crumpled to the floor.

The song finished with a series of yellow and green explosions that sent one of the drummer's arms—still clutching his percussion hammer—spinning into the seats.

Then it was over. The shaking and vibrating stopped. The smoke cleared. The crowd roared. Erik Heimlick dashed back on stage. Blood dripped from his mouth, eyes, and ears. "The beautiful dead Ültra child of your nightmares has thus spoken!" he screamed.

The crowd began chanting something that sounded like *hard horn—lard corn*.

Father tore off his helmet, ran up the stairs, and threw his arms around one of the singers. "Fuck," he said, tearfully, "I needed that!"

Nineteen

Walter took off his helmet and glanced at me with a fearful frown. "Too loud," he said.

His nose was smashed and bleeding. "Walter," I said, shocked that I would have to tell him, "your nose is broken."

Looking down cross-eyed, he grasped the bone and wiggled it back and forth.

"Don't do that!" I said, revolted.

Leaning in, he smiled. "The ARU takes all pain away."

"You better go see one of the hospitality girls."

"Michael," said the director, sitting on the edge of Father's chair, "you look fantastic in your suit. Love it!" As he spoke, he peered all around, as if pleased with his work. With a nod, he added, "Come with me. It's time."

Father was on stage still hugging and shaking hands with Anüs. And after I told Walter to have his nose checked again, I followed the director as we headed to the black door at the side of the stage.

Taped-down wires covered the floor. Assistants shouted orders and questions and ran in all directions. "Damn it! I'll be right there!" replied the director to his screen. "Back in a second!" he told me, before he dashed off.

A woman almost ran into me. Then two men carrying a big metal drum rushed by. Afraid of being blown up, I stepped beside the clear sound baffles that lined the stage.

"And now," I heard the announcer intone, "please stand, scream, and join me in welcoming the implausible host of the best and most popular celebrity interview channel show—with a very naughty and nautical theme—yes, it's Milo Holly from *Celebrity Research Yacht!*"

Across the shiny icelike stage, Milo in his whites and captain's hat skipped down the far stairs. He looked like he was trying to imitate a carefree boy returning home after the last day of school. When he came to the front of the stage, he grasped the large silver mike and screamed, as if he had just lost his mind, "We're charting a course for even more implausible Ültra!"

Behind the baffles, the crowd roared like a huge passing Bee Train. After Milo droned on about himself and RiverGroup, he introduced the next band. "With implausible pleasure, implausible pain, and implausible implausibility, I give you the greatest Ültra band since the last one on this very stage, the stark-raving hot Dark Cästle of Poünd!"

From all three staircases came the members of the band, wearing the same sort of bizarre pirate costume as Father, with short-sleeve jackets, shirts with big flopping orange sleeves, and overstuffed codpieces. Instead of Father's wooden sandals, though, they wore huge, black rubber boots that were a half-foot thick and made them waddle like ducks. A man with a bumpy, misshapen skull wheeled in an enormous, black harp with a human skull atop the column. Another man had a metallic electric cello strapped to his chest and played the strings with a blowtorch. Still another held a pneumatic saxophone that vibrated in his arms like a jackhammer. The rest played rocket and mortar drums. The last to come on stage—the leader, I guessed—who looked like he had just come from an emergency room, with tubes running from his mouth and nose, wore a curved, florescent green keyboard around his waist, like a peplum. As he screeched lyrics, the giant video screen lifted away to reveal the jet-powered organ I had seen them constructing before. When the leader began playing runs on his keyboard, fifty-foot flames shot from the pipes.

They were loud, but not unbearable behind the baffles. When I turned to see if I could find the director, fifteen feet back, in the shadows beside a stack of blinking electronics, stood a man in a black suit and glasses.

I started toward him and the closer I got, the more I was sure that it was Father's freeboot. His gristly skin was the same. So was his hole of a mouth and his single nostril.

"You damned bastard," I said, "I hate you." He didn't move a molecule. Behind his dark glasses, I couldn't even tell if he was looking at me. "You hear me? Get out." He still didn't move, and it was like the arteries in my body weren't filled with blood anymore but gasoline. I pulled my arm back to whip it at him.

"Michael!" said the director, grasping my arm just before I brought it forward. "What's going on?" His breath was salty and sour, his eyes, wide and concerned.

The anger I had felt slowly became dismay and horror. I had just about blown myself up. It was the same madness I had felt when I'd screamed at father minutes before. The freeboot was gone. I worried that father had brought him here to kill me.

"Hair and makeup," enthused the director, as if he were afraid something was wrong with me. "We're ready for you! You all right?"

"Yes," I said, stepping back. "Sorry. I—I was confused."

"Drink too much carrot?" he asked, with a nervous smile.

"None," I said as I glanced about, wondering where the freeboot had gone.

The director led me behind the stage were it was quieter and fewer people ran around. Crates of machines, amps maybe, sat humming, their green power lights throbbing to the distant beat. Then he stopped suddenly and I bumped into his back.

"Oh no!" he said. "We're not supposed to see you!"

Before him, stood Elle. Her face was again pink, her nose black. Her hair was the same white-blonde seafoam and protruding from it were two rounded pink ears—maybe pig or raccoon. The material of her huge, white wedding gown was shiny, stiff, and awful, like polyurethane. On it hung a dozen glassy, undulating red and orange spots, each five inches wide. Her eyes were big with surprise. "Oh, look at you," she said, her voice squeaking, "you're the *bestest* of the *bestest!*" After one of her tittering jungle-bird giggles, she grabbed one of the polka dots from the front of her gown, held it up, and said, "Look, my cervix agrees!"

As the director dragged me away, while telling a gaggle of assistants to get her back to wardrobe, I decided that those polka dots had been camera views of her insides. I felt nauseated and wanted to go wash my hands a dozen times. We came to a row of black fabric tents not much bigger than outhouses.

"Could be bad luck, that," chuckled the director, as he turned to me. "They say it's a bad omen to see your bride before the ceremony." Opening the door to one of the tents, he said, "Go on in. Take a seat. Relax and refrigerate! Someone will be with you."

The room was five-foot-square. In the middle, an inflatable orange chair sat before a navy stand where I saw a multitude of hair products, makeup, and various face and neck stretchers. On top of the stand was a large square mirror with red, blue, and violet vanity lights all around.

For a minute, I stood looking down at my nitrocellulose suit. Like I had done before, I ran my hands over the material and watched it fluoresce, like instantly rusting and unrusting metal.

Sitting, I closed my eyes and thought of Nora, her dark eyes and her full lips. I imagined her in her dressing room getting ready. She would be watching the show on a small screen while her coiffeur, makeup artist, and fashion consultants helped her dress. They probably assumed she was going out. Maybe she told them she was having a cream coffee at the SunEcho, or attending a silence concert of Love Emitting Diode.

No, I decided, she was not watching. She would be keeping an eye on the clock and at maybe two in the morning, she would ask her people to go. Sitting alone before her black and white iMirror, she would take a tiny sip of poison from a black goblet. She'd only have to wait for a few beats before the chemicals stopped her heart, and like a powerless space capsule, she would drift forever into the cold and black.

Taking the vial from my pocket, I held it to my chest. Please, Nora, I thought, reconsider. Go on and forget about me. Live another life.

A shiver of recognition shook me. Father's voice was nearby and his tone was urgent and pleading. Standing, I pushed open the door and peeked out. Five feet away, he stood before green-face Jun, the aluminum-shirted LETTT brothers, the *Om Om* president of iip-2, and the aneurysm CEO of SLT.

"Come on!" he said to them, as he combed his awful stringy, marshmallow-filled wig from his face. "We're about to announce the *secret* secret! And I know it's what you all really want!"

Putting his hands on his hips, Jun asked, "What is it?"

"Go on back to your seats," coaxed Father. "You're gonna be shocked."

"Just tell us," said Jun, his tone as bored as his expression.

"It's a surprise, but you'll like it. I promise."

"I have no patience," said Aneurysm.

"If I just tell you, that'll ruin the secret!" He paused as if sure they would change their minds. "Fucker cakes!" he said. "Fine! I'll spoil it for you—Xavid is going to be the next RiverGroup CEO."

Xavid? That creepy idiot? I couldn't believe Father was making him CEO. Besides that, Xavid was a fake, he didn't have anything to do with the family.

"Your hairdresser?" asked one of the LETTT brothers, stunned.

"He's a damn good hairdresser!" said father, with a laugh. "And he's been our COO and CFO for the last couple of days.

Yeah, I know he's not a Rivers, but the guy can work the code! Besides, my son can't do it. He's useless."

While the clients eyed one another, as if not sure what to think, I felt stung. Father had said as much to my face, but it felt worse that he had told all of them.

"I don't like it," said the *Om Om* lady.

"Why not?" asked Father. "Xavid's lard. He's Ültra. He loves all the great bands and everything."

"I was hoping for real news," said Jun.

"We got that, too! We're going to demo the Ribo-Kool stuff."

"From what I've seen, they're garbage," said one of the LETTT brothers as he folded his arms over his aluminum chest. "I'm not interested."

"Don't be ridiculous!" said Father, wiping his temple with one of his sleeves. "Ribo-Kool is lard! I checked them out. Their stuff is amazing."

"Hiro," said the *Om Om* lady, shaking her head slowly, "don't patronize me."

"I'm not! Not at all!" His tone was pinched and uncomfortable. After he managed to swallow, he laughed. "See! You *do* hate me. That's why I'm making Xavid CEO. You can still hate me, but *I'm* not RiverGroup." His eyes darted at their unhappy faces. "Don't you guys get it? It's like a switch-a-roo!" As he mimed some fast-handed magic trick, he got his big sleeves tangled.

"We don't *hate* you," said the *Om Om* woman, primping her too-tight brown suit.

"You keep promising," complained the other LETTT brother, "but you never deliver." The brothers turned to go.

Father jumped in their way. "Wait! Guys! We're in the middle of the big show. Go on back to your seats. Enjoy yourselves. There's lots of lard surprises."

"The freeboot shooting was too much," said the first brother.

"*That* old news?" asked Father with a laugh. "We're way

beyond that."

"You have never explained how the freeboot got a certified RiverGroup identity. Forget the other crazy shit. It got the one thing in the world it shouldn't have."

"It was those MKG puds!" he fired back. "They shot Michael. Everyone knows it!"

"*No one* knows it!" corrected Jun.

"Do you have proof?" asked the *Om Om* lady.

"Almost," he said, his voice small.

"We need proof," she said.

"Prove it, Hiro," echoed one of the LETTT brothers.

Pointing his fat index finger he said, "Believe me. I'll prove it." Then his hand fell to his side. "I just need more time. A couple of weeks. Maybe a month …"

The LETTT brothers glared at him as if they'd had it. After they eyed each other, they stepped around him and walked away.

"You butt bombs!" he said after them. "Go on! Get out of here. And those shirts are like *so* last year! Guess you bombastic butter creams didn't notice, but Anüs doesn't wear them anymore!"

The *Om Om* CEO wiped her bloody lips. She looked annoyed and frustrated. "When you have proof, talk to me." With a frown, she added, "I'm sorry," and followed the brothers.

Father tightened his lips like he was holding in a convoy of profanities.

Jun said, "MKG's new product is quite compelling."

I was stunned to hear Jun mention Nora's company. It felt like he was cutting Father's heart in two with a scalpel.

Father's face turned pink. "And after all I did for you … you plastic pussy! You rotten brain cake!" he said, regurgitating Erik Heimlick's curses. Flinging his arms he added, "Go on! Go kiss Gonzalez-Matsu's stinking ass!"

"Hiro," shot back Jun, "I kept telling you to explain what happened. Give me a plausible answer! Give me anything! You never gave me bug fuck!"

I thought Father was going to up the screaming ante, but then a small, sickly smile appeared on his face. Dropping to his knees, he said, "Please, you have to stay with us! I'm begging you here."

"Hiro!" said Jun, grimacing as though his face underneath might be the same green as his makeup. "Get up! You're being disgusting."

"Listen," he continued from the floor, "we're gonna rage all night! Alüminüm Anüs is staying. And DJ Furious Molester is back! Remember him from the old days? He's got a new ass!" Father's laugh was like the squeak from a balloon. "I'm telling you, the guy's undomesticated! He's shitting everywhere!"

I felt ashamed. And as Jun and Aneurysm eyed each other, then bid Father good luck and headed off, I, too, had to turn away. Only minutes before I had thought him happier than I had seen him in years; now, when I heard a dozen fleshy thuds, I knew he was beating the floor with his fists.

For a minute, he lay there, berating the clients, their companies, their favorite bands, and Ültra songs. Finally, he got up and aimed his remaining wrath at his documentary cameraman who had been filming the whole time. "Turn that off!" he screamed. "Get out! I never want to see you or that film of my fucking life again!"

The silver-hair director stepped before him. "Hiro," he said, "get it together. The show is still going! Poünd is about to finish, and you're on for the crowning ceremony."

"Go away!"

"Look at me," said the director, grasping Father's shoulders. "Take a deep breath. Come on now. Exhale the bad …" He blew out. "And inhale the good."

Ignoring him, Father dug into his shorts and pulled out a handful of hay from his codpiece. "God, my balls itch. I think there's fleas in this shit!"

"Come on … breathe the good in … and the bad goes away … "

Pushing open the door, I stepped out.

Father jerked backward, as if frightened. "What do you want?"

"In …" continued the director, "… and the bad goes out …"

Before we were both dead, I wanted to tell him what I knew. "You stole Maricell's jawbone."

"Who?"

"In good … out bad." The director smiled and glanced back and forth, as though trying to get both of us on his breathing schedule.

"She's part of Tanoshi No Wah!"

"Tanoshi no shit!" Father's face went lax. "Who cares?" He spread his pumpkin arms and shouted, "You just missed it, but RiverGroup has died a glorious, lousy, stinking, miserable, rotten death!"

"You stole bones and organs from my brothers and sisters!" I said.

"Yeah?" he asked, waving his handful of codpiece stuffing about. "So?"

"It's illegal, wrong, and awful. You did it because you wanted me to be some perfect Ültra dancer, like you could never be!"

"What rancid lard are you talking about?"

"Mother told me you did it to make me perfect."

"That's your mom again. A trillion percent wrong!"

"Then why did you do it?"

For a second, he stared at me. Then whipping the hay in the direction the clients had gone, he shrieked, "Because of those stupid assholes!"

His skin was blotchy, and his eyes, wild. I glanced where Jun, the LETTT brothers, and the rest had gone. "Because of them? What's that mean?"

As though imitating a cockatoo, he said, "Hiro, we want you to have a son who can take over in case you fall over dead, you stupid bastard!" Glaring at me, he snarled, "You were supposed to be the succession plan! But a fat log of good you did me!"

I wasn't even supposed to be a dancer. Instead, I was like the buildings, furniture, or machinery that made RiverGroup work. I told him, "I'm sorry I didn't make you all the profits you wanted. But why did you *maim* my brothers and sisters?"

"Maim!" he sneered. "All aboard the exaggeration train!"

"It was worse than that! Why did you do it?" I demanded.

"You want to know?" He stepped closer. "You really want to know?" Just as he seemed about to bellow, his lips trembled. His eyes watered. He turned away, and seemed to be struggling not to melt into a full-out sob.

This had happened before at the club in Kobehaba and the time I had fallen from the Loop. I couldn't recall what had triggered it then, but this time, he looked like he was truly on the edge of collapse. Not sure I wanted to know, I asked, "What's the matter?"

"Nothing!" he snapped. "You're so ignorant, you probably don't even know about the war with those pharmaceutical slubber bastards! But I fought them."

"I do, and congratulations," I said flatly. Half the family members had been affected by the biological toxins released in the cities, although now no one admitted it. "What does that have to do with me and my half brothers and sisters?"

"I was this close to death." He squished his index and thumb together. "Yeah, you can tell all your friends! They turned your dad's balls into mutant raisins." Around us a dozen of the leotard-wearing stage workers had stopped to watch. I thought he was going to yell at them, but then as if he were pretending to be thrilled, he said, "You heard me! I'm a genetically poisoned freak from the war! I'm not a real man anymore. Go on and stare your hearts out." To me he added, "This isn't something you tell your clients." He spoke as if it was a joke, but clearly he knew it wasn't funny. "They don't want to invest if you can't reproduce. And they wanted someone handsome to take over. At least not the freaks I could make."

I always thought of Father as a beast for what he did and said, but this was the source of his anger and craziness—he was broken inside. It made so much sense I wondered why I hadn't thought of it before.

"Very tragic, indeed," agreed the director, grasping our hands like two children, "but please follow me. The show must continue!"

"I don't want to!" growled Father, pulling away.

"Ratings!" said the director, as if that were the holy word. "We're having a hell of a show! They love it."

Father let out a big sigh. "It's a disaster. Like everything I ever made."

"No! The crowd is sucking it down faster then greased slut cakes! They love you, Hiro. This is your real audience, not those stuffed hams who just left."

"They were the whole reason for this," said Father.

"Forget them! You are a performer. I've been filming your life for years, and I know. That's what you are—a performer. A real star."

Father looked up at him with a glimmer of hope.

"The director's right," I said. "We have to finish the show!" If he didn't go back on stage, my plan was done, but letting Nora and the world see how I felt was part of it.

"Well," said Father, flipping one of his hands over as one might turn a burger "… I do like acting …"

"Of course you do! You were born to be before the camera. The eye loves your face. The ear cherishes your words. The heart suffers your feelings!"

"I guess so," he said, like a dry sponge absorbing a last drop of water. Then smiling, he looked the director in the eye. "I'll do it for you."

"That's it! Now you're going! And they do love you! I know they do. Come on." Assistants opened the door in the sound baffles, and we stepped onto the strangely ornate glacier of a stage. A smoky, jet-fuel haze filled the air. The director led us to the front where the shiny blue floor was covered with a craze of cracks, scorch marks, and bits of paper and trash. The huge curtains were closed, but I heard strings, a dreary rhythm, and several voices chanting something about palpitations, kitty cakes, and pussy willows. It was the same group I'd heard at my promotion date with Elle.

"It's illegal," I said, picking up where we had left off, "to cut and paste people."

"It is," he agreed. While he had been near collapse a minute ago, the director's words had lifted him, and he held his head up as if filled with a form of pride. Not the real stuff perhaps, but a pride for the sake of pride. "But real parts are so much better than the grown ones. And we had *lots* of real parts."

"Stay with me!" said the director, eying us with concern. "Concentrate. This is an important section of the show." He nudged me toward a small, white-taped x on the floor. "It's a little showmanship! Some razzle dazzle." He placed Father four feet away. "In thirty seconds, the curtain will open. At first, the house voice thinks it's the wedding, but it's the CEO crowning. Xavid will come down that set of stairs."

"I thought this was the wedding!" I said.

"That's next."

"But this is just Father and me?"

"Yes," he said. "The Beavers will be singing on either side, but it's a simple quiet moment … an ebb to the flow. It's just the two of you … then Xavid comes down."

It wasn't what I planned, but I couldn't wait any longer.

The director gazed at me as if horrified.

"What?" I asked, afraid he had read my thoughts.

"Where's your makeup? You didn't get makeup!" He called over a man who began dabbing my face with a huge sponge. "Look into the cameras. Smile. Be calm. If you get stuck, look for me stage right. I'll help you." The makeup man powdered my nose three more times. Before he ran off, Father asked him for all the sponges he had. After he handed them over, Father stuffed them down his codpiece.

As the curtains parted, I saw a hundred rows of tables and chairs on the old dance floor and all the seated Ültra freaks. In back fifteen balconies were filled with thousands more. In the glare of the yellow, violet, and blue stage lights, I couldn't see them, but I could hear them and feel their heat. Three transparent screens hung beyond the stage. On them blinked blue words. *Stand still.* High above, rings of colored spots shot shafts down through the haze like a million-legged spider. Then lasers began scribbling words and lyrics all over the walls and floor—as they had in Father's car. I saw *dead orgasm, rip it red,* and *crush më* among the vibrating scrawl. On the steps on both sides of the stage, stood the singing Beavers. The closest one on the right held a long note while he rubbed one of his paws over his crotch. Atop his head the linty fur was highlighted in a large yellow light.

"Aren't they cute?" asked the announcer. "They're The Pipsqueak Beaver-boys! They are everyone's favorite band, and check out their derrieres!" Half the crowd cheered, the other booed. But when the Beavers turned around and bent over, the cheers overtook the catcalls.

"I thought crowning Xavid would be an ass-saver," said Father, with a sigh.

"Xavid is Chesterfield's brother," I told him. "And neither of them are part of the families."

Father gazed at me bewildered. "Where do you get this butt fluff?"

"Is this the part of the show when Michael Rivers becomes a man?" asked the announcer. "Is this when some super-lucky girl becomes his sex-slave wife? Or are we stretching out the show with one more RiverGroup business announcement?"

The Beavers began singing the wedding march a cappella.

"I was at the Kez *compound.*" I emphasized the last word because it was so wrong. "There is no Ribo-Kool. There's nothing. Walter told me they're not even Kez. They're Noodle

… or something. Xavid stole identities for them."

"Shh!" I heard the director say from the side. "Quiet! Wait for your lines!"

"Who is going to come down the stairs?" asked the announcer. "Could it be a beautiful and raunchy girl—someone to make Michael happy a thousand dirty ways?"

"Oh, my, gosh!" said the announcer with a phony laugh. "I'm sorry, that's not a luscious and slutty girl for our beloved Michael, it's RiverGroup's own COO and CFO, Xavid Xarry! Yes, that's right, this is a super-secret surprise! One of special interest to all you partners, subsidiaries, and affiliates."

Beavers—double tempo appeared on the prompters, and when they sped up to a cartoony frenzy, the crowd laughed.

Father stared at me as though I was insane, but I thought I saw a hint of fear.

"When were you at the Kez compound?" he asked over the din.

"Today! It looks like the slubs."

"Bullshit!" Shaking his head he added, "Xavid checked them out."

"Xavid lied to you! He's not part of the families!"

"After a fabulous run," continued the announcer, "as the greatest CEO the world has ever known, our beloved and yet deeply hated Hiro Bruce Rivers is going to relinquish that coveted title."

"Squid shit!" said Father, rolling his eyes at me. "Xavid's lard!"

Maybe father would never understand or admit his mistakes, but at least I had told him what I knew.

"Serving with RiverGroup for more than two years," said the announcer, "Xavid has shown amazing loyalty, fearless determination, and hot, relentless love—the one thing that every great CEO needs. But before we welcome Xavid into our greedy corporate hearts, let's give a much-earned standing ovation to our squealing, bawling Ültra baby of agony, the hard, long, and fat Hiro ... Bruce ... Rivers!"

I could see people in the front rows stand and clap. Some pumped their fists. Others hollered. Father waved a pumpkin arm slowly. He spoke, but I couldn't hear.

"What?" I asked stepping closer.

"There were a lot of ugly babies." He smiled and pretended to point at someone he knew. "One had five nostrils. Another had chicken wings for legs. Some had brains but no skulls. Others had skulls but no brains."

While I could picture the horrors he described, he seemed more nostalgic than sorry. I told him, "You're a monster!"

The prompters said: Hiro—*Thank you! I love you all!*

With a sardonic smile, he eyed me. "I am a monster, but then again, so are you."

"Not by choice."

He laughed. "Me neither."

"Your lines!" shouted the director. "Hiro, say your lines!"

Now the prompter read: Hiro—*I loved you the best I could. But my love just wasn't good enough.*

"You *made* me!" I told him. "I didn't choose to be like this."

"I didn't choose either!" he barked. "Don't you get that? They poisoned me."

"It's not the same at all."

Shaking his head, he said, "It's completely, absolutely, and totally identical!"

"But why did you have to hurt Nora?"

Now he scrunched up his face as if he had never heard anything so absurd. "I didn't hurt her. Every three seconds it's something else!"

I heard the director off-stage saying, "Hiro! Your lines! Say your damn lines!"

"You did hurt her," I said. "You cut off her toe!"

Shaking his head, Father spoke, but the house voice drowned him out.

"Your love is good enough for me, Hiro! And we will all miss you, very much. But from this day on, the mighty RiverGroup will hereby be shepherded by the very talented code bastard, Xavid Xarry. And that means for all of you who what to vomit in Hiro Bruce Rivers' mouth, he's not the man to blame anymore and whatever bad things he presided over are now officially gone with him!"

I studied Father's profile as he stared forward. The bright lights flattened his face and made him look younger, but now all I could see—or imagined I could see—was the flawed DNA in each of his cells. And in that instant, I was angry, and disappointed, but I didn't hate him like I thought I should. Maybe there was no such thing as the pure hate I wanted to feel, or maybe I came upon that opposite dot of emotion right in the middle. Or maybe I'd just felt that he had heard me—even if he couldn't yet respond. He was, after all, my father and whatever he had done—easily a million terrible things—maybe I was about to make a worse mistake.

Then, loathing my sympathy, my pity, I turned to check how close Xavid was, to see if I could include him, but he was still fifteen feet away and walking one step at a time. *Now*, I told myself. I couldn't wait any longer. Bending my knees, I stepped toward Father. Then out of the corner of my eye, I saw another figure come from the opening at the top of the stairs on the left. It was Joelene.

She wore my grey jacket over her underwear as if she had just come from the dungeon. Her curly hair was matted and dirty. Her skin was mottled with bruises, and in the lights they were vivid shades of purple and hunter green. Bright blood ran down her chin.

She sprinted down the stairs three at a time like an athlete. And although I could see that she was going straight for Xavid, all I could do was watch.

"The hell?" said Father softly, as if he hadn't had time to inhale and fill his words.

Completely unaware, Xavid slowly continued toward us as

though wading through three feet of water. "Thank you all," he said to the audience. "It's an extra-extraordinary day of exhilaration for me!"

From the bottom step, Joelene leaped into the air and straight-legged Xavid's neck. His head was knocked so far back, his face disappeared and his chin became the highest point of his body. The sharp, bony crack filled the PartyHaus as everything else went silent. For a second, even with his neck obviously snapped, he just stood there. The seal pelts all over his blue and orange color-blocked suit vibrated as if from aftershocks. Then he fell forward and crashed three feet away.

Joelene stood beyond him breathing hard. Her ribs were visible when she inhaled. Her left hand was bloody. Her pinky and ring fingers had been cut off.

Twenty

A single drop of blood gathered at the end of Joelene's middle finger. It grew to the size of a kidney bean, broke away, and splat on the crackled blue stage. The dot was perfectly round and in the shiny, convex surface, I could see pinpoints from the colored spotlights above.

I had been about to kill Father, Xavid, and myself, but the brutality of what just happened—the palpable snap of bone—made me nauseous and fearful. And as I gazed at Xavid's body, I felt shaken that his death had been so violent.

Another drop of Joelene's blood gathered on her fingertip and hit the floor. Now two circles rested a half an inch apart. Her breathing was slowing. I wondered if she had been hit in the mouth for the red on her chin.

"Improvise!" said the director from the side of the stage. "Invent! Do something good."

One of the Beavers let out a high-pitched yowl like a strange, exotic bird. The crowd cheered. Someone nearby shouted, "Kick 'em all dead!"

More drops had fallen from her hand. Two formed a figure eight. Joelene was watching me. Her expression was at once angry, victorious, and surprised, as though she had been hoping to kill Xavid, but couldn't believe she had.

"Come on," she said. She was gazing at me, and as much as I was glad she was alive and out of the dungeon, my Joelene wasn't a killer. She knew the fighting arts—she had put Mother in a headlock in a half-second—but this wasn't my thoughtful, gentle advisor. "We're going." Her voice was heavier and harder, and I thought of that time I had heard her swearing early that morning.

"Please bear with us," said the announcer, "we are experiencing technical difficulties. This is not a breach."

Someone screamed in pain. In the audience I saw a chair fly through the air, hit a man in aluminum pants, and flatten him. A woman in lavender feathers climbed onto one of the tables as if to dance or proclaim something. As she tore off her plumage, someone knocked her down. She fell onto her head.

Above, a prompter screen read: Michael—*I have promised my full support for Xavid Xarry and pledge to …*

When I turned back to Joelene, the floor beneath her hand was now a puddle of dots. "What is going on?" I asked her.

"Please remain in your seats and refrain from violent conflict," said the house voice. "We'll be right back with the exciting conclusion to this year's show." The curtains began closing. The crowd booed and hissed.

"God damn fuck!" yelled Father as if he had finally regained his volume.

His words seemed to energize Joelene. She leaped toward me and put her right arm around my neck. "You're my hostage," she said quietly. "Play along."

She wasn't hurting me, but her grip was rigid like steel. I stood still, afraid that if I tried to pull away, I would explode.

"Do as I say!" Joelene said to Father. "Don't move or Michael dies."

A gold crown covered with sparkling blue and orange jewels hit the floor about a foot from me, with a tinny thunk as if it had been dropped from high above. A handful of the gems popped out and scattered like glittering beetles. The thing rolled past Xavid's pelt-covered body and stopped a foot away.

"Security!" cried Father. "Xavid is down! Get that woman!"

I felt heat on the side of my face. A huge crawling amoeba of yellow flames spread across the curtains. Clouds of black smoke dimmed the lights.

From both sides of the stage, half a dozen people rushed toward us. They wore cobalt leotards with the word *security* on their chests. Forming a circle, they surrounded us. They all stood in the same crouched-and-ready position like they were from a tennis academy, and their faces were pale, young, and afraid. Beside Father was his freeboot all in black.

"Let my boy go!" said Father, his eyes panicked. "Just let him go!"

"Keep back!" said Joelene as she jerked me toward her. "I can crack his neck in an instant!" As Joelene gestured with her right hand, I could see bite marks in her flesh. She had chewed off her pinky and ring finger to escape the cuff in the dungeon! I thought of Walter's nose and the ARU.

"Careful," I told her, afraid she would knock the suit and blow us up.

"Back off you fucking idiots!" shrieked Father at the security people. He grabbed one of them by the collar and whipped him to the ground.

The crowd roared as the fire ate the curtains away and they could see again. High above, flames engulfed several spotlights. One exploded with a shower of white sparks that arced down like the sizzling petals of fireworks.

The prompters now read: Hiro—*Xavid is a man of many talents, who we have brought into our family to help us ...*

"What are you?" I asked Joelene.

"Corporate assassin."

Her answer should have shocked me. Maybe I was beyond shock. "You destroyed RiverGroup," I said, glancing at Xavid's body.

"Come on, lady," yelled Father, who had obviously forgotten her name, "let him go and take me!" In his right hand, he held a clear fashion gun. A neon green bullet glowed in the chamber.

It wasn't until I opened my mouth that I knew what I was going to say. "*You* had me shot."

"Not *shot*," she corrected, as she maneuvered us toward the front of the stage. "Precise medical explosives." Glancing about, she said, "Once the fire subsides, we'll slip into the audience, and exit through the east wing."

"Why did you hurt me?"

"'Best way to ruin the company," she began. Then she smiled a bloody smile and I could see bits of muscle and skin between her teeth. "But I promised you, and we're going to MKG."

For an instant everything froze. The curtains were mostly burned away. A layer of acidic smoke hung in the air. In it violet, yellow, and red beams swirled from above. Through it I couldn't make out the channel cameras but knew they were there. On the other side Nora sat in her dressing room. She was watching. I could feel her obsidian eyes on me.

Joelene had done it. In the middle of all of this, my advisor had done exactly what I had wanted. I was going to join MKG and be with Nora.

A huge, black electronic gizmo fell from above and crashed into the stage like a fallen satellite. Joelene yanked me back, as a blast of sparks shot from it. A burnt-plastic smell filled the air. The audience was howling for more blood.

"… Uh … yes," I said, barely able to speak. "Let's go to Nora."

The prompters said: Xavid—*and part of my job will be destruction … in order to revive this mighty company…*

In the audience, tables and chairs were being overturned. Ültra freaks ran in all directions. Two goo-covered hospitality women were smashing a man over his head with hearing helmets. A couple in polka dots fucked like dogs. A woman cried for them to go faster.

"Forget the dead man." I heard the director yell. "Read your lines!"

"Give us room!" shouted Joelene. She waved at Father with her bloody hand. "Give us a path out or Michael dies!"

Father fired his gun. A man fell on his back a foot from Joelene and me. He wore a green jacket with holes for his black-painted nipples. Only his right nipple was spurting blood like a water fountain.

"Keep the fucking audience back!" Father yelled at the security people. "Knock 'em off the stage."

Another audience escapee in a glowing violet suit, a blinking shirt, and a marshmallow wig like Father's ran at me. "Business fame!" he hollered. One of the security men threw himself onto Fame, and the two of them tumbled down the steps at the front of the stage.

Father said, "Give my son back!"

"We just want out!" said Joelene as she scouted the audience, as if looking for a safe route out.

"Let up," I told her. I was not going to make it alive in my nitrocellulose suit. She raised her elbow, and I began frantically unbuttoning the jacket and tugging off the sleeves.

"You can go, lady, but give us Michael!"

"What are you doing," Joelene asked me.

"I have to take this off."

"And now," said the house voice, as a distorted drum began pounding, "it is my super-amazing and spectacular honor to welcome you to the thirty-third annual RiverGroup product show and Ültra extravaganza. As you —" The voice and drum turned into screeching feedback and stopped.

"Take it off!" barked someone. Others laughed and applauded.

I lay the jacket on the stage and as I began undoing my pants, looked toward the channel cameras. "Don't drink the poison!" I told her. "I'll see you soon!"

The prompter said: Michael—*I am happy to let Xavid take my place as* … The screen was smashed with what looked like a pair of aluminum pants thrown through the air. Shards of glass showered down on the audience.

"Strip it off, golden boy!"

"Make me beg your balls!" wailed someone close.

"You can go free!" said Father again. "Just release Michael! We won't hurt you if you do."

Joelene stooped for the orange jacket.

"Leave it," I told her. "Let's go!"

She picked it up and sniffed it.

"Put it down!" I said. "Come on!"

Her eyes met mine. Next she was balling up the jacket into a wad the size of a cantaloupe. "You were going to kill him," she said, with a grin as though she thought we were the same evil, commercial assassins.

"No!" I told her. "Let's just go. Let's go to MKG!"

Father fired another shot.

The bullet hit Joelene's abdomen right in the middle of a smooth green bruise. Her body wobbled. For an instant there was a small, dark hole three-inches northwest of her bellybutton. Blood, as thick and dark as cola syrup, welled out and ran down her front. It spread into her green underwear and down her thigh. From there, it turned around her kneecap, and continued toward her bare foot.

"Get away from my boy!" said Father, taking a step toward us.

She tightened the balled jacket and muttered, "Fucker." Her eyes were ecstatic and furious like someone who wanted to kill. She was insane.

I had slipped off my pants and held them before me. "You did it," I told her, afraid of what she was going to do. "You ruined RiverGroup. You got me Nora. Let's go!"

She reared back like an old-fashioned baseball player. The clear gun in Father's right hand fell two inches as his eyebrows tightened over his nose.

"No!" I screamed. "Joelene, don't do it!"

Her weight shifted forward. She launched the wadded-up jacket. It spun backward, and one sleeve came unfurled as it flew. With a backhanded swing, I whipped the pants at her. An instant before the jacket hit Father, the *Adjoining Tissue* pants struck Joelene's back. The white explosions flung me twenty feet.

Epilog

Sitting up, I adjusted my company tie, glanced around the table, tried to refocus on the names, numbers, timelines, and locations that were being discussed, but my concentration was as settled as a droplet of quicksilver. Soon, I picked up the moon-wool tweed samples and began to flip through them. When I came to the 2x2 twill that I had picked out for the product show tomorrow, my eyes defocused on the smooth, dark charcoal. In the last year, I had learned a lot about grey. Maybe more than I cared to.

Originally, of course, I had been attracted to grey because I assumed it was the opposite of Father's garish colors, the reverse of his style and manner, but it was much more complicated than that. In fact, because its parents were black and white, no color in the spectrum was the offspring of such complete opposites, and as such no other tone could ever represent and compass the vast distances between those extremes, that of light and dark, life and death, and good and evil.

More important, grey was not the escape from the world I had wanted, nor was it the negation I had desired. All I had to do was close my left eye and see the grey spine of the world. Everything was grey. Color was nothing but a thin veil of deceit on top.

Setting down the cloth samples, I focused on my half brother again.

"I have been in contact with one of the members of the Ültra band, Stinkin' Dead Ünicorns, who feels strongly, as many of us do, that Hiro's death should be avenged." Rex, my armless half brother from Tanoshi No Wah, wore a sleeveless maroon frock, vest, and a black tie. The screen beside him now showed the diagram of a theater with a red circle around a front seat. "This man, whose name I am not going to reveal, is one of the drummers who plays the new Nalor 450mm munitions tom. As you may know, that specific drum has caused dozen of fatalities at recent concerts." Returning to his chart, he drew a line from the stage to the circled seat. "Despite the dangers of this new drum, in an interview yesterday, Mr. Gonzalez-Matsu insisted he will sit in the front. So, what we are proposing …"

As Rex continued, my eyes gravitated toward the distant gleam of Ros Begas, the geometric high-rise towers silhouetted against aquamarine, the gaudy flickering signs, blinking spires, all connected with flowing arteries of red and white light. Then the dots began to coalesce, the shapes turned hazy, and the city became one amorphous glow.

I thought of her.

Like I had many times, I recalled the moment when the door of her Loop car slid back and she stood inside in her gown. Since we were off the system and the cameras in her car were disabled, no footage existed. But that made it more special, more rare, if unfortunately more vulnerable to the corrosion of memory.

I could still conjure the color of her skin in contrast to the iridescent grey of the bodice and the hazy white edge of her skirt that deepened to a glistening black in the center, the calm of her muted irises, and the smooth, moist watermelon of her lips. Sometimes though, without the help of video or images, it was difficult to exactly recall the shape of her hairline, how her eyebrows curved, or the precise timbre of her voice.

And although it had been a year, almost every morning, while I lay in that semi-dream state at dawn, I would often feel her chenille-covered fingertips on my back or gently squeezing my throat. Sitting up, hoping to see her beside me, I would only find the wrinkled landscape of the empty sheets.

After the product show, I sent a hundred messages to Nora, but they were all returned unanswered. The channels were filled with wild speculation and the foursome on *Intellectuals and Soup* debated whether she was even still alive. Every few weeks someone thought they spotted Nora at Slate Gardens, SpecificMotor 505, or the SunEcho, but after careful study, they were all fakes—no doubt some of the same young women from the auxiliary room that day. In *Pure H*, a new advertisement for plutonium buttons appeared. Instead of the beautiful dead couple, now a man lies alone. And although his palm is bloody, as though he had held her hand, she is no longer near.

Even as I worked twelve- and fifteen-hour days to try to rebuild RiverGroup, my heart was dismal and motionless. And I began to worry that if she were alive—which I desperately believed—she had rejected me. It was bad enough I had once worn gold and danced to killer beats, now the world also knew that I was the stitched-together collage of a Pharmaceutical War freak.

Then, the day before, Nora made an appearance on *Celebrity Research Yacht*. She wore a simple bias-cut charcoal one-piece, with wide flat-fell princess seams, a v-neck, and a slender gold scarf. Her hair was shorter and the ends were tinged with black. And while she answered Milo's silly questions with her usual succinctness—giving out no information other than that she was alive, I could tell that she had changed in a million ways, that her eyes were a darker shade, her face a little rounder, and her cheeks a deeper blush. And yet, despite all the differences, she was Nora—my Nora. At the end of the show, her dark eyes met the camera's stare, and she touched the cloth of her dress where she had once touched the button of her jacket.

Immediately, I got a team of analysts together to decipher her message, but the hunt for clues was unnecessary, as later that day it was announced she would attend the Intel-Sunbeam Ironing and Renovation Invitational. I redirected the team to set up a covert rendezvous.

"So, Mr. CEO," concluded Rex, obviously irritated that I had been daydreaming, "that's the scenario."

"Sorry," I said. "I got the strategy if not all the details."

He asked, "Shall we go ahead?"

Two days ago, I would have immediately said yes, but now that I knew she was alive I didn't know. To delay, I asked the others, "What do you think?"

Around the hammered-silver and sugar maple table sat Mom, Mason, Ari, the girl whose skin looked like scrambled eggs, my tailor, and Walter Noole. We were in what had become our conference room on the fifteenth floor of the PartyHaus. The black toilets had been removed, and so had the ornate and pastel couches and easy chairs, but cobalt tiles still covered the floor, walls, and ceiling. Mom complained it was gloomy and cold, but I liked it.

"The risks," said Mason, nodding thoughtfully. "Are they worth it?" He wore a tuxedo-like black suit and glasses. Out of his ratskins, he had become a distinguished gentleman and presided over a popular game show on channel 43,001 at dawn each morning.

"No," said Mother, shaking her head. "Rex, I'm sorry, but you know I don't like it. We've been about positives. This is purely negative." Mother now wore her hair short. It was frosted a light strawberry, and although I wasn't sure it worked with her tanned complexion, it was better than before. Her tailored charcoal suit was beautiful and made her look both strong and yet delicate in a way she never had before. "I think we should forget it and go to the ironing show. I'm sure no one wants to miss Maricell's singing."

"Have you really thought it through?" asked Mason, eyeing Mom.

"I have!" she replied. "It's destructive. That's why I hate it."

"The question is," began Ari, leaning forward, "will it win us customers?" She was always the pragmatist.

"Definitely," said Rex. "Most of our customers are still Ültra and they want blood." Shrugging, he added, "We've been weak for a year."

"The plan is very mean," said Walter, who sat beyond Mr. Cedar on my side. "But what they did was very mean, too." Frowning he added, "I'm not sure what to do." It turned out that Walter had an amazing gift for coding, and while he was still learning his way, I had given him the job of chief code officer.

Mr. Cedar, who often spoke last, sat back and twisted his single beard hair. "Does it jeopardize your future with Nora?"

"That can't be part of a business decision," I said.

"It has to be," he countered.

"It does not! It cannot. She has nothing to do with the business." Even I could hear the overtones of denial in my voice.

"That's maybe the best reason not to," said Mom, her voice softer, as if she was hoping the notion would just fade away. "Let's table it and go. We're going to be late."

"I need a decision," said Rex.

"We're not interested," said Mom.

"Wait!" I said, pushing back my chair. "If we can't increase our percentages, our creditors aren't going to keep us going. We've got to be courageous."

Rex spoke toward Mom. "If all goes well, his death alone will make the product show a success. I get questions about retaliation from our clients all the time." Softer, he added, "A lot of them still love Hiro."

Sitting back, Mom said, "It shouldn't be like this! I hate how the families do business like savages. When we toured the slubs, we never were like this."

"It was worse!" said Mason. "It was much worse out there."

"It was," agreed Ari.

Standing, I stepped toward the windows. An hour from now, I was to see Nora off the system during the ironing invitational. What would I tell her? What could I possibly say?

When Mom came to my side, I looked up as though I had been staring at the lights of the city. Actually, I had been gazing down toward the far end of the oxygen gardens at Father's headstone. It might not have been visible except the ground lights were on and, a couple of months ago, I had spread a handful of mutant carrot seeds, and their tops formed a thick black patch.

After the product show last year, I retreated from the world. I lived in my dressing room and while I did nothing but burn a lot of gen-cotton shirts with a Schiaparelli-Firemaster Jr. that I had sent out for, I told myself I hated all of them, especially Joelene. When a family commission found she was born a freeboot it was clear that she had deceived, betrayed, and used me. Worse, she had killed Father at just the moment when I had started to see him for what he really was—a flawed, frantic man who had let the company disfigure his heart. Maybe in the future, in a few years from now, I would be able to forgive Joelene since she had done so much for me, but clemency wasn't yet in me.

A month after the show, one morning, after I scorched the collar of another shirt, I started to cry. I fell to the floor and wept so hard I could barely pull air in my lungs. Once I had picked myself up, I headed to the technology building and walked into the code lab, where I knew there was still activity. The thirty workers stood and began to clap, but I told them to stop.

"I know almost nothing about the business," I told them. "But in my Father's name, I'm going to try."

I became CEO of RiverGroup and began working the long hours that he had. Five months later, after weeks of negotiations, the *Om Om* president of iip-2 agreed to return thirty percent of her business and that felt like a new beginning. But it was only that. RiverGroup wasn't first anymore. We weren't even second. We were fifth behind MKG, KodeKing, XL8, and Budget-Crypt. And currently, the only moneymaking part of the company was the Tuesday, Friday, and Sunday night rages at the PartyHaus where Maricell sang, and many of Tanoshi No Wah performed.

Even after all the hard work we had put in, we were struggling, and without something daring and dramatic, I doubted we would make it another year.

"It's just not good," said Mom, quietly. "It really isn't. You know how you felt … how you still feel."

I thought of Father's last moment, the confusion and bewilderment he must have felt as the jacket flew toward him. Sometimes I thought I was being sentimental to imagine that things would have changed between us. But documents that Xavid had left indicated that he had issued the order for the freeboot to cut off Nora's toe. I don't know if that truly exonerated Father, but maybe it had in my heart.

"RiverGroup will be fine without retaliation," she continued. "I know Mr. Gonzalez-Matsu is not a good man. Everyone knows that, but where will it end?"

As I had before, I wished that the morning I'd heard Joelene's cursing I'd told Father, and that somehow together we discovered that she was working for MKG. What we would have done, I wasn't sure, but anything that changed the past seemed preferable. "Gonzalez-Matsu planned it for years," I said, as if that made it doubly bad.

Mom whispered, "Think about her."

"That's all I used to do," I said, trying not to raise my voice. "That was exactly the problem. I only thought of her. If I had done something else, just once, then Father would still be here."

"Don't blame yourself!"

Whipping around, I told Rex, "Go ahead! Kill him."

Rex nodded once and turned to go.

"Wait," I said, as I pictured Nora alone in her dressing room after she had gotten the news of her Father's death. "Hold on … I don't know …"

"I'll go ahead," said Rex. "If you want to stop, let me know within two hours."

The Intel-Sunbeam Ironing and Renovation Invitational was being held in the new massive single-crystal ConEmFuKo building in Ros Begas. Ninety-five thousand fans had gathered. Most sat below in theaters seats; the balconies were filled with corporate boxes. The RiverGroup boot was on the far right, MKG's, was in the center. Through the black glass, I could see nothing, but this was the closest I had been to her in a year. I thought I could feel her presence, her warmth, her being, her heart, but the truth was, I wasn't sure.

Mother sat on my left, Mr. Cedar, right. In the seats in front of us were Mason, Ari, Walter, and another of my half brothers.

We had arrived just in time for the opening ceremonies, and now, far below, Maricell sang. She wore a long, creamy yellow dress, which highlighted the black speaker in the middle of her chest. Her hair was arranged elegantly, her eyes, glowing. She looked gorgeous and happy. When I invited all of Tanoshi No Wah to the compound, I offered to pay for corrective surgery. Later, Mom explained that that was an insult. What worked out, after I apologized, was my proposal to let them stay in the compound if they worked for RiverGroup.

Maricell was singing the Intel-Sunbeam corporate anthem, and while it wasn't a favorite—corporate songs all sounded the same to me—her interpretation was warm and emotional. We, and many below, stood and cheered at the end.

"She looks so good," Ari said to Mom, tearfully. "And she's so happy now!"

"She is," she replied as she massaged Ari's shoulders, tenderly. "It's wonderful how someone can grow in a positive and healthy atmosphere."

I suspected her remark was pointed at me.

"I don't like it either," I told her, again. "But I think it must be done."

Mom ignored me. Now her tactic was silence.

As the stage was prepared for the ironing, Walter and Ari headed off to get snacks. The rest of us sat quietly for several minutes. On the stage, I saw the silver-hair director. Tomorrow, he was going to produce our product show.

"I just hate it," said Mom, as if she couldn't hold it in any longer.

"Yes," I said, wishing we didn't have to keep discussing it. "I hate it, too."

My tailor twisted his beard hair, sadly. "What do you think her reaction will be?"

I hadn't yet even tried to fathom it. "I don't know."

"She could use it against RiverGroup."

"She'll hate you," she said. "Who wants their father killed? Even the fathers you two had. She's got to be loyal to him, even if she detests everything else."

"All right!" I said, louder than I meant. Closing my eyes, I said, "I'm sorry, Mom, but please, this isn't easy. I am wrestling with it."

"Obviously, you're not."

Rubbing my face, I just wished everything would go away.

"Who's who?" asked Mason, turning toward us.

He asked because the two ironers had come out on the stage. They were, of course, Fanjor and Isé–B. Only a point separated them, but unlike all previous times, Isé–B was ahead. All he had to do was tie Fanjor in the final race, and he would be crowned the new champion.

While Mr. Cedar explained the ironing to Mason, I gazed down at Isé–B in my powerglasses. Before, I had completely identified with him. I was still a fan, still wished for the clarity for competitive ironing—in fact working my own iron was one of the few relaxing things I did anymore—but the complexities of business had taken me from attending many competitions.

Putting down the powerglasses, I told myself I couldn't do it. I couldn't have Nora's father killed. It was awful, especially for her. As soon as I'd thought that, though, I felt livid that he had been the cause of so much pain and wrong, and I felt like I wanted to strangle him myself.

"We miss anything?" Walter wanted to know, when he and Ari returned.

Eyeing his snacks, Mother asked, "Should you be eating those?"

After popping several redheads in his mouth, Walter said, "These are the new Frix mini sluts." Quoting their slogan, he added, "Forty percent less tar and saturated fat, but all the original debauchery!"

"You're so weird!" said Ari with a giggle, as she sat beside him. Her voice was filled with that sort of faked disgust that hides affection.

A horn blew. The ironing was about to begin. And seconds from now, I would be meeting her. My fingertips began pulsing my heart beat so hard.

"Who's who?" asked Mason again.

"The black one is Isé–B. The other in yellow is Fanjor," said Maricell, as she came into the booth. She sat beside my tailor as we all congratulated her on her singing.

The starting gun fired. The ironers grabbed their shirts and headed to their boards.

Mr. Cedar tugged on his beard hair twice. That was the signal. I stood.

Maricell asked me, "Where are you going?"

"Uh … er … restroom," I stuttered.

Exiting our booth, I turned left, rushed past the concession stands and souvenir shops, and headed through a door labeled *equipment*. Inside was a series of control panels and several workers watching various screens. On one I could see the two ironers working. Black smoke chugged from Isé–B's Schiaparelli-Firemaster, but Fanjor's short jabbing motions made it look like he was already ahead.

Through an unmarked door at the other end of the equipment room, I started climbing metal stairs. After ten sets, I came to a roof exit. Outside, in the blazing heat and light, stood Pheff in a near-white suit. He held up his hand.

"What's the matter?" I asked.

"Wait," he said, peering into a small screen. "Hold on … be patient …"

"Pheff!" I said, frantic, "tell me. What's going on? She on her way? She not coming? There something wrong?"

"Wait for the system to be shut down." Lowering a hand, as if timing it, he said, Aaaand … go!"

Running as fast as I could, I sprinted for another rooftop doorway one hundred yards away. There, I tore open the door and flew down the stairs. Finally, I came to a platform before metal elevator doors.

As I tried to catch my breath, I wondered what would happen. A year stood between us. I knew I had changed. Maybe she wasn't the same either. And then there were my terrible plans for her father. Should I tell her? What would she think? What would she feel? Would she slap my face or try to choke me to death right here?

The doors weren't opening. Why was this taking so long? This wasn't good. They were supposed to open immediately. I began to panic that I had been double-crossed or that her father had discovered the plan.

From below, deep in the building, I heard a roar. It was the audience. Someone had just won the coveted Intel-Sunbeam. Maybe it was Isé–B.

The doors opened. Jumping back, ready to hit the floor and try and roll away from fashion gun fire, I saw that it was just her.

Inside the scratched utility elevator she stood in a beautifully simple near-black dress. The fabric looked like a plutonium glazed 2x2 alloy twill, and a bias carbon ribbon finished the scooped neck where, from a rhodium chain, hung two black satellite pearls. Her hair was like it had been on *Celebrity Research*—shorter and with tinges of black as though she too had escaped fire. On her feet she wore matt-black, handmade HIFI pumps. It pained me that the right was obviously thinner than the left.

Tears ran from her dark eyes down her cheeks, and at first I thought she was hurt or sick, distraught, or that something was terribly wrong. But as I parted my dry lips to speak, to tell her how much I missed her, how I loved her exactly as before, she smiled, and I understood that the tears were for joy.

Bending, slowly, she picked up a charcoal bassinet. Beneath a soft, nano-wool blanket, she had brought our baby.